Colin Falconer was born in north London, not far from the home of Tottenham Hotspur Football Club. A promising career as an elite football player was tragically cut short by the fact that he wasn't very good at it. After a short stint working in radio and television, he became a full-time novelist and has so far written over twenty novels that have been translated into twenty-three languages. The DI Charlie George series draws on his London roots and is his first foray into crime fiction. Colin Falconer is a pseudonym.

Also by Colin Falconer

The Charlie George series:

Innocence Dies
Lucifer Falls

For more information about Colin Falconer books, go to:

colinfalconer.org

ANGELS WEEP

COLIN FALCONER

CONSTABLE

CONSTABLE

First published in trade paperback in Great Britain in 2020 by Constable

This paperback edition published in 2021 by Constable

A CIP catalogue record for this book
is available from the British Library.

ISBN: 978-1-47213-268-0

Typeset in Sabon by Initial Typesetting Services, Edinburgh
Printed and bound in Great Britain by Clays Ltd, Elcograf S.p.A.

Papers used by Constable are from well-managed forests and
other responsible sources.

MIX
Paper from
responsible sources
FSC® C104740

Constable
An imprint of
Little, Brown Book Group
Carmelite House
50 Victoria Embankment
London EC4Y 0DZ

An Hachette UK Company
www.hachette.co.uk

www.littlebrown.co.uk

For Janet. So glad you married my brother.
Thank you for a lifetime of enthusiastic support.

Never say you know the last word about any human heart.

Henry James

CHAPTER ONE

The worst thing is when you know they're there, when the fear is so bad you start to gag. You know that if you can't stop, you'll choke. You tell yourself it's not really happening; try and pull yourself into the dark.

It gets so that you're not really in your body any more, like you're floating on the ceiling, watching yourself down there, all curled up into a ball. That way you don't feel anything. Knowing what's about to happen, before you can escape out of your body, that's what really does your head in.

So you keep swallowing it down, the bile, as he gets closer. In your mind, you run away, think about other things. You go to another place, a place far away where he can't find you, no one can. You pull the darkness over your head like a blanket. Please. Just leave me alone.

He gets closer and you can hear him breathing, hot and fast. He stinks. You're trapped, and he's right there, outside the door, and there's no way of getting away.

1

CHAPTER TWO

Charlie parked the car and looked at his watch: three in the morning, as good a time as any to slip into God's waiting room. No other cars in the car park, just his and the nurses'. He dragged himself out from behind the wheel, way past tired, made his way towards the splash of light from the foyer. He punched the security code into the keypad and went in.

If you had a dead body, the job would keep, you could close your eyes for a few hours at least. But when you knew your victim might still be alive, there was no way you could rest, even for a minute. Nothing to reasonably achieve before the rest of the crew gets back in, but you keep worrying and worrying at it anyway, can't sleep for thinking about the one thing you might have missed.

The foyer was the size of a football pitch. The nurse at the reception desk peered at him over the top of her glasses. She looked calm, but that expression on her face, he knew her finger was hovering over the alarm button.

'Can I help you?' she said, when he was still only halfway there.

What was her name again? Anna, that was it.

'Morning, Anna,' he said.

'It's Hannah,' with a frown.

'Right. I'm here to see Mrs George. I'm her son. You rang me earlier.'

She looked at her screen. 'That was at one o'clock.'

'I couldn't get away.'

2

'She's asleep now. We managed to get her settled.'

'Well, I'm here now. Can I see her?'

'Don't wake her up.'

'Why would I do that?'

'She's in Room . . .'

'Two oh three. Yeah, I know.'

The door to her room was half open; almost seventy and she still couldn't sleep alone in the dark. He remembered all the beltings he got as a kid for asking to have a light on. *There's no such thing as monsters.*

Oh yes there is.

She had a night light; Ben had bought it for her. Charlie stood in the doorway and looked around. Christ, looks like the London Dungeon in here, he thought, all her holy martyr pictures on the walls. Michael must have brought her a few more since the last time he'd been in. No wonder she needed a night light.

Ma lay on her back, her mouth open, her teeth out. Her hair was getting thin. When did she get so ancient? She wasn't really all that old. The doctors reckoned it was the Alzheimer's.

He'd asked them how people got it; they said it was just one of those things. But was it, was it one of those things? Or was it getting slapped upside the head every Saturday night from the old man? He'd read in the papers about old soccer players having a greater incidence of dementia because of those big leather footballs they used to head all the time. If you could get Old Timer's from that, then what were her chances? His old man's fists were a lot harder than a wet football; he knew that from personal experience.

He kissed her on the forehead. 'Hello, Ma. It's me. How are you then, all right?'

She was well away. He undid his coat and sat down on the chair by the bed. It was nice to get some peace and quiet at last. This was the proper business. First minute all day he'd had to himself.

'Sorry I didn't get in earlier. I had a Gold Group meeting with the brass about this missing girl. Then I was staring at the computer all night, mostly witness statements, trying to figure out if I've missed something. It's like trying to do the *Times* crossword, only a lot bleedin' harder, know what I mean? Time got away from me.'

He stroked a wisp of white hair off her face. He supposed she wasn't so much old as worn out, poor old thing. It did that to you, living in fear twenty-four hours a day. Funny, this, her losing her memory. Well, ironic, more like. She'd spent most of her life trying hard not to remember, just to stay sane.

'They reckon the first forty-eight hours is when you have to find them,' he said aloud. 'If they're still alive, that is. They call it the golden hour. I don't know why; it should be the golden weekend.' He checked his watch. 'I've got till midnight.'

He leaned back in the chair, closed his eyes. Twenty-one hours. Not a chance in hell.

No, can't start thinking like that, must stay positive.

'See, thing is with this job, you're always second-guessing yourself. If it all goes pear-shaped, I'll be thinking about this later, wondering if I could have done things different. And I know I'll think of something. Only I want to think of it now, not when it's too late. Or maybe that's the Mick in me, always feeling guilty, even when it's not my fault.'

There was a *Daily Mirror* lying on the bedside table. He picked it up. The girl's picture was there on the front page, smiling at him. 'Looks like a nice young girl, don't she? Not Mother Teresa, I don't suppose, but just out having a good time, and now look. Only nineteen years old. It's not right. Her car broke down the other side of Wandsworth Common. She called her boyfriend to come and get her, and while she was waiting, some bloke in a white van got out and grabbed her. She shouldn't have got out of her car, should she? But that's hindsight, we can all be clever with hindsight. Someone saw it, saw the whole thing, got the rego and everything. But here's the thing: the number

4

plate he reckoned he saw belongs to a vicar in Dumfries. Easy to make a mistake, I suppose; it was dark, and the van had its lights off. But Jesus Christ.'

Would have got a belt round the ear for blaspheming, once. He still wouldn't have been surprised if she'd opened one eye and given him a swift backhander. But she was right out of it. She looked so peaceful when she was asleep, not agitated any more.

'Done everything right, I know I have. But it'll be down to me if we find her wrapped in plastic in a skip. No one will say it, but they'll think it. *I'll* think it.'

He stood up and went to the window. Pitch black out there, he couldn't see a thing. He went back to his chair, then got up again, couldn't help himself.

'We checked all the sex offenders in a two-mile radius of where she was grabbed. You wouldn't believe how many we found. Reckon half of London's criminally deviant. We think the van is a Ford Transit. What we do, see, is we check all the roads that lead to where she was taken, then all the roads out. There's cameras everywhere now, not like in your day. But you can't find a vehicle if you don't have a registration, unless it's a pink and white Batmobile. You want to know how many Ford Transits there are in London? Still, you don't want to hear my troubles. What was it you used to say? Laugh and the world laughs with you, cry and you cry alone.'

He turned away from the window. 'It's bloody murder, this. Because I can't stop thinking: she's out there *somewhere*. What is he doing to her right now? And her poor parents. I bet they're not sleeping. So why should I? I know that doesn't make any sense, because my guv'nor expects me to be wide awake and ready to do my job when I get into the office in the morning.'

He stood over the bed, stroked her arm.

'By the way, Ben's organising a surprise party for you next Sunday. He said not to tell you. I said, what's the point of not telling you, how is she going to remember a surprise birthday

5

party when she doesn't even remember who she is? I said to him, Ma could organise the party herself and it'd still be a surprise. No disrespect.'

He looked at his watch. He should go home and try to get some sleep. No point hanging around here.

'They rang me up earlier, reckoned you lost your purse again. Always losing your purse, aren't you, you silly bugger. I keep telling you, you don't need your purse in here, it's like one of those cruises you always wanted to go on, everything's paid for. But I suppose I'd better find it, seeing as how I'm here.'

He started going through her drawers, looking in all the usual places, under her unmentionables, as she called them, behind the ancient portable television she had on a stand in the corner.

Next he pulled open all the drawers in her dresser. It was full of old photograph albums. Quaint. Some of the old ducks in here showed off their grandchildren by flicking through the gallery on their iPhones. Not his mum. She still preferred the old-fashioned way; on the good days, anyway, when she remembered she had kids.

He found Michael's baby book. There was a lock of his hair and a record of his first word. *Mum.* Well, Michael was always a traditionalist. The fact that there even was such a book surprised him. Perhaps their family had been normal once.

He looked for a baby book with 'Charlie' written on the front, but there wasn't one. No prizes for seconds, he supposed. He found a handful of Kodak wallets with negatives and prints, held together with an elastic band.

There was a photo of him in his soccer kit, the Arsenal shirt his old man had bought him. He'd never forget that shirt, it had 'O'Leary' printed on the back. Who was he kidding? O'Leary had been a proper player back in the day. Charlie had been more like Tony Adams, shouting at the referee and kicking lumps out of the other team's centre forward.

The big surprise was finding Mr Rocastle, the teddy bear

he'd had as a kid. It was fair tatty now, had lost an ear and an eye, looked more like a robber's dog than anyone's teddy. Bit like its original owner. He used to carry that thing around with him everywhere when he was a kid, until his old man told him only nancy boys had teddy bears.

He couldn't believe she'd kept it.

He tossed it back in the drawer. No sign of the purse. Where had she put it last time? He opened the freezer compartment of the little refrigerator in the corner, where she kept the milk.

Bingo.

He put it on her bedside table and flopped back into the chair next to the bed. Mustn't think about the girl any more, he thought. She would wait until morning, which by the way was only three and a half hours away. He should be getting off in a minute.

He didn't remember falling asleep. He'd promised himself he wouldn't. He dreamed he was watching CCTV on his laptop and the driver of a white van got out and started strangling a young woman right there in front of him. He tried to stop him, but his legs were too heavy and he couldn't move.

A nurse woke him at a few minutes after six, shaking him by the shoulder, said he'd been shouting in his sleep and frightened his mother. He apologised and left. He had to get back to the office. He looked at his watch as he ran across the car park.

Eighteen hours of his golden hour left.

CHAPTER THREE

Daniel Howlett came down the stairs, his hair still wet from the shower. He looked like a model, she thought, with his long dark hair and brooding eyes. Funny how Ollie was the spitting image. He was a real heartbreaker, was Danny, until he opened his mouth. Then it was your soul he more or less tore apart.

He leaned over her, took a bite of her toast, put the car key fob in his pocket. He was wearing his Hugo Boss shirt and chinos, immaculate as always. He looked her up and down. 'Is that what you're wearing?'

'What do you want me to wear round the house?'

'Not that. You know what I like. Something a bit more feminine.'

'I'll go and change.'

'No point, I'm going out now.'

She cut up some more toast for Ollie and put it on his plate. 'You were late home last night.'

'Was I?'

He checked his look in the hall mirror.

'Where are you going?'

'I'm playing golf with Taj and a couple of other blokes from the office. Taj has got us in at Walton Heath. Always wanted to play there.'

'What time will you be home?'

'I don't know. I won't be late. Ania will be here at seven.'

'Ania? Tonight?'

He checked the weather app on his phone, fetched his rain jacket from the hall cupboard. 'Don't tell me you've forgotten.'

'I've got a lot on my mind.'

'Like what?'

'Everything. What are we going to do with Ollie?'

'Ines can look after him, can't she?'

'It's her day off.'

'Call her, tell her you need her tonight. She won't be doing anything anyway.'

'She said she's going into London. With her boyfriend.'

'She's got a boyfriend? She looks like Ozzy Osbourne.'

'She's going to one of her meetings or rallies or something.'

'What is it this time, Save the Shark?'

'I don't know. Climate change, I think.'

'Climate change. Another name for the weather.'

Sarah wiped Ollie's face with a damp cloth, poured some apple juice into his sip cup and clipped on the lid. She put it down in front of him. 'So, you want me to ring her?'

'If you can make time in your busy day.'

'What shall I say?'

'She's always complaining she doesn't have enough money.'

'Can't we just put Ania off for tonight?'

'Worst comes to the worst, we'll leave Oliver in his room, give him something to help him sleep. What's that stuff you use on the plane? Phenergan or something. He'll be all right.'

'The doctor said the Phenergan is only for when he's sick.'

'Giving him drugs is good training. Get him used to living in London.'

Ollie knocked his sip cup over and the lid came off. The juice spilled and dribbled off the table onto the tiles. He started bawling. Sarah tore off a strip of paper towel and got down onto her knees to clean it up.

'I'll be home before seven,' Danny said and walked out.

The plasma TV was turned on in the other room, on mute, the breakfast news; more about the poor young woman who had been abducted in Wandsworth. There was shaky video of a car skewed across the road with the driver's door wide open, police patrol cars with flashing lights, blue and white tape. The vision changed to a police conference room, a tough-looking man in a sharp suit reading from a script while news cameras flashed, a ticker scrolling across the bottom with numbers for the police incident room and Crimestoppers.

Somewhere, the detective said, a woman was being held prisoner.

Ollie started to cry.

CHAPTER FOUR

Nice out here in the country. When she turned off the A12, there were lanes with hedges and fields and animals, white signposts with pretty names like Ingatestone and Margaretting. Sometimes Sarah thought she'd like to just drive, not to go anywhere, just stay in the car and never have to stop and talk to anyone, or do anything.

She reached his turn-off, but she didn't want to see him yet, it was too soon, so she pulled over to the side of the road and turned off the engine. She wound down the window. She could hear birds and a tractor in a field, the sound of insects in the hedgerow.

She looked in the rear-view mirror. Ollie was asleep in his car seat behind her. Easy to pretend he was normal when he was like that; he looked so peaceful, like any other little boy.

She closed her eyes, the sun on her face, dappled through the oak trees. A car went past and sounded its horn. She only had two wheels on the road, what was their problem? People, she thought. No one gives an inch any more.

Better go, he was expecting her.

She started the engine; the radio was playing the end of a Bruce Springsteen song, about a man with a wife and kids who went out for a drive and never went home again. Almost two hundred thousand people went missing every year in Britain, or that was what she'd read in a magazine she'd picked up in the doctor's surgery. I wonder how many of them never want to be found?

She liked the last verse best.

Ain't nobody like to be alone.

The gravel crunched under her tyres as she pulled into her father's drive. Liked living out here, he did, playing the country squire. Back when they lived in Hackney and he was out driving cabs every day, he always said he'd like to live in the country one day. She never thought he'd actually do it.

Danny had raised his eyebrows when he first saw it: two storeys, big stone fireplace, love seat round the back and a new Range Rover Sport parked out front. Nice bit of garden too, almost half an acre, a gazebo with a weeping willow, fruit trees, even some old raspberry cages. Mum would die if she saw it; well, she would have if she hadn't already passed.

He came out in a cardigan. Look at him, it'd be wellies and a flat cap next, start gobbing on about Brexit and Pakis.

'Hello, sweetheart, haven't seen you for ages, thought maybe you'd gone abroad and hadn't told me.' He held out his arms as she got out. 'Doesn't your old man get a proper hello, then?'

She hugged him, leaning in but making it quick, before she could get caught up, then pushed away again.

'Where's my little Ollie?'

'He's in the back. He's asleep, don't wake him up.'

He leaned in and ruffled Ollie's hair. It woke him up. 'Ollie, look who it is. It's your grandpa.' He unbuckled his seat belt and lifted him out. 'I think he recognised me. He smiled.' He tossed him up in the air. 'Hello, Ollie!'

'Careful, you know he gets car sick. He'll throw up all over you.'

'Come on in, I'll put the telly on for him.'

There was a hall table inside the front door with half a dozen framed photographs, all of her: her first day at school; playing teddy bear's picnic in the garden of their two-up, two-down in Hackney; in a school hockey uniform with braces on her teeth; blowing out the candles on her sixteenth birthday. Danny had called it her shrine. He'd only been here once; her dad had never invited him back.

12

I don't want that bastard ever setting foot in my house again.

She followed him into the kitchen.

'How's Daniel?' he said.

'Same.'

'You two been fighting again?'

'Why do you say that?'

'It's written all over your face.'

'Wasn't anything.'

'Doesn't hit you, does he? If he ever hurts you, I'll be round there so fast it will make his head spin.'

'He won't hurt me, Dad.'

'What was it about this time?'

'It doesn't matter. Just marriage stuff.'

'Where was Ollie when all this was happening?'

'Dad, Ollie's fine. He wouldn't understand anyway.'

'Whatever you say. Do you want coffee? I just got one of those machines with pods.'

'For God's sake, you didn't?'

'What?'

'They're crap for the environment. The pods end up in landfill.'

'Well, that's why we have land. What about a cup of tea, then? I've got special tea bags, guaranteed not to make the ice caps melt, it says so on the packet. I'll put the kettle on.'

She checked on Ollie. He was sitting cross-legged on the carpet in the living room, watching *Small Potatoes* on CBeebies. Dad had done it nice, she'd give him that; restored the timber fireplace, bought himself some black leather sofas, real expensive ones, a view of the gazebo through the French windows.

When she looked up, he was standing in the doorway, smiling. 'Lovely, eh?'

'Yeah, it's proper nice.'

'Better than living in Clapham.'

'Bit far out is all.'

13

'You don't have to live there. Honest, I don't know why you're wasting your time with that . . . prat.'

'Stuck with him now. Sometimes I wish I'd been more like Jackie.'

'Come off it. You want to live in a grotty little flat in Romford?'

'At least she's got a career.'

'A career! She's a bloody nurse.'

'And no one tells her what to do.'

'Why don't you leave him?'

'How can I?'

'People get divorced all the time, sweetheart. You could walk away with half, you'll be all right.'

'Half of what? You know how much the mortgage is on our place in Clapham? Danny is up to his eyeballs.'

'That's what he tells you. I'll bet he has enough squirrelled away somewhere.'

'He'll never let me go, Dad.'

'You're not scared of him, are you?'

'Maybe. A bit.'

'You don't have to be. Come home. I'll look after you till you get yourself sorted.'

'No, Dad.'

'Your room's just like you left it.'

'I'm not a little girl any more. Anyway, you know I can't.'

'Don't say that. Look, I know you and me, we had some problems when you were a teenager and that, but I've changed now, I'm different. Everything will be all right.'

'I'm not coming home. I know you mean well, but it'll only start up again, you know it will.'

'Oh sweetheart,' he said. He put his arms around her. 'Don't cry. Everything's going to be all right. I'll look after you.'

'I don't want you to look after me!' She untangled herself. 'Don't.'

'No one will ever love you like I do, you know that. Ever

14

since you were a little girl, I've only wanted the best for you. Your uncle Joe, he'd say to me sometimes, "Tone, you're a soft touch when it comes to that girl. Twists you right round her little finger." Remember we used to sit down and have a tea party with all your teddy bears on the living-room rug. Remember?'

'Yeah, I remember, Dad.'

'"Grown man," Joey used to say, "playing tea parties. Who'd have thought? If your mates down the pub could see you now."' The kettle whistled in the kitchen. 'I'd better get that,' he said.

Sarah picked Ollie up off the floor. Christ, he was heavy. She walked out with him and put him in his booster seat in the back of the car. She fastened his seat belt and jumped in the driver's seat, flicked on the central locking.

Her dad came rushing out. 'Love, where are you going?'

She felt herself choking up. Don't cry, she thought, don't give him the satisfaction.

'Love?' He banged on the window, ran after her as she was driving away. She caught a glimpse of his face in the rear-view mirror. She dug her nails into the palm of her hand. She shouldn't have come today, it was a mistake.

Everything was just one big fucking mistake.

Sarah had Ollie in a sling. He was way too big for it, but it was the only way she could carry him around these days; he screamed if she left him in the pushchair too long. She sat down on a bench to wait for the bears to come out. There was only one of them today, playing on the tyre swing.

Ollie reached out a hand.

'She looks cuddly, doesn't she, Ollie? But you wouldn't want to go down there. She's really fierce.' Sarah made a growling noise and curled her hand into a claw. 'They'll eat you all up.'

He thought that was funny.

She liked it here: no one to stare at her, no one to worry her or touch her. Just her and Ollie. It was the best time, during the week. There were not so many people.

15

She still felt a bit shaken up. There had been a woman with a little girl in the souvenir shop when she was buying their tickets. The girl wasn't much older than Ollie and she was staring and staring.

Then she said: 'What's wrong with him?'

'Nothing.' Sarah had taken her tickets from the woman at the desk and hurried out. She was only a little girl. She didn't know not to say things like that. But it hurt, just the same.

She avoided crowds whenever she could. She avoided most people, even her friends; well, they were Daniel's friends mostly, his banker mates and golf buddies and all the yummy mummies. They thought they were being supportive, telling her how great she was. They used to come around and make a fuss of Ollie, tell her how he would catch up, just give it time. *Soon he'll be walking and then you'll wish he wasn't.* Did they ever stop to listen to themselves?

They talked about her as if what she was doing was special. But she wasn't special and she didn't want their pity. She coped because she had to, because there wasn't any other choice.

She and Danny had taken him to a paediatrician in Harley Street, who told them he had global developmental delay. And that was all Danny heard, 'delay'. He didn't get it. He didn't want to get it.

'I'm sorry you had to listen to Mummy and Daddy fighting this morning,' she said to Ollie. 'I've seen you looking at us sometimes. Everyone thinks you don't understand, but you do, don't you? I can see you in there, looking out. I reckon you do know. You know something's not right. Thing is, Ollie, your daddy doesn't really want me; he just doesn't want anyone else to have me.'

Another bear came out of the bushes. It stood up on its hind legs and scratched its claws on the bark of the nearest tree, then joined its mate in the pool.

There was a sign on the fence, with a laminated newspaper cutting about the bears. They'd been rescued from a zoo in Romania where they had been penned in a cage with metal bars and cement floors, half starved. They had mostly survived on the porridge that local people brought them because they felt sorry for them. Milwood had asked for donations from the public to help pay for the cost of bringing them back to England and building the enclosure. Their new home had a rope bridge and a swimming pool and three quarters of an acre of woodlands for them to roam in. Sarah had given a thousand pounds towards it, straight off her credit card. Hadn't Danny hit the roof when he saw that on the bank statement. She thought he was going to have a stroke.

But it proved something, didn't it? It was possible to do it. The bears had escaped, even though it had seemed hopeless for them once, and look at them now with their shiny coats and little paunches, playing in the sun.

She looked down at Ollie. Such a beautiful boy, with his dark eyes and long eyelashes. You'd never know there was anything wrong when he was still like this. He jumped out of her arms and started shouting at the bears, no sounds you could really recognise as words. He tried to take his shirt off and she made him put it back on again.

She sat him back on her knee.

'If anything ever happens to me, Ollie, you'll be all right. You know that, don't you? You probably wouldn't even notice if I wasn't here, I reckon. Your dad would take care of you. He wouldn't like it, but he would. He'd organise everything, anyway. You'd probably have to go and stay with Grandma. You remember Grandma? She reckons she can do a better job than me anyway, she tells me so all the time.'

He looked at her so seriously that for a moment she thought he understood.

'I lost my mum when I was about your age, did you know that? I don't even remember her all that well any more. Sad, isn't it? Not remembering. But that's what happens. You forget, and life goes on. It's not so bad really. Not like I worry about it all the time. Got other things to worry about now.'

17

Her throat closed up and she couldn't talk any more.

On the way out, she went in the shop, thought she'd buy Ollie a toy, keep him occupied on the way home. 'Have you got any of those little blue bears?'

The girl gave a shake of the head. 'We're waiting for stock.'

Sarah thought she might try and sell her a furry yellow fox or a pink deer. But she didn't. Totally didn't care. Just stared at her, at Ollie, from behind the counter. The door opened, the bell rang, a woman came in with a pushchair and two normal, noisy, walking kids.

I have to get out of here, Sarah thought.

She carried Ollie to the car.

She started driving. It was five minutes before she realised she was heading in the wrong direction. She turned on the radio, looking for some music. Instead it went to the news, the usual rubbish, Cliff Richard, Brexit, Theresa May, the heatwave.

There was more about the missing girl. Evie Myers, her name was. The road where she was taken, it was only a mile from where they lived. Sarah pulled over to the verge, Bluetoothed 'The Teddy Bears' Picnic', turned up the volume, to keep Ollie happy. Was today the day?

She switched on the GPS, started to log in an address in Croydon, changed it to the train station instead, in case anyone snooped around in the car later.

She could walk to the house from there.

CHAPTER FIVE

Danny got home on time that night. Only time he ever managed it, when Ania was coming.

He went upstairs to get changed, came down wearing an Italian linen shirt and brown cords. Such a beautiful man, she thought, but that was the trouble with beautiful people: they were so lovely to look at, it distracted you, stopped you from seeing how ugly they were.

He gave her a look. 'Don't you ever change out of that tracksuit? Put a dress on, for Chrissakes.'

They both heard the taxi pull up outside. A few moments later, the doorbell rang and Ania's face appeared on the security camera. 'Forget about it, it's too late now,' he said.

He opened the door. She stood on the doorstep wearing a short black dress, pumps and perfume.

'Ania,' he said.

CHAPTER SIX

Charlie's inside DS, Dawson – 'the skipper' – was already at his desk when he got in. He was scrolling through a PNC database and taking desultory bites out of a carrot stick.

One of the DCs, Wes James, grinned at him. 'They look brilliant,' he said.

The skipper gave him a sour look. 'Wife's idea. Not enough making me go to the gym, now I have to eat rabbit food.'

'You haven't been to the gym in weeks.'

'That's because I injured my glutes doing squats.'

'Your what?'

'My glutimus maximus muscle.'

'It's gluteus,' James said. 'And in your case, gluteus enormous.'

'Okay, that's enough,' Charlie said. 'That's bullying in the workplace, that is. Give him a break, Wes, you can't take shots at a bloke when he's eating carrot sticks. Skip, how are we doing on the MOs? Anything?'

The skipper shook his head. He had been going through a list of MO suspects, local scrotes who had previous for sexual assaults or abductions, but although the computer had thrown up several names, none of them owned a white van. The DCI had wanted them brought in for questioning, but Charlie had resisted. If Evie Myers was still alive, he didn't want to panic her abductor, or drive him underground.

The helpline had been inundated on Saturday, but now the calls had slowed to a trickle. His team had spent two days knocking on doors, following up on leads from the public and getting nowhere. Most of them had hardly slept, Charlie himself hadn't been home since Evie had been taken, had worked all weekend until the small hours, grabbing a couple of hours on the camp bed in his office the first night and then, last night, dozing off in the armchair in his mother's bedroom at the care home.

His head ached, his eyes were sore, his neck was killing him.

All they had was a single eyewitness; he had been over a hundred yards away, in the dark, saw a masked man throw Evie into what he thought was a white Ford Transit van. They'd been able to trace it on CCTV cameras for almost a kilometre before it disappeared south of Brixton railway station. The ID on the plates had been no use to them; they'd either been altered, or their eyewitness had made a mistake in the dark.

'We have been visited from On High,' the skipper muttered, nodding in the direction of the doorway.

The DCI pointed a finger at him and went into Charlie's corner office. The skipper leaned towards him and lowered his voice. 'If God and Detective Chief Inspector O'Neal Callaghan both walked in at the same time and said they needed to talk to you urgently, which one would you go to?'

'The one who writes my performance review,' Charlie said.

He followed his guv'nor in and closed the door. The DCI was examining Charlie's pot plant, which had recently died. That was the fifth one this year. 'Where are we with Operation Loxley?'

'I've made finding the van our priority,' Charlie said.

'Charlie, tracking down and sighting every Ford Transit registered in the local postcodes will take weeks. We don't have that much time.'

He wasn't going to argue about that. Ford Transit vans were commercial vehicles, and many of those registered to local companies were also being used in other branch offices all over London. But it was still their best hope.

'With respect, sir, we don't have that many leads. What I'm

hoping to do is tie an MO suspect with a white Ford van. I think that's a better use of time and effort than doing these endless house-to-house walk-ups and press appeals.'

There was a knock on the door, and it edged open. It was the skipper.

'Sorry to interrupt. Think you might want to have a look at this, guv.'

'You found a match?' Charlie said.

'Looks like it.'

'Get in,' Charlie said.

The government loved acronyms, and MAPPA was one of Charlie's favourites. It stood for Multi-Agency Public Protection Arrangements, which, roughly translated, was an online register with the details of anyone who had committed a serious crime. His intel team had been searching the system for anyone in that area of south-east London who had been released from prison in the last six months for a similar offence.

The numbers thrown out by that particular enquiry had been unwieldy; the MO had been too broad, and the specified radius too wide. So Charlie had run another search, extending the time frame and restricting the search area to a one-mile radius of Wandsworth Common. This time they came up with a name: Billy Cogan.

Parm, his intelligence officer, was waiting by the skipper's desk. She handed Charlie a printout of Cogan's intelligence record, an inch-thick pile of A4 paper. It was a grim history of domestic assaults, drugs and sexual offences. In April 2013, he had been convicted of the attempted abduction of a seventeen-year-old girl from a bus stop in Stockwell. He had been released fourteen months ago.

A further search of national computer records had revealed his address, his known associates and his ride. He had one vehicle currently registered in his name – a 1998 Ford Transit.

'I'll organise the warrant,' the DCI said.

'Just a minute, sir,' Charlie said. 'I think we should hold off on arresting him for the moment.'

'What for? We grab him, let Crime Unit go through his van, all we need is one speck of blood, one hair and we've got him.'

'Got him, but not got her.'

Charlie could feel Parm and the skipper watching him; he could see they agreed with him, but he also knew they were glad it wasn't their call to make.

'Sir, let's put surveillance on to this first. We get a visual on where he lives, do a covert search as soon as we can. If Evie Myers isn't there, we put a lump on his van. Then we can track him on GPS and he'll lead us to her.'

'That's a dangerous game, Charlie.'

'What if she's not inside his house when we grab him? His brief will tell him to say nothing; all he has to do is wait out the ninety-six hours and then we have to let him go. By then Evie Myers will be dead.'

'You think she's still alive, do you, Charlie?'

'I won't give up on her while there's still a chance.'

'What if we can't make a covert search? What if he stays indoors the whole time? He could be torturing her to death in his back room while we're sitting in our cars drinking coffee and reading the newspaper.'

'Give it twelve hours.'

The DCI looked pained. He looked up at the ceiling, playing it forward in his head. Whatever they did, this could go tits-up.

'On your head,' he said, finally, and headed back to the lifts to get the warrants and the surveillance crews organised.

The skipper shook his head. 'This goes wrong, guv'nor, he's going to hang you out to dry.'

'Tell me something new,' Charlie said.

An hour later, Charlie, Dawson and the DCI were all crowded into his corner office. Charlie's new deputy walked in, and the DCI put his hand out. 'You must be DS Grey,' he said.

23

'That's right, sir.'

'Good to have you on board.'

Charlie looked at Dawson and raised an eyebrow. What was that all about? The DCI was not known for taking an interest. After six months, most of the newbies were lucky to get a grunt, and a *Haven't I seen you before somewhere?*

Charlie put his Nokia on the desk. The surveillance crew were already on their way to Cogan's terraced house in Stockwell. The surveillance commander, Amory, was directing the operation from his command car, and had promised to keep Charlie up to speed on his mobile.

As soon as he heard the default ringtone, he answered and tapped the speaker key so they could all hear it. They were in position, Amory said. They didn't yet have a visual on Cogan.

'This could take a while,' Dawson said. 'Who wants a cup of tea?'

'You know I hate tea,' Charlie said. 'I'd rather drink bleach.'

'Don't think we've got bleach. Shall I send out for some?'

Grey said he'd like tea, and Dawson gave him a look, not sure if he wanted to fetch and carry for the newbie just yet. 'I'll join you,' the DCI said, and winked at DS Grey.

It was a face-saver. 'Right you are,' Dawson said, and went out.

Dawson was on his third mug of tea when the Nokia buzzed again. That was quick, Charlie thought. He imagined he'd be through a whole box of PG Tips before they finally got some action. He snatched it up.

Amory reported that Cogan had come out of the house holding a plastic bucket full of chemicals and industrial-strength detergents. He'd already got to work scrubbing the bench seat in the back of the van. 'Do you want us to intervene?'

'He's trying to clean away the evidence,' the DCI said.

'It's still too early to go in, sir,' Charlie said.

'We have to protect the forensic trace.'

'What we want is Evie.'

Amory cut in. 'What are your instructions?'

'It has to be him,' the DCI said.

'Sir, I'd strongly advise we hold off.'

'No, Charlie, we can't let him clean that van.' He reached across the desk and picked up the Nokia. 'Amory, this is DCI Callaghan. Arrest the target. I repeat, arrest the target. I want that van protected for evidence at all costs.'

'Affirmative.'

Amory hung up. The DCI handed Charlie the phone. 'It's the right call, Charlie. He who hesitates is lost. You have to be proactive.'

He walked out.

Grey and Dawson looked at Charlie. 'For once,' Charlie said, 'I won't mind being wrong.'

CHAPTER SEVEN

'When we went in the house,' Amory said, 'we did find a young female, but it wasn't Evie Myers. Her name was . . .' he checked his notebook, 'Desiree Chantelle Winterbottom. She said she was his girlfriend. She was sitting on the sofa watching *Dr Phil* and eating a packet of Wotsits.'

'How does a bloke with his record get a girlfriend?'

'She's probably got form as well. Charlie, you should have seen her. Covered in tatts and half a dozen rings through her nose. Scared the life out of me.'

'Didn't she come out when she heard you arresting him?'

'There's people getting arrested all the time round that way. She didn't seem that bothered.'

The DCI came out of Interview Room 2 with a face like thunder. He stormed past Charlie and Amory and got in the lift. A few moments later, Cogan came out with his brief. He smirked at them as he walked past.

Dawson was last out of the room. 'What happened?' Charlie asked him.

'He's in the clear.'

'Alibi?'

'Friday night he was in King's having his haemorrhoids fixed. Reckons he's going to sue us for wrongful arrest.'

'Haemorrhoids?'

'Painful. I had to get mine done a couple of years ago.'

'Too much information,' Charlie said.

He waited until Cogan and his brief were on their way out of the building, then went back up to the incident room. The DCI was standing at the far end under the plasma TV, his hands in his pockets, watching Evie Myers' parents latest televised appeal from the media room at New Scotland Yard.

'Someone out there must know something. Please, if you can help in any way, we want you to come forward and contact the police.'

Mr Myers paused for a moment, looked like he was trying to swallow a stone. He took a deep breath, forced himself to go on.

'She has been missing now for over two days. Her mother and I are praying that we will get our little girl back safe and well. It's breaking our hearts not knowing what's happened to her. Please, if you have her, don't hurt her . . .'

That was it. He couldn't finish. Catlin, the media officer, gently took the piece of paper out of his hands and finished the prepared statement.

'Next time,' Charlie said, 'we can't rush it, sir. For Evie's sake, we have to hold off.'

The DCI gave him a look. 'We won't be finding her alive now,' he said and walked out.

CHAPTER EIGHT

Danny watched the reflection of the late-afternoon sun gleaming on the glass towers above Canary Wharf. The river was slick as mercury. Everything looked cool and clean and promising; contrails spread in white feathers across the blue sky.

He'd read somewhere that those white feathers contributed to the build-up of greenhouse gases. It showed you what a deceptive bitch a sunny day could be.

On the other side of the glass, two dozen traders murmured into headsets, rubbed their eyes and stared at the endless flow of data on their screens. Danny knew what it was like: four screens, three phones, living on caffeine and high-octane greed. He'd always lusted after the office with the view, one just like this. He'd thought that would be the end of the constant grind.

But it had been just the start.

The problem was, you needed so much to break even these days. Apart from the house in Clapham and the holiday home in Brittany, there were the two cars, Ines, his pension contributions, his tax bill, parking fines. It was a wonder there weren't more homeless.

His whole life was spiralling out of control. He felt like one of those magicians spinning two dozen plates at once; sooner or later, one of them had to fall. In his case, the whole lot was toppling over with a crash all at once.

He rearranged his desk: the blank yellow legal pad, the engraved Montblanc pen his mother had given him for

28

Christmas, the coffee mug from the Schönbrunn market, his Caffè Nero loyalty card.

He touched a button to lower the blind. The window to the trading room turned opaque. They couldn't see what he was doing from out there anyway; this desperate need for privacy, it was all in his head, he supposed.

He turned to one of the monitors, and with a few clicks of the mouse brought up the account he was looking for, closing the screen when one of his traders tapped on the door wanting to know if he was coming for drinks after work. He nodded without really thinking. He was still trying to digest what he'd just seen.

When the door shut again, he reopened the screen. A cold, greasy sweat oozed out of his body. He sprang to his feet and went to the window; instinct, he supposed, some ancient fight-or-flight reflex. He couldn't breathe and his heart was beating too fast. Christ, he hoped he wasn't having a heart attack.

Breathe, Daniel. You'll think of a way out of this. You always have before.

The account was an artefact, had originally been set up to balance trades at the end of the day. Taj in Compliance had found a way to delete it from the system but keep it open for trading.

Danny had gone long on the Australian dollar against the yen, closed his position with a handsome profit and hid the funds in the account; he'd then gone short on the US dollar, and in a few weeks he and Taj were looking at a profit of over seven million each.

They had agreed they would close out. No one in the company would ever have known. But then Danny heard some brokers talking up prospects for the euro in a bar in Hoxton. He'd done a little research of his own and taken a position. He hadn't told Taj because he knew he'd bottle it. That's my trouble, Danny thought. Every time I see daylight, I have to go back, push things just a little further. Can't help myself. Love that adrenaline rush, always have.

He went back to his desk. The figures on the screen started to blur.

His gamble on the euro had wiped out their profits and then some. He had held the position over the weekend, thinking it would recover, but now they were looking at losses close to ten mil. They would have to cover that loss with another trade or end up in prison. This severely limited his options.

Fuck, what was he saying? His options weren't just limited; he was *trapped*.

The phone rang. He snatched it up.

'What the fuck.'

'Settle down. It's all right.'

'What do you mean, it's all right? What have you done? We're twenty-five down.'

'I can make that up by the weekend.'

'We were supposed to be getting out. We agreed. What were you doing getting into euros?'

'I said don't worry, I'll sort it.' He hung up, went back to the window. Christ, there was a smell coming off him, sweat and something else. This wasn't supposed to happen. Not to him.

His iPhone rang. He checked the ID, straightened his shoulders and picked up. 'Hello, Mum.'

'Hello, Danny. Not disturbing you, am I?'

'Just in the middle of something at the moment.'

'I won't keep you. Just checking that you and Sarah are still all right for this weekend.'

'This weekend?'

'You're coming up to stay? We arranged it last time.'

'Did we?'

'Have you forgotten?'

'Let me check my diary. I'll get back to you.'

'Katie's coming down. It'll be lovely, so long since we've all been together.'

'Sounds brilliant. Look, I can't talk now, but I'm sure that will be all right.'

'We'll see you then.'

'Bye, Mum. Love to Dad.'

He hung up, stared at all the people down there in the square, scurrying like ants. Look at them, all those little lives, little secrets. He wondered what his mother would say if she knew about his secrets. Kate had blabbed to her about him and Sarah, but she only knew the half of it. She had no idea how far in the hole he was. She thought he was raking it in, like his brother-in-law, fucking Peter Perfect.

No one knew.

'No one really knows anyone, do they?' he murmured.

You've been asleep, dreaming. It was a dark dream, hands clawing at you in the dark. You were trying to run, but you were up to your knees in sand, and no matter how hard you pumped your legs, you couldn't get away. It's all you want, to get away, but you can't, you can't.

Just pretend this isn't happening. Get outside your body and come back when it's safe, then it will be like it hasn't really happened to you. If you don't remember, then you can't remember how much it hurts.

CHAPTER NINE

Danny got a cab home; you couldn't trust the Tube this time of night. Besides, he was bone tired and he'd drunk too much. He needed his bed. When he walked in, he saw a splash of light from the kitchen, heard the refrigerator door close, the clink of a wine glass.

She was sitting at the breakfast bar, drinking, with that look in her eyes.

'What are you doing?'

'Waiting for you to come home.'

'How much have you had to drink?'

'Just a couple of glasses. Small ones.'

He dropped his briefcase on the worktop, found the bottle in the bin. 'You drank the whole bottle?' He looked up at the clock, some stupid skeleton thing with Roman numerals; it was either five to one or five past eleven. Late.

'What about Oliver?'

'He's asleep.'

'What if he wakes up? Call yourself a mother.'

'I needed something to relax me.'

'Relax you from what? You don't do anything.'

She threw her wine at him. The glass was almost full. It shattered on the tiles.

'Clean that up,' he said.

She didn't move.

'I said, clean it up.'

He started towards her. She grabbed her car keys off the

worktop and ran to the door.

'Sarah,' he said, and went after her, but it was half-hearted really; he knew where this was going. By the time he got outside, she had already climbed into the Lexus and was gunning the engine.

'Get out of the car, Sarah.'

He grabbed for the driver's door, tried to pull her out. She pushed him away.

'Get out of the car!' A light flicked on in an upstairs window across the street.

Sarah jammed the car into reverse. The half-open door hit him as she shot out of the driveway, knocking him onto his back. The car fishtailed, leaving rubber on the road as she sped away.

Danny sat up, clutching at his ribs. Well, that was a nice show for the neighbours. They'd get talked about. People weren't used to that kind of chav behaviour in this part of town.

He got to his feet a little gingerly, went back inside, made coffee in the *macchinetta*, tried to clear his head. He lifted his shirt to inspect the damage. Lucky the bitch hadn't broken his ribs.

He wondered how long it would be before he got a call from the police.

Sarah gripped the wheel so hard her knuckles were white. That look he got in his eyes sometimes, it scared the life out of her.

There was a tall kerb at the next corner, and she hit it hard as she turned. She over-corrected, lost control and hit it a second time. The dashboard lit up and the ABS warning light started flashing. There was a grinding noise coming from the front left wheel. She pulled over, stopped the engine.

Her heart was hammering in her chest.

She put her head on the wheel; she needed a moment to gather herself. When she sat up again, she saw her face in the rear-view mirror, a complete stranger.

33

She wound down the window to get some fresh air. It was so quiet out there, she could hear the high-pitched yipping of a fox somewhere on the common. The sound sent shivers through her. There were only a few street lights. The moon hung low over the trees. There looked to be no one about, but you could never tell, not in this city. Nowhere was safe, ever.

A siren wailed somewhere in the distance.

The engine ticked as it cooled. Her phone started ringing in her bag; she glanced over and saw from the ID that it was Danny. As if he cared. She reached for it, out of habit, and there was a moment, even then, when she thought about answering. The hold he had on her.

Her finger hovered over the screen, then she flipped right to left, rejecting the call.

Get a hold of yourself, girl. You know what you have to do.

She rang AA Road Assistance, and after they had taken down her details, she put the phone on the passenger seat and got out of the car. There was a CCTV camera mounted on the wall of the wine bar at the end of the road. Big Brother is watching you, she thought.

She glanced at her watch, then looked up and down the street, expecting to see headlights. There was nothing, just someone on the common, a man, urinating against a tree.

She thought about getting back in the car and locking the doors. Checked her watch again. She saw headlights, and a white van drove past. The brake lights blinked on, and the reverse lights glowed white as it backed up.

The driver jumped out, threw open the van's side door and came towards her. She put up both her hands, as if she could somehow protect herself from what was coming. Suddenly there was an arm around her face and another around her arms, pinning them to her sides.

She thought about Ollie, fast asleep in his bedroom. She wondered what he would make of this in years to come. She would probably never know.

There was a rag over her face, and she felt herself being dragged backwards. She kicked her legs, flailing at the air, knew she was about to pass out. This was how they had described it on the news: a car abandoned in the street, door wide open, a woman overpowered and thrown into a white van. Her last thought was: No one is ever going to see me again.

CHAPTER TEN

'The state of you,' the DCI said. 'You'd frighten a dog out of a butcher's shop.'

'Thank you, sir. Good morning, sir.'

'Same MO, same van, same everything. I'm officially making this part of Operation Loxley. Don't look at me like that, Charlie.'

'My team are exhausted.'

'This could be the break you've been waiting for.'

'I'll need more people.'

'I've already broken the bank.'

'I appreciate that, sir, but this could turn into a proper clusterfuck.'

The DCI gestured to the CCTV camera on the wall of a wine bar about a hundred yards away. It was pointed straight at them. 'You should have this all on digital. It's a slam dunk, Charlie. I've already informed the Homicide Assessment Team that this is going to you. Find the perp, he'll lead us to this woman and the other one he grabbed. I could train a monkey to do it. I want a full report at 0900.' He went back to his car, his Mercedes-AMG umbrella keeping him dry.

He accelerated through a rain puddle as he drove away and splashed the uniform protecting the cordon. The constable looked at Charlie as if it was his fault.

'The wally with the brolly, mark two,' Charlie murmured.

Net curtains twitched on the other side of the street. They

wouldn't have to watch the breakfast news this morning, it was happening right outside their windows.

Jack, the crime-scene manager, nodded a greeting. He held up the blue and white cordon tape and Charlie ducked under.

CS techs in blue overalls were crouched down next to a burgundy Lexus, pointing at something in the footwell. A photographer was using a flash to take pictures of the left front wheel.

'You look like you've had a night on the town,' Jack said.

'I haven't had a good night on the town since Noah built his first boat. What have you got?'

'The Lexus has a broken tie rod. Would have been impossible to steer. I imagine that's why she stopped.'

'How did that happen?'

'Hitting the kerb at speed would have done it.'

'Got anything promising?'

'Not yet. Rain doesn't help. Got some personal effects from inside the car, not much else. Apparently, he grabbed her about there.' Three of his techs were on their hands and knees, checking the wet bitumen for fibres. 'I'll let you know if we find anything.'

'Is my new DS here yet?'

A shake of the head. 'Haven't seen him.' Jack walked away.

Charlie went over to Hoeness, a DS from the local borough CID, shook hands. 'Do we know who she is?' he asked.

Hoeness checked his notebook. 'Sarah Howlett. Twenty-three years old, blonde hair, five foot seven, last seen wearing a grey Adidas tracksuit and pink Converse trainers. We've spoken to her husband. Apparently they had a domestic in the early hours of the morning and she stormed out, took the car. They live about a mile from here.'

'Did she let him know the car had broken down?'

He shook his head. 'The AA logged a call requesting assistance at 1.13 this morning. When they got here, the car was unattended.'

'Was it them that called us?'

37

'There was an eyewitness. No, really, there was.'

'Someone saw this?'

'Trouble is, he's a bit pissed. On his way home from a big night out.'

'Where is he?'

'In the patrol car over there. There's two uniforms trying to get him sobered up.'

Charlie got into the car, out of the rain. The sergeant was in the front and a constable was in the back; she kept nudging their witness to keep him awake. The atmosphere in the car was pungent with the smell of booze and wet clothes.

Charlie introduced himself to the uniforms. 'This is Mick,' the sergeant said to him, nodding at the bearded young man in the back seat. 'He's been out celebrating with his mates. He's at university. It was his birthday yesterday and he's still pretty happy about it.'

'That's lovely, that is. Happy birthday, Mick. How old are you?'

'Twenty-two.'

'Great age. Old enough to drink, young enough that your liver still works. What are you studying at university?'

'Anthro . . . anthrop . . .' There was a long pause.

Charlie got tired of waiting. 'Anthropology?'

Mick nodded.

'Had a few, have you?'

'A couple.'

'Where have you been tonight?'

'No idea.'

'Where's your mates?'

'No idea.'

'Do you know where you are?'

'I'm in a police car.'

'Where is the police car?'

'No idea.' Mick's chin sagged onto his chest.

'Should you wait until he's sobered up?' the constable said.

38

'No, he won't remember anything then. I'm speaking from bitter experience.' Charlie shook Mick's knee. 'Tell us about the girl.'

'The girl.'

'The girl you saw getting abducted.'

'Ah.'

'Try and remember, Mick. This is important.'

Mick's face twisted into a grimace of concentration. 'Her car was . . .' He took a breath.

'It was broken down.'

A nod. 'I think . . . I think she was calling someone.'

'She was on the phone?'

Another nod.

'In the car?'

'No, no, no, no, no.' A shake of the head.

'Where then?'

'She got out.'

'All right, then what happened?'

'There was a van. A man came and grabbed her.'

'You saw all this?'

'Clear as . . . clear as . . .'

'Day.'

'That's the one.' He started to snore. The constable slapped him, none too gently, and he woke up, looking around as if nothing had happened. 'What?'

'Mick, try and concentrate.'

'I will.'

'Now, this man, did you see his face?'

'He had a mask on.'

'What kind of mask? Like a Donald Trump mask? A Kabuki mask, what?'

'What's Kabuki?'

'It doesn't matter. What kind of mask was it?'

'I know what you mean now. Kabuki. It's that Japanese opera thing.'

'Mick, forget about Japanese opera. Concentrate. What sort of mask was it?'

'It was like a mask that robbers wear.'

'A ski mask? Right. What did you do?'

'I tried to stop him.'

'Then what happened?'

'I don't remember. I might have fallen asleep. When I woke up, they were gone. There was some policemen and this nice fella who said he'd fix my car. But I don't have a car.'

'How did you get that cut on your head?'

Mick put a hand to his forehead and stared at the blood. 'I'm bleeding,' he said.

'There's an ambulance waiting over there, they'll take a look at that,' the sergeant said to him.

'Is there anything you can remember about the van?' Charlie asked. And then he added, when Mick seemed puzzled, 'The one he put the girl in.'

'It was white.'

'Anything more than that?'

Another shake of the head.

'Who called it in?' Charlie said to the sergeant.

'A car came past at . . .' he checked his notebook, '1.20. He saw the Lexus with its door wide open and Mick here lying on the road in front of it. He thought it was a hit-and-run and called 999. The AA came along a couple of minutes later. By then Mick was awake and shouting about how the girl had been grabbed.'

'I did,' Mick said.

'How did he get the cut on the head?'

'Maybe the kidnapper whacked him.'

'I'll get one of the crime-scene team to come over. If our perp hit him, there might be evidence. When they're done, take him over to the ambulance, and make sure he doesn't go anywhere; one of my team will be over to the hospital to interview him again when he sobers up. Are you all right with that, Mick?'

Mick was snoring again.

Charlie went to look for Jack. He was standing by the Lexus and signalled for Charlie to come over. The interior light was on; he pointed out the car keys, still in the ignition, a pink teddy bear on the key ring. Then he pointed out the child's car seat in the back.

'Some kid's going to be missing his mother.'

'Nice car. Find anything?'

'A recyclable coffee cup with the name of a wildlife park, a child's sip cup and a parking ticket from last week.'

'What about her phone?'

Jack handed him an iPhone in a pink case with a decal of a Moschino teddy bear. Charlie put on a pair of forensic gloves and turned it on. There was no PIN.

'Happy days,' he said and took out his Nokia, called the skipper.

'Now then.'

'Morning, skip.'

'It's the middle of the night.'

'It's half past five. You should be out jogging.'

'I'm taking selfies to leave on the fridge so my wife and kids remember what I look like.'

'Stop your moaning and get a pen.' Charlie read him the number from the phone. 'I want you to call Parm, get her into the office right now. I want full telephony, soon as.'

'Good as done,' the skipper said. He read back the number and hung up.

Charlie checked through the phone. The last call had been at 1.13 a.m. An 0800 number. That would have to be the AA. Jack held out a Faraday bag and Charlie dropped the phone in. 'I'll send it straight over,' Jack said.

Well, Charlie thought, he'd filled his boots now, no mistake, thanks to the DCI. Two women's lives in his hands.

He looked up and saw Grey signing in with the uniform on the other side of the cordon. 'Where have you been?'

'I was asleep,' Grey said, like that was some excuse, as if sleep was owed to anyone in his squad. 'Another one, guv?'

'The DCI says it is. Young woman in a car, breaks down, some geezer in a white van stops and snatches her.'

'Anything?'

'There's an eyewitness in the ambulance over there, I don't know how much use he's going to be. Get one of the team down here, stick with him until he's sobered up, get a statement out of him. I'll have the skipper sort the CCTV, and we'll need a door-to-door right along that side of the common. Maybe someone else saw something.'

'What about you, guv?'

'I'm going to have a chat with her husband.'

'Want me to ride along?'

'Might as well. According to the DCI, this is a gimme, so we better get it done quick smart.'

He went back to his car, looked up at the CCTV camera. It had a grandstand view of the abduction; a Hollywood director couldn't have positioned it better. Sod's law said it wasn't working.

CHAPTER ELEVEN

She heard the grinding of metal on metal, someone shouting. It was so loud it hurt. She wanted to cover her ears, but she couldn't move. Finally, it stopped. She heard beeping, knew that sound, the dial pad on a mobile phone. Something familiar, at last.

Everything coming to her through a fog.

She tried to speak, but her tongue seemed too large for her mouth. She couldn't make sense of anything. Perhaps she was dreaming.

She heard footsteps crunching on gravel, saw the glow of a cigarette. She tried to call out to them, please, I'm here, come and help me.

Please.

Once you wouldn't have brought your granny down here, but these days the houses had been bought up by would-be-if-they-could-be's spending their bonuses putting ballrooms in their basements, giving all their readies to burly blokes from Cracow and Lodz. Half the houses in the street had a skip parked out the front and scaffolding on the pavement. The terraces had all been built at the turn of the century from London stock brick. There was an odd couple at the end of one of the rows, three-storey affairs with French windows, probably built back in the fifties to plug the gaps after the Blitz.

When Charlie and DS Grey arrived, there was a shouting match going on; some bloke had got through the cordon and was yelling up at the window of one of the houses, while two uniforms tried to steer him in the other direction. They were going about it softly, softly.

He went up to them and showed them his warrant card. 'Problem, is there?'

'Sorry, sir,' one of the uniforms said. 'He claims to be the missing woman's father.'

The man looked to be in his fifties, lots of grey hair and self-importance. He reminded Charlie of Nigel Farage, so he was immediately prepared to dislike him, but then he thought, no, steady on, he might be a nice bloke underneath all that grey cardigan and outrage.

He turned around and stared at Charlie. 'Who the fuck are you?'

Charlie showed him his ID. 'Detective Inspector Charlie George, Major Incident Team. What's going on?'

'I should never have let her marry that bastard.'

Charlie looked over his shoulder, where the camera crews were jostling each other to capture it all for the entertainment of Greater London. 'Perhaps you could come and sit in the car over here while we sort this out.'

'Are you in charge of the investigation?'

'Yes, sir, I am.'

'Then what are you doing here? My little girl's missing, why aren't you out looking for her?'

'Sir, everything possible is being done. But this doesn't help.'

The man pointed a finger back at the house. 'That bastard knows something, I know he does.'

'You mean Mr Howlett?'

'What was my Sarah doing out on her own at one in the morning?'

'Do you have evidence implicating your son-in-law in Sarah's disappearance?'

'Yes, I do. He's a cunt.'

'I'm afraid that doesn't constitute hard evidence.'

The look on his face, Charlie thought. He's out of control, there's saliva on his chin. We need to get him sorted before this goes any further. 'What's your name, sir?'

'Jones. Tony Jones. All right?'

'Thank you, Mr Jones. Perhaps you could wait in the patrol car. We can talk things over after I've done here.'

Charlie nodded to the two constables and they led Jones over to the X5. Well, that was a bright start.

The Howletts' nanny let them in, a small child on her hip. She looked startled, dowdy and very young. Dealing with all this was not in her contract from the agency, he didn't suppose.

The first thing he noticed was that the house smelled like a garden. There were flowers everywhere; he breathed in a heady scent of jasmine and fresh-cut roses. Now that's nice, he thought, a bit of class. Any chav can have a ninety-squillion-inch plasma TV, but fresh flowers in the house say something about a person. There was a yoga mat in the living room, a vintage movie poster of Bette Davis smoking a cigarette in the hall.

It made him want a fag.

He clocked the sash windows, high ceilings, timber floors. The fireplace looked original. Glass doors led onto a patio; proper *Ideal Home* stuff, this. The TV was on in the living room. What was it with children's TV presenters? Charlie thought. They all acted like they were on bugle; he could see it now, a line up each nostril in make-up then rush onto the set and start raving about the song Jemima wanted to sing and the letter Q.

The nanny led them through to the kitchen. For a boy who'd grown up in Walthamstow, the LED downlights and German appliances were intimidating. Daniel Howlett was leaning on the granite worktop, the sleeves of his striped business shirt rolled up, a Rolex the size of a soup plate on his wrist. He was good-looking in that male model sort of way that made you want to smack him with something substantially heavy. Nothing effeminate about him, though; he looked like the sort of bloke who could handle himself.

'Christ, more cops,' he said as they walked in. 'What are you doing? She isn't here. Did you come to check under the bed?'

'Mr Howlett, I'm DI Charlie George, I'm heading the investigation into your wife's abduction. This is DS Grey. Do you mind if we ask you a few questions?'

'How many more times? I've already been through all this with the rest of your lot.'

'They were probably local borough detectives. I've taken over the investigation.'

'What is it now? You want to go through her knicker drawer?'

'Mind if we sit down?' Charlie perched himself on one of the stools on the other side of the breakfast bar.

Daniel Howlett took a sip from a mug of coffee. The child started crying and he gave the nanny a sharp look. 'Can we get him out of here?' he said.

The help disappeared into another room. Daniel sighed, and rubbed his face with his hands. 'You want coffee, tea? We've got some lapsang souchong somewhere. Or you can have some of this. Rwanda Buliza. Only one supplier in the whole of London. It's from the Rulindo district in northern Rwanda. Don't think we have any instant.'

'I don't drink instant, Mr Howlett. I have my own blend, a company makes it for me; they're from the Shoreditch district in east London. But I'm fine. By the way, I met your father-in-law outside.'

Daniel gave him a look; he didn't like people talking back at him, clearly. 'Lucky you. Cheeky cockney sparrer, isn't he?'

'That what you call him, is it?'

'I've called him other things, time to time.'

'He thinks you have something to do with Sarah's kidnapping.'

'Of course he does. He tried to implicate me in the death of Michael Jackson and the assassination of JFK. Sarah breaks a nail and he thinks it's my fault.'

'You don't get on?'

'Oh, is it that obvious? The detective who was here before said you found her car near Clapham Common.'

'It was abandoned. We have CCTV images that show her being abducted.'

'Then you should be able to find the man who did this, right? You just read the plates, ring up Swansea and there you are.'

'Can you tell me what happened last night, sir?'

'As I have already told your underlings a hundred times, I got home late from work. Sarah was still up. I suspect she was waiting for me. She was in the mood for a fight.'

'How late is late?'

'I don't know the exact time. Around one.'

'What was the fight about?'

'The usual.'

'What's the usual?'

'Are you married, Inspector?'

Charlie shook his head. Daniel shrugged his shoulders: *Well, what's the point of talking to you, then?*

'Enlighten me.'

'I may have accused her of not being a very good mother.'

'That seems a bit harsh.'

'Does it? I come home, and she's drunk a whole bottle of wine. With my son asleep upstairs. She's supposed to be responsible for him.'

'Do you normally get home late?'

'I work long hours. This place doesn't pay for itself; it's rather expensive, even for London.'

'And you were at work until one o'clock?'

'No, I was at work until eight. Then I joined some of my colleagues for a drink at the Arbitrager. Do you know it? It's near Liverpool Street.'

'They'll verify that, will they?'

'I've given their names to the other detective.'

'What happened after you fought?'

'In her characteristically restrained way, she threw a glass of

47

wine at me, then grabbed her car keys and ran out of the house. She got in the car and drove off.'

'Did you try to stop her?'

Daniel pulled up his shirt and showed them the bruises on his ribs. 'She almost ran me over. As I told your other drone, she's done this before. She drives away to make a dramatic point, I suppose, and then comes home when she's cooled off. Frankly, I'm sick of all the drama.'

'When were you aware that she was missing?'

'The front door bell rang at God knows what time, and there's two cops on my doorstep breaking the happy news.'

'And what were you doing?'

'Well, I was asleep.'

'You weren't worried about her?'

'I needed some sleep, I had an important meeting today. A meeting that I shall have to cancel, by the looks of things.'

'You were here from the time she left until the local police alerted you to what had happened?'

'We have a young son, as you saw for yourself when you came in. Where else would I be?'

'Do you have any reason to think this was not a crime of opportunity?'

'What does that mean?'

'Has she talked to you about anything that may have alarmed her recently? Has she received any threats? Has anyone been following her?'

'Don't be ridiculous.'

Charlie resisted the urge to reach across the granite breakfast bar and tip Howlett's specially sourced Rwanda Buliza over his perfect hair.

He took a deep breath instead. 'Well, thanks for your time. DC Sanderson is on his way. He's our family liaison officer; he'll keep you up to date with the investigation.'

'What do you mean, he's on his way? You mean he's coming here? Coming here to do what?'

'He can answer any questions you have, assist in every way possible. Being the victim of serious crime is a very stressful experience.'

'No, thanks.'

'Sir?'

'I don't need a babysitter. If I do, I'll ring the agency. I'd rather just be left alone, all the same to you.'

Charlie stood up. 'As you wish.' He turned to go, but then, as an afterthought: 'By the way, does your wife have any other phones?'

'She's got an iPhone. I think she took it with her last night. I tried calling it, but it's switched off.'

'Yes. We have that one in our possession already.'

'Good. Can I have it back, then?'

'It's still undergoing forensic investigation. It will be returned in due course. That was her only phone?'

'Yes, why?'

'Does she have a laptop?'

'What the hell do you need that for?'

'It's routine.'

'Detective, if I understand you correctly, there's some nutjob out there who's grabbed her out of her car, and you have the whole thing on CCTV. Why the hell would you need to check her computer?'

'Is it a problem?' Charlie said, and smiled.

Howlett put down his coffee mug and went into a small room off the hallway. Charlie saw him pulling leads out of the wall. He came back in carrying a MacBook and slammed it down in front of him.

'Knock yourself out.'

'Could we have your laptop as well, sir?'

'What?'

'As I said. Routine.'

'No, you may not have my computer, or anything else belonging to me. I do not see what possible assistance my digital

49

footprint can be with all of this. Do I need my solicitor present for these conversations?'

'That is entirely up to you, Mr Howlett. Do you think you do?'

'I know how you people work.'

'And how is that?'

Daniel tried to stare him out. Oh, I can do this all day, Charlie thought.

'Just find the man who took my wife. All right?'

'One more thing, Mr Howlett. How long has your nanny worked for you?'

'What has Ines got to do with this?'

'I'd like to talk to her for a few minutes, if that's all right.'

'Is it really necessary?'

Charlie smiled. When Daniel realised he wasn't going to back down, he went to the door. 'Ines! Ines, can you come in here a moment, please?' She came in, still holding the child in her arms. 'These men want to ask you some questions.'

She was like a rabbit caught in the headlights. She stood by the door, looked like she was ready to rush out again at the slightest sense of alarm.

'This is Ines. Our son's name is Oliver,' Daniel said.

'Hello, Oliver,' Charlie said.

'Don't expect a reply,' Daniel said. 'He's got global developmental delay. If we're lucky, he may be able to say "Mummy" by the time he's eighty-five.'

'I'm sorry,' Grey said.

'Why should you be sorry?'

'My nephew was diagnosed with it. That's very hard.'

'Thanks.'

'I'd like to talk to Ines on her own, if that's all right,' Charlie said.

'Seriously?'

'Just need a couple of minutes.'

'Her English is rubbish,' Daniel said, and Charlie saw her flinch.

'I'm from Walthamstow, so I'm not exactly fluent myself,' he said.

Daniel sighed, and Charlie noted the look that passed between him and Ines. Then he got up and walked out, shutting the door behind him.

Charlie leaned in. 'Ines, is it? My name's Detective Inspector George. I'm in charge of the team looking into the disappearance of Mrs Howlett last night.'

Ines looked embarrassed and frightened in equal amounts. She stared at the tiles, still bouncing the child on her hip. He took her through several routine questions, but she didn't have a lot to add to what he already knew.

She was reticent about the state of the Howletts' marriage; he supposed she was worried about being disloyal to her employers.

Or it might be something else.

'Señora Howlett is very sad lady. Always cry.'

'Do you think she was depressed?'

'Maybe. I don't know.'

'When was the last time you saw her?'

'Saturday night. I leave here normal time.'

'She seemed fine then?'

Ines nodded.

'You didn't see her yesterday?'

'Is my day off.'

'When did you find out about Mrs Howlett's disappearance?'

'This morning. Señor Howlett ring, ask me to come early, say there has been terrible thing happen.'

Daniel came back into the room. 'Everything all right? Got a full confession out of her?'

'You know, Mr Howlett, we're all on the same side here.'

'Then why doesn't it feel like that?'

Charlie stood up. 'One of my detectives will drop by later today and get your statement, if that's all right.'

'I'm sure you'll have found her by then.'

51

As they were leaving, Grey nodded at some shards of glass in the corner of the kitchen; a tea towel with wine stains on it had been thrown in the sink. It looked staged.

'By the way, has your wife any medical conditions?'

'You mean is she crazy? All women are crazy.'

'That's not what I meant.'

'She has PMT. But we've never had to call an ambulance for it.'

'Thanks, Mr Howlett. I'll be in touch. If you need anything, don't hesitate to call.' Charlie gave him his card.

'You're going to keep him away from me, right?'

'Your father-in-law?'

'I swear to God, you'll be investigating another crime if he tries to set foot in this house.'

'It's natural that he's worried about his daughter,' Charlie said, and he and Grey let themselves out.

The sun was up when they left the house. Looked like it was going to be another hot day. As they walked back to their car, Charlie heard the whirr and click of cameras, a TV cameraman running along the footpath behind them getting footage.

'So, what's global developmental delay?' he said to Grey.

'It's an umbrella term. In my nephew's case, the poor little bugger wasn't actually delayed, he was intellectually disabled. Took my brother years to work that out.'

'How old is he now?'

'Ten.'

'What do you make of Howlett's attitude about it?'

'I think he's just embarrassed by him. Don't you?'

One of the constables got out of the patrol car. 'All right?' Charlie said.

'He's a bit worked up. Had to give him some first aid.'

Charlie slipped into the back seat next to Tony Jones. He was breathing into a brown paper bag. 'What did that mongrel say?' he gasped.

'His wife is missing, sir. He's very upset.'

'Upset, my arse. He doesn't give a shit, that bastard.'

'Mr Jones, when did you find out your daughter had been abducted?'

'I was having breakfast, the telly was on. Can you believe it? My little girl goes missing and he doesn't even ring and tell me.'

'Perhaps he wasn't thinking straight. I'm sorry you had to find out this way.'

'Some lowlife has my little girl. Why are we sitting here? Why aren't you out doing something?'

'Where do you live, Mr Jones?'

'Just outside Chelmsford, don't I?'

'So how did you get here?'

'My car's over there.'

'That's a long way.'

'Just over the hour with a bit of low flying.'

'Are you going to be all right to get home?'

'Go home? While my little girl's out there somewhere? You got to be joking. I'll get a hotel or something.'

'What about Mrs Jones?'

'Ain't no Mrs Jones. She left us a long time ago, her. We were all fine till Sar married that douchebag in there.'

'Have you got family you can call?'

'I'm all right. I don't need anyone fussing. What I need is for you to find my daughter!'

'There's a team of thirty detectives working on your daughter's case, Mr Jones. I assure you everything that can be done is being done.'

'What did he tell you? Why wasn't she home last night?'

'He said that he and Sarah had an argument.'

'Another one! They're always fighting, those two. I don't know what she ever saw in him. I warned her, didn't I?'

'Do you know what they fight about?'

'Probably the fact that he can't keep it in his trousers. I kept telling her she should come home, get away from him. She

53

should have listened. If something's happened to her, I'll never forgive myself.' He breathed into the bag again. His hands were shaking. 'How come he knew before I did?'

'He is her husband,' Charlie said.

'I'm her father. Don't that count for anything?'

'There are protocols,' Charlie said. 'He's next of kin.'

'That busy little prick is no kin of hers. You know what he does for a living? Stock market. Seven figures a year for screwing retirees out of their pension funds. Not only morally questionable, but he's a right sexual deviant too.'

Interesting, Charlie thought. 'In what way deviant?'

'She told me, he asks her to do things.'

'What sort of things?'

'Stuff,' Tony said, and suddenly looked as if he wished he hadn't said anything. 'That poor kid in there. Having to grow up with him as a father.'

'Mr Jones, when was the last time you saw your daughter?'

'Sunday. She brings little Ollie up to see me every couple of weeks.'

'You never come down here?'

'He doesn't like it. We've never got on.'

'I see. What do you do, Mr Jones?'

'I'm a retired businessman.'

'Look, I don't think it's a good idea for you to stay in London. How about I get one of my detectives to take you home? You're not in any condition to drive. I'll liaise with him, keep you updated on our progress throughout the day. Okay?'

Tony nodded. The bag inflated and then sagged.

'Have you got family who can come and stay with you?'

'I'll be all right.'

Charlie got out, rang the skipper, told him to get Sanderson to come down. He was good at doing the ministering angel bit, was Sanderson, had done all his FLO training. It could be useful; he might be able to get some background on Tony Jones and let him dish the dirt on Howlett as well.

There was something not quite right here.

Danny Howlett watched Charlie get into his car. Still a crowd of reporters down there. Hadn't they got better things to do? Ines came in, carrying Ollie on her hip. 'What did you tell them?' Danny said.

'Nothing, Señor Howlett. I tell them you are good man.'

'Did they ask about . . . the visitors we entertain sometimes?'

She shook her head.

'Sure about that?'

'I not want to get you in trouble.'

'How can you get me in trouble? I haven't done anything wrong. Do you think I've done something wrong?'

Ines looked scared.

'Our friends are our private affair. They have nothing to do with my wife's disappearance.'

He felt a vibration in his jacket pocket. He took out the phone, stared at the screen. His hands were shaking, for God's sake. 'I'll have to take this.'

He went upstairs to his study, shut the door.

'I can't right now,' he said into the phone.

He stared at the calendar on the wall next to his desk. Sarah had ordered it, one of those online companies that let you design them yourself with your own little family snaps. She'd pinned it up there at Christmas, when she was still trying to be reasonable, and not a crazy bitch.

'I said, I can't. It's impossible. You'll have to wait until tonight.'

He hung up. The phone immediately started buzzing again. He threw it across the room in a fit of anger. Christ, Danny, get a grip. He scrabbled for it on the carpet, stared at the screen. Please don't be broken, please, please. What are you doing? The last thing you need now is to break the freaking thing.

He just needed time to think.

Ollie was having one of his episodes downstairs. For God's sake. Shut up. *Shut up.*

He closed the door, scrolled through his music files on his iPod, found some jazz, Tom Harrell's *Art of Rhythm*. He sat down, closed his eyes, took some deep breaths. Those days the market went crazy, this was what he did, it was why he was so good at his job; when everyone was screaming into their phones and punching their desks, he always knew to take a step back, give himself a moment to think things through.

Not the end of the world, Danny boy. Have to roll with the punches is all.

His iPhone rang. It was Kate. He'd better take it. 'Hi, sis.'

'Danny, how are you doing? I just heard the news. You poor man.'

'I'm all right.'

'I'm getting the train down. I don't care what you say, you can't go through this on your own.'

'Do *not* do that. All right? I'm fine. Last thing I need is you having hysterics all over the place.'

'I won't have hysterics. You can't be alone through all this. I'm your *sister.*'

'You will have hysterics. I'll end up having to look after you while you cry and carry on. I'm calm, I'm fine. I don't need anyone here.'

What she wants, he thought, is to be on the television, have the press take photographs of her coming in and out of the police cordon, be the centre of attention, as always.

'But I worry about you being on your own at a time like this. What about Oliver?'

'Ines is taking care of Oliver.'

There was a long silence. 'On the news it said it was the same man who took that other woman.'

'Apparently.'

'You know if there's anything I can do—'

He hung up.

He went to the window and looked down into the street. He thought about the trip he and Sarah had taken to South Africa, not long after they were married. They'd gone to the Kruger, and once, out by a waterhole, they saw some vultures and hyenas fighting over the carcass of a buffalo, flapping and squabbling over the bits of entrail. Not much different to that lot down there. What do you call more than one journalist? A flock? A rabble?

Couldn't go anywhere while they were all camped outside. So what the hell was he going to do?

CHAPTER TWELVE

Charlie took the tiny steel elevator to the third floor of the Essex Road station.

Not yet seven o'clock and his squad were already at their desks. They still had actions from the first investigation; now their workloads would be effectively doubled. They all knew they weren't going to be seeing much of their beds until this was sorted.

When he'd started working Major Crime, there had been twenty-six teams covering the London area; now there were eighteen and about half the number of detectives. Meanwhile, Charlie and his team were supposed to catch a growing population of villains. It was like expecting Arsenal to win the Champions League with a five-a-side team.

Evie Myers' face smiled out at him from the whiteboard, alongside the crime-scene photographs: an abandoned Vauxhall Corsa, the driver's door yawning open.

Charlie headed for the long conference table at the end of the room, threw his jacket and his policy book on one of the chairs and tossed his takeaway coffee cup in the bin. The team got up from their desks and gathered around in a rough half-circle so he could bring them up to speed.

'As you all know by now, there's been another abduction. The same MO, so it's landed in our in-tray. We have been asked to run the two investigations concurrently.'

He waited for the moans. He was surprised that there weren't more.

'Our victim's name is Sarah Howlett. She's married, twenty-three years old, she has a son aged four. She is married to Daniel Howlett, an investment banker with Dillon and Rowe, in the City. I've interviewed him at his home in Clapham; he told me that he and Sarah had a domestic last night and she left the house in an agitated state in their Lexus.'

'What was the row about?' James said.

'He said he'd been drinking with friends after work, got in about one. He said she was drunk when he got home, and he accused her of being a bad mother.'

'That's pretty rich,' one of his DCs Lubanski said, 'given that he'd been out drinking all night.'

'If that's where he was,' her partner, McCullough, added.

'Well, we can soon check that.' Charlie looked at the skipper, who noted it down to be actioned.

'That's pretty late to still be rowing,' James said.

'It's pretty late to be getting home from work.'

'Unless you're a cop.'

'What's he like?' Lubanski asked Charlie.

'Not exactly the devastated spouse. I think he sees his wife's disappearance as more of an inconvenience than a personal tragedy.'

'Did he give us much?'

'To be honest, I was expecting a little more cooperation. He declined the offer of family liaison; he also refused to surrender his laptop.'

'Is he a suspect?'

'Definitely.'

'For the Evie Myers investigation as well?' someone asked.

'I have found no connection between Howlett and the abduction of Evie Myers. But the DCI has ruled that the two crimes are linked, so they both now form part of Operation Loxley.' He let that sink in.

DC Singh raised a finger. 'So, guv. What did Howlett do when his wife didn't come home?'

'He went to bed.'

'He wasn't worried about her?'

'He said she'd done this sort of thing before and he's sick of all the drama – his words.'

'That sounds a bit cold.'

'Well, he's an investment banker,' Charlie said. 'There's also a nanny, who looks after the little boy.'

'What's her name?' James said.

'Ines Goncalvez, Spanish, early twenties. They employed her through an agency.'

'Let's get rid of the elephant in the room,' Dawson said. 'Any chance Howlett has been playing hide the sausage with the hired help?'

'Unlikely. She looks to be more the studious type than a Penelope Cruz.'

'Did she hear the fight between the Howletts?'

Charlie shook his head. 'She's not live-in, goes home about six every night, so she only found out what had happened when Daniel Howlett called her this morning. Didn't get much out of her, to be honest. We'll need a translator when we get a proper statement. Now for the good news.' He pulled up a file on his iPad, and the grainy images came to life on the electronic whiteboard behind him. 'Luckily for us, we have CCTV of the abduction. There was a camera about a hundred yards away outside a wine bar, angled towards the road. It's not Cineworld, but you can pretty much make out the whole thing.'

The images were grainy and indistinct. As the Lexus pulled into the kerb, the time stamp on the right-hand corner of the screen showed 01:11. Sarah Howlett did not get out of the car until 01:15.

'What's she doing?' Dawson said.

'Looks like she's waiting for someone,' James replied.

'She called the AA before she got out of the car,' Charlie said. At 01:17 she disappeared off the screen.

'Now where she's gone?'

'Maybe she needed to pee,' Lubanski said.

60

She reappeared at 01:19:23. Thirty-three seconds later, a white van came into view. It slowed down, disappeared off the screen for several seconds, then reversed back towards the Lexus. A tall figure in a ski mask jumped out of the driver's side. Sarah didn't move.

The driver grabbed her and pulled her towards the van.

'What is he holding?' James said.

'Could be chloroform,' Lubanski said.

'Takes forever to work, that does,' the skipper said.

'How do you know?'

'I've tried it on the kids.'

'The skipper's right,' Singh said. 'People don't just pass out straight away, like they do in those old movies. Takes a couple of minutes.'

'She could have fainted out of fear,' James said.

They watched as Sarah was bundled inside the back of the van. As it pulled away, Mick stumbled into view. He tried to grab the handle on the passenger door, tripped on the kerb and face-planted on the road.

'Ouch,' someone said.

'That's our eyewitness,' Charlie said. 'Believe me, he didn't feel a thing.'

'Does this clown have a name?' Dawson asked him.

'Michael Donnelly, or Mick as he prefers to be called; he's a student at Middlesex University. His heart's in the right place – as you can see, he did try to intervene. However, he was severely intoxicated.'

'Did he give a statement?'

'I interviewed Mr Donnelly briefly at the crime scene. He seemed convinced that he saw Sarah Howlett making a phone call before the van pulled up.'

'Could have been checking with the AA?'

'The thing is, we found her iPhone in her car. But from that CCTV footage, she didn't get back in the car. So what phone was she using?'

Dawson shrugged. 'You said yourself, young Mr Donnelly were pissed.'

'Intel can tell us a bit more when we've done the telephony. I checked her phone myself this morning at the scene. Her last call was to the AA at 01.13.'

'What about the van? Have we checked the registration?'

'The plates were stolen from South Croydon yesterday afternoon.' Charlie picked up his iPad, brought up a map of the area around the crime scene on the whiteboard. 'First job is to track every possible access and egress, pick it up on any ANPR cameras in the area within the time frame.' Charlie pointed to his two most senior DCs. 'Wes, Rupe, get on to that as soon as the meeting's finished.'

He pulled several images of the van from the CCTV and enlarged them.

'Looks like a Ford Transit. And see, there's damage to the front right bumper and there's no wing mirror on the passenger side, plus the left headlight isn't working. Canvass the area for CCTV inside a half-mile radius. See if we can work out which direction the van went. We may be able to track it from the irregularities, even if they changed the plates again.'

James scribbled a note in his book.

'Let's get hold of that friend of yours at Ford, Wes, see if he can narrow it down to model and year. Long shot, but we'll see what he can tell us.' Charlie went back to the crime-scene map. 'We also need to do a house-to-house. Every one of these places along this road here, they look right over the common; someone might have seen something. And I mean every one of them. If they're out, go back again, keep going until we've talked to everyone. Skipper, can you action that?'

'Done,' Dawson said.

'Where are we on the Evie Myers investigation?'

'We found her phone,' he said. 'Some homeless bloke was using it. Reckoned he found it ditched in a skip. The uniforms say he was playing Candy Crush when they picked him up.'

'Do we know where he found it?'

'Wandsworth Common. Near where she was taken.'

'That doesn't help. How are we doing on local sex offenders?'

'Seven still on the list that we haven't yet eliminated. One of them owns a white Ford Transit. We've sighted it. It doesn't have the dent on the right front like that one.'

'Are we sure this is the same perp?' James said.

'Both abductions involve young women whose cars broke down beside the road. Both were kidnapped by a masked individual in a white van and both seem to be crimes of opportunity.'

'Why has he taken another girl so soon after he took the first one?' Singh said.

'We won't know that until we find him.'

'Malik called in,' Dawson said. 'The Sarah Howlett abduction has been all over the morning news. Evie's parents have seen it; he doesn't know what to tell them.'

'Well, if the kidnapper's out hunting again already, it doesn't sound like good news. So best to say nothing.'

'Can we have another look at that CCTV?' James said.

Charlie brought it up again on the screen.

'Why didn't she ring her husband instead of the AA?' Singh asked.

'They'd had a big row,' James said. 'Would you?'

'I'm always having rows with my missus,' Dawson said. 'I'd still ring her and ask her if we needed milk on my way home. Rowing, it's part of being married.'

'Thanks for that insight and making me glad I'm still single,' Charlie said. 'Could be she rang him and he didn't pick up. Telephony will tell us about that. Anything else? No? All right, the skipper will action your jobs for the day. Don't make any plans to go to the ballet tonight; we'll be putting in a few hours on this one. Questions?'

There weren't any. As Charlie watched his team go back to their desks, he wondered what Evie Myers and Sarah Howlett were doing right now; whether either of them was still holding on.

As the meeting broke up, Charlie saw the DCI standing in the doorway, and he didn't look best pleased. How long had he been there? He crept around the place like the Ghost of Christmas Past; Charlie hadn't even heard his chains rattle this time.

The DCI followed him into his office.

'Sir?'

'You didn't sound very enthusiastic, Charlie,' he said.

'I thought I maintained a positive but professional demeanour.'

'We've been chasing dead ends the last forty-eight hours. This latest development is a heaven-sent opportunity.'

'I don't know that heaven-sent is the word I would have used.'

'We have CCTV of the crime being committed.'

'It's a long way away, the perpetrator is wearing a ski mask and he's using stolen plates.'

'We've got two women snatched off the street right in the middle of London. We need a result.'

'I'm sure they'd like one as well,' Charlie said.

'I'm relying on you, Charlie,' the DCI said, and somehow he made it sound like a threat. He turned for the door, then turned back again, as if he'd had an afterthought. 'How's your new DS working out?'

'Too early to say, really.'

'I knew his father. Couple of years above me at school.'

'Which school was that, sir?'

'St Michael's. In Oxford. Heard of it, have you?'

'I've heard of St Michael. He's Prince of the Heavenly Host.' He almost added, *a bit like you, sir*, but stopped himself.

'I used to be President of the Old Boys' Association.'

'I didn't realise you knew Grey's family.'

'You don't have to know everything,' the DCI said as he walked out. 'Keep me up to date on his progress.'

Great, Charlie thought. Multiple abductions and now nepotism: what a great start to the week.

CHAPTER THIRTEEN

Dawson had taken over the important business of organising coffee and muffins. Lubanski and McCullough were staring at CCTV files, drinking endless cups of coffee to keep themselves awake. Grey was typing up Michael Donnelly's statement; their eyewitness had been able to remember much less sober than he had when he was drunk, which Charlie didn't find surprising. A pathologist had tried to explain to him once about the effects of alcohol consumption on the brain, and why people had blackouts after a big night. It was something to do with transfer encoding from short-term to long-term memory.

Most of the team were out following up the actions thrown out by the HOLMES system and the morning's briefing: interviewing Daniel Howlett's family and work colleagues, gathering CCTV, finishing off the house-to-house near the common.

Charlie put on his jacket and came out of his office. 'Get the car keys,' he said to Grey.

'Where are we headed?'

'I want to talk to Sarah Howlett's sister myself. She lives on the Fenchurch Street line somewhere.' He checked her file on the computer. 'Romford,' he said. 'I had an uncle who owned a boozer in Romford. He burned it down for the insurance.'

He felt Grey staring at him as they went down in the lift. He wondered what was on his mind.

'Been hearing a lot about this DC Lovejoy,' the DS said finally. So that was what was bothering him. Been listening to too much canteen gossip in his first week.

65

Charlie nodded and didn't say anything.

'She made quite an impression in her first couple of months in the squad. Hope I can emulate her.'

'You wouldn't want to emulate her too closely. She got herself quite badly injured.'

'Is she still on sick leave?'

'Yeah. She's still got a hole in her foot and it won't heal.'

'When is she coming back to work?'

'I don't know. Soon, I hope.'

They left the cool of the building and went out to the car park. July in London. Used to be you could rely on a bit of rain; these days London was hotter than a slave ship. Global warming, he supposed. The Tories blamed it on the EU and immigrants.

With Grey at the wheel, they drove out through Dalston and Hackney, past the Empire, all done up now. He'd gone there to see Jo Brand and Harry Enfield when he was younger.

'Saw *The Revenant* there. You seen it?'

'No, guv.'

'Leonardo DiCaprio gets eaten by a bear.'

'Not a happy ending, then?'

'He doesn't die. The bear eats him, but he doesn't die.'

'That's not very likely.'

'Well, he doesn't eat *all* of him. He just chews bits off. But in the end, he gets revenge.'

'On the bear?'

'On Tom Hardy. It's complicated.'

'What happened to the bear?'

'He stabbed it. I didn't like that bit. Can't stand violence, me, especially to animals. Bear hadn't done anyone any harm.'

'You said it ate him. Leonardo DiCaprio.'

'Well, he deserved it, for making that horrible film with Kate Winslet about the boat.'

'My wife loves that movie,' Grey said.

Charlie brought up the Arsenal website on his phone and

glanced at the homepage, but then switched it off again. He couldn't really concentrate on anything until he found Evie and Sarah. It felt wrong even thinking about anything else. It was different from a homicide; someone could murder Winnie-the-Pooh, and no matter how sad it was, there was nothing you could do about it. But an abduction, you could still change the outcome, right up until someone called the pathologist.

He scrolled through his Google newsfeed, and there it was, four or five down after some crap about Trump and Brexit: a picture of Sarah's car, behind the blue and white police tape and the constables in their high-vis jackets: *Police have confirmed that there has been another abduction. The victim's name is Sarah Howlett. They are appealing for witnesses to come forward.* There was a Twitter handle and a hotline number at the bottom.

His phone rang in his pocket. Wagner, 'The Ride of the Valkyries'. He'd been meaning to change the ringtone to the Arsenal club song, but he was so depressed after the previous season he'd changed his mind.

He looked at the screen. It was Ben. He hoped it was good news.

He picked up. 'How's the Wolf of Wall Street?'

'I'm in pretty good shape for the shape I'm in. I saw you on the news this morning. That woman who went missing. You were standing in the background with your magnifying glass and deerstalker.'

'I'll give you an autograph next time I see you. What's up, Ben?'

'Did you go and see Ma Saturday night?'

'Yeah.'

'How was she?'

'It was late. She was asleep.'

'Did you find her purse?'

'How did you know about the purse?'

'Arlington House left me a message.'

'It would have been nice if you could have gone out there instead of leaving me to do it. I was busy.'

'I'll try and get over there tonight. Did they say how she's been?'

'The same. All downhill from here, Ben, she's headed to la-la land one marble at a time.'

'She's too young for all this. Can't get over it. She should be doing senior aerobics at the church hall and knitting for her grandchildren.'

'Look on the bright side, she's only got one grandson, and he'd rather have a Troy Deeney Watford shirt.'

'Want to ask you a favour, mate. You know Will's arriving today?'

'No, I'd forgotten. Work is mad, mate. I forget what day it is.'

'I know this is a bit sudden, but can he stay with you?'

'Are you serious? I told you, I'm in the middle of a major operation here.'

'You're the only option.'

'Why can't he stay with you?'

'Mate, I've got a nice place.'

'Thanks.'

'You know what I mean. If he makes any kind of mess at your gaff, it won't matter so much, will it? Anyway, I've got a girl staying with me.'

'You've got a what? You moved a woman in?'

'On a temporary basis.'

'Bugger me.'

'I don't want her to get the wrong idea about me. Will's great and everything, but you know, he's a drug addict. It's only for a few days. You're hardly ever home anyway.'

'God's sake, Ben.'

'I'll give him the spare key. It's in the usual place, right?'

'Do I have a choice?'

'Thanks, mate. You're all clear for Mum's party, right?'

'I'll do what I can.'

'Mate, you promised. She's not going to be seventy every day of her life.'

'Last week was our on-call week. I didn't think it would carry over, but this is exceptional circumstances. What can I say? I will do my best.'

'I'm relying on you.'

'Not you as well.'

'What?'

'Never mind. I've got to go, Ben.'

'Right. One other thing. Are you going to watch the Arsenal game on Saturday?'

'Were you listening to a word I said? I got a proper flap on here.'

'It's the first game of the season.'

'It's a friendly.'

'No such thing.'

'It's just another season. You know what's going to happen. This time next month we'll be dreaming about winning the treble, then come January we'll lose to Doncaster Rovers in the Cup, go out to Dynamo Bokwurst in the Europa League and finish sixth in the table. It's better not to dream at all.'

'You're such a miserable bastard, Charlie. See you at Ma's party.' Ben hung up.

'Problems?' Grey said.

'My family are all mad,' Charlie said. 'What are yours like?'

Grey shrugged. 'Fine.'

Fine: Charlie supposed that meant no drug addiction, no domestic violence, no history of paedophile uncles or little brothers throwing themselves under trains. And Grey's old man had gone to the same school as his DCI.

They didn't really have much in common at all.

Her eyes blinked open. She tried to sit up, but she couldn't. Her arms were pinned behind her back, and there was a terrible pain in her wrists. She couldn't feel her hands.

It was so hot. She could feel her heart banging painfully inside her ribs. It took a conscious effort just to breathe. If she stopped concentrating on dragging air into her lungs, she was sure she'd die. She rolled onto her side, trying to relieve the pressure on her wrists.

She stared at the bare metal ribs of the van. She could hear birds, insects. Where was she?

She squirmed into a sitting position, peered at the digital clock on the dashboard: 2:20. She wriggled across the floor, kicked the doors as hard as she could, called out for help. Her voice sounded as if it was coming from a long way away. The effort exhausted her. She gave up.

Minutes drifted into hours, hours were mere glimpses. She dreamed, she woke.

Help me. Someone. *Help me.*

CHAPTER FOURTEEN

They always put betting shops in poor areas, Charlie thought. You weren't supposed to say 'poor' any more, you were supposed to say 'lower socio-economic', but it meant the same thing. Whatever they called it, it meant you had more betting shops, more skateboarders on the pavement, more graffiti, and more people reading the *Daily Mirror* at the bus stop.

There were a few people up and about, most of them walking dogs. At least they looked a bit happy about it, the dogs. You could always rely on a dog to see the bright side.

Sarah's sister lived in a studio flat over a bathroom centre. They were renovating the shop next door and the front looked like a building site. On the plus side, it was walking distance to the railway station. Cheap if not cheerful, and handy for work.

Jackie didn't look anything like her sister. Nature had somehow seen to it that Sarah got the looks, and Jackie had been blessed with the independent streak. She had just got home from her shift, was still wearing the light blue uniform of an NHS staff nurse. According to intel, she worked in the neonatal unit at Queen's Hospital.

'It's not much,' she said when she invited them in. She was right about that; it was cold, the washing machine was next to the refrigerator, and you couldn't get milk or put your delicates on soak without hitting your head on the dormer ceiling. A long way from granite worktops and German kitchen appliances.

But then that was Britain, wasn't it? Fifteen million quid a year for Mesut Özil to sit on the bench at Arsenal and sod all for someone to save your baby's life.

Jackie sat on the end of her single bed in front of a bar heater while Charlie and Grey got the only two chairs. She handed them mugs of tea. Charlie hated tea, but he never said no. People relaxed more if you had a cup of something in front of you.

'Just finished my studying. Now I've got a proper job, I'll set myself up with something better.'

'Your dad doesn't help you out?' Charlie said.

She made a face. 'We don't get on.'

'I'm sorry to hear it. Does he get on with Sarah?'

'Could say that.' She put her face in her hands. 'Sorry.' She took a moment to pull herself together. 'I can't believe this. I keep pinching myself. You are going to find her, aren't you?'

'We're doing everything possible,' Charlie said.

'When was the last time you saw your sister?' Grey said.

A shrug. 'We're not close. Never have been. Chalk and cheese, me and Sar. She was always Daddy's little girl.'

'And you?' Charlie said.

'Do I look like a daddy's little girl?'

'I don't know. What does one look like?'

She studied him over the top of her mug. She's making up her mind how much she wants to tell me, Charlie thought. Fully editing it. 'State of mind, I suppose,' she said eventually.

'You grew up in Hackney?'

'Until he won the pools.'

'Your father?'

'Yeah. Mum never got the benefit; she took off when me and Sar were only little. Hardly remember her.'

'She's deceased, I believe.'

'Yeah. She was an alcoholic. Did he tell you?'

'No, he didn't.'

'It was the three of us most of our lives. If you listen to him tell it, it was just him and Sar. When he won the pools, we all moved out to Essex. You been to his place? Bell End Mansion, I used to call it. Suddenly he thought he was too good for the rest of the family. Got all posh, didn't he? Sold his cab and bought himself a cardigan with leather patches on the elbows.'

'He told us he was a retired businessman,' Grey said.

'Well, driving a cab is a business, I suppose. I mean, cabbies do all right, but they don't make the kind of dosh you need to buy a place like that, do they?'

'When was the last time you saw Sarah?'

'Just after Christmas. She caught the train into London and we met up in that funny little pub other side of Blackfriars Bridge.'

'The Black Friar.'

'Is that what it's called? We called it the triangle pub.'

'Eight months. That's a long time not to see your sister.'

'Suppose it is. He never liked it, see, never liked her doing anything on her own.'

'Your father or Mr Howlett?'

'Danny boy. Yeah. Possessive, isn't he? It's like he owns her. She's used to that, mind.'

'Why is she used to it?'

She made a face. 'I thought you said you'd met my old man?'

'How would you describe your relationship with Mr Howlett?'

'I don't have one. He's your average City-boy wanker, all cock and cocaine. Sar was just his type. She's eye candy and doesn't answer back.'

'So you're not his biggest fan?'

'No, that would be him. Sar thought he was sophisticated. I thought he was proper up himself. You know what private-school tossers are like.'

Grey cleared his throat but didn't say anything.

'Is she happy?'

'She's proper miserable. It's the marriage from hell. Used to do my head in listening to her go on about it.'

'Do you love your sister?' Grey said.

That's an interesting question, Charlie thought. I wonder what she'll say. He watched her go through another full edit before she answered.

'Wouldn't hurt a fly, Sar. She's proper nice. Too nice, you know what I mean?'

'Too nice?' Charlie said.

'Well, when I heard what had happened, I wasn't surprised. She's always been one of those women. Bad stuff happens to her.'

'Like Mr Howlett?'

'All the men in the world and she picked him. Makes you laugh.'

'Why does it make you laugh?'

'She only went with him to get away from the old man. She was dead young, too, when she married Danny. She was already pregnant, did he tell you?'

'No, he didn't mention that.'

'It wasn't a love match, then?' Grey said.

'Oh, she loved him all right, at first. Life and soul of the party, Danny. Everybody loves him till they get to know him. In the end, he turned out to be just like dear old Dad. For Sar, it was like out of the frying pan into the shit.'

'Why doesn't she leave him?' Grey asked her.

'She did try.'

'What happened?'

'Showed up on my doorstep one afternoon with little Ollie. *Can I come and stay with you?* Of course, didn't take long for him to find out where she was. One day when I was out at work he came and got her, threw her and that poor little boy in the car and drove home. Gave her a good hiding later.'

'He physically abuses her?'

'He abuses her every way, I'd say.'

She drank her tea, chewed her lip, her eyes darting around the room. Charlie kept quiet. Sometimes silence was the best question there was.

74

'She was good at running away, was Sar. Lost count how many times she ran off when we were teenagers. Sometimes she'd go and stay at a friend's house. Dad would do a ring-round, go and bring her back. Once, she caught the train to Margate, showed up at our Auntie Janet's. She had to drive all the way back up to Essex with her.'

'You never wanted to do the same thing?'

'I weren't scared of him. Besides, if I'd run off, he would have just changed the locks and rented out my bedroom.'

'Back to Danny,' Charlie said. 'That time she came here. Was that the only time she tried to leave him?'

'I don't know. Maybe. Every time I talked to her, which wasn't often, like I said, she was always on about it.'

'On about it?'

'How she wished she could go somewhere and start all over again, clean slate. Leave everything behind.'

'But she never did.'

'She said he'd find her, no matter what. You know what blokes like him are like.'

'She's frightened of him?'

'She said to me once, "Danny will do for me one day."'

'Those were her words?'

'Yeah, I remember clear as anything.'

'How would you describe her, your sister?' Grey said.

Jackie thought about it, then reached into her bag and took out her purse. There was a dog-eared photograph in the insert; she handed it to Charlie. 'It's not a very good photo. But I like it because it sort of captures her, know what I mean? Took it at Oliver's birthday party a couple of years ago. I don't think she knew I was behind her; caught her by surprise, sort of. That's her, really. Always smiling, but every now and then she got this sad look. No one can cover up all the time, can they?'

'Don't suppose they can,' Charlie said, and handed back the photograph.

'I suppose when your husband and your old man are both

complete pricks, that's enough to make you sad. But her problem is she's too nice about it. Not like me. I don't put up with
shite like she does.'

'Have you been in touch with your father?'

'What, like recently?'

'Since Sarah was abducted.'

She shrugged her shoulders.

'How did you find out about your sister's disappearance?'

'Saw it on the telly.'

'So you haven't spoken to him?'

'I rang him when I heard, see if he was all right. Should of
known better. He more or less said he wished it was me they
took. Something like that.'

'That must have hurt.'

'I'm used to it,' Jackie said, and gave Charlie a look: *Don't
you feel sorry for me, copper.*

'You said you saw Sarah at Christmas. Was that the last time
you spoke to her?'

'We talk on the phone sometimes, when Danny's at work.
Not often. We don't have much in common any more.'

'When was the last time?'

'Maybe a couple of months ago.'

'Was she worried about anything?'

'The usual. Her kid. Her husband. She basically hated her
life. You been to their place, right? In Clapham?'

Charlie nodded.

'I know what you're thinking. You come here, look at this
dump, and there's her, living in that la-di-da house in Clapham.
But I tell you what, I wouldn't swap with her for quids.'

'Did you ever have any reason to believe she was in danger?'

'You think this was planned, like?'

'We have to look at all possibilities.'

'She's living with Danny. That's dangerous enough, my opinion.' She leaned in. 'Want to know what I think?'

'Absolutely.'

'I think it was him. I think he paid someone to knock her off.'

'That's quite a serious allegation, Jackie,' Grey said. 'Do you have any evidence to support it?'

She shook her head. 'I just know it.'

'Why would he do that, do you think?' Charlie said.

'Because he's a complete fuckin' psycho. Because he doesn't want to give her half of what he's got if she leaves him. Because he wants her insurance money. You do know how much he's got her insured for?'

'Yes, we do.'

'There you are, then.'

Grey looked at Charlie, as if this was news. No, Charlie thought, she has an agenda. I'm not discounting our Mr Howlett, but I'm not convinced, not yet.

He stood up to leave. 'Thanks, Jackie. We'll be in touch as soon as we have any news.'

'Do you have someone you can stay with?' Grey said. 'You shouldn't be on your own at a time like this.'

'I've been on my own all my bleedin' life.' She gave him her hard-nut look.

Grey shrugged. Charlie left her his card and they went back to the car.

'You know, it's occurred to me,' Grey said, as they made their way back down the A12, 'that our Sarah Howlett might have planned this. That it's all fake. You heard what her sister said: how she talked about running away, making a fresh start.'

'We can't rule it out. But it's not easy, disappearing.'

'But people do it.'

'I know. Funny, innit? People think that if they go somewhere else, suddenly everything's going to be good again. But wherever you go, you have to take yourself with you, don't you?'

'I suppose so,' Grey said.

'I mean, things that happen in your life, no matter how bad they are, you have to look at the upside. Suppose you have a rough childhood; even that can be a good thing, in a way. Makes you resilient. Know what I mean?'

'Did you have a rough childhood?'

'Wasn't great. My brother, for instance, he dwells on all the bad stuff. He was one of them that ran away. Fat lot of good it did him.'

'Where did he run to?'

'Australia. I mean, how's that safe? No matter where you go over there, there's something wanting to eat you.'

'Maybe he just wanted a fresh start.'

'It's not a fresh start, it's a change of scenery. My other brother, Ben, he always says if you want to sort out your problems, look in the mirror. They all start and end right there. Mirrors don't change their reflection with geography.'

Charlie's Nokia buzzed in his pocket. It was Dawson.

'You far away, guv'nor?'

'We'll be back in about half an hour.'

'Only Wes thinks he's got something you might want to take a look at. Could be important.'

'Get in,' Charlie said, and told Grey to put his foot down.

The incident room was busy, officers keying data into computers, calling up witnesses on their mobiles, eating muffins and watching CCTV. The usual glamour. Uniform cops were coming in and out with footage they'd collected.

Dawson, DC Singh and a couple of other DCs were gathered around James's desk, staring at his monitor. James was tapping at something on the screen, and they all looked animated. When Charlie went over, they made room for him. 'What's the story, Wes?'

'That witness who saw Evie Myers get taken, he was sure he got the plates right, yeah?'

'Well, it was dark. Easy to make a mistake.'

'But when we interviewed him, he seemed so certain about it.'

'Maybe he was right, and they'd been altered.'

'Exactly. What if he doctored the plates himself?' He pushed his work pad towards Charlie. 'The witness said he saw OF53 TEP. But it's dead easy to change most of those letters and numbers just a little bit; all you need is some black adhesive tape. Don't have to be Banksy.'

'And?'

'Well, what if our witness made just one mistake with the numbers or the letters? So I tried every combination I could think of and ran them through the computer looking for a match, any crime reported for any of those combinations within a one-mile radius of where Evie was abducted. And I got this.'

He opened a CCTV file on his screen and Charlie watched a white van pull up at a service station pump; a young man in a beanie got out, filled up and then took off without paying.

'Where did this happen?'

'A Shell in Herne Hill.'

He enlarged the image so they could all read the registration tag: OF58 TEP.

'Have you run it?'

'The plates are registered to someone in Manchester, a Ford Puma. So I rang a mate in CID in Stockwell, sent him this.' He rewound the file, zoomed in on the driver's face as he stood at the pump. 'He took one look, knew him straight off.'

Dawson passed Charlie the printout. Charlie shuffled through it. Christopher James Markham, twenty-three years old, born in Herne Hill. His criminal record was for minor offences: receiving, petty theft, drunk and disorderly. He'd never incurred a custodial sentence, but he was currently on remand for an alleged assault on a young woman near Stockwell Tube station.

There was an address in Brixton. He lived with his mother, no siblings. He belonged to the National Front. He was unemployed.

He owned a Ford Transit van, registration CF58 TFP.

'So, he alters his plates when he goes to nick a tank of petrol,' Charlie said. 'He's got the dodgy plates when he abducts Evie Myers. Our witness saw an 8 instead of a 6.'

'Run it back again,' Dawson said. He pointed to the van's passenger-side mirror. 'In the Sarah Howlett abduction, the mirror was missing.'

'The CCTV from the service station was captured the night before Evie was taken. He could have had a shunt any time over that weekend.'

'He'd have to have balls of steel to use the same van two days later.'

'Used stolen plates the second time. Means it was premeditated.'

'Maybe,' Charlie said. He looked down at the printout. *Christopher James Markham.*

'Do we pick him up, guv?' the skipper said.

'What for, petrol theft?'

James logged in to Google Maps and brought up a Street View image of Markham's house in Brixton. 'Evie and Sarah could be in there,' he said.

'Or not,' Charlie said. 'What, he's keeping two girls tied up in his bedroom with his dear old mum downstairs watching *EastEnders*?'

'He's got to be our man, guv,' Singh said.

'Thing is, Rupe, our priority is not catching the bloke who snatched Evie and Sarah; it's finding Evie and Sarah. Suppose we get a squad of armed police and bust in there with the big red key. We still got the same problem we had with Cogan. What if Evie and Sarah *aren't there*?'

'We make him tell us where they are.'

'And how do we do that? It wouldn't be in his interests to tell us. We don't do waterboarding in the Met, unfortunately; all he has to do is get a brief and keep shtum, and he's off the hook. He pleads guilty to stealing a tank of unleaded and then we have to let him go.'

Charlie tapped Markham's file on the edge of the desk, gave himself time to think.

'Wes, have we got anything back from your mate at Ford on the van used in Sarah Howlett's abduction? If it matches Markham's, then we're definitely in business.'

'Nothing yet,' James said. 'He's still looking at the CCTV.'

'I'd better go upstairs and talk to the DCI,' Charlie said.

So much for Automatic Number Plate Recognition, he thought as he went up in the lift. It was brilliant when it was first introduced. But it was always the way: find some new technology to make it easier to catch the villains, and almost straight off some crim figured out a way around it. He'd read a report that said one in twelve cars on the roads now had stolen or cloned plates. Most people did it to avoid parking or speeding fines. You didn't even have to go under the counter; a lot of crooks did it themselves. Black Adhesive Tape United 1, Digital Technology Rovers 0.

The DCI looked surprised to see him. He leaned back in his ergonomic chair and folded his hands across his middle.

'Charlie. Well, well, well. That was quick. "Always hope but never expect." Shakespeare, wasn't it?'

Just say yes, Charlie. Say yes and try and make him like you.

'No, sir.'

'No?'

'I think it's a meme on the internet.'

The DCI leaned forward, frowning. 'It's good how you know all these things, Charlie. What have you got for me?'

Charlie slid the printouts across the desk. The DCI shuffled through them.

'Is this our boy?'

'We have enough for an arrest warrant.'

'Then what are we waiting for?'

'Petrol theft.'

'What?'

'I've got him bang to rights for fifty litres of unleaded at

81

a Shell in Herne Hill. But the link to the abduction of Evie Myers is only circumstantial. We can nab him for the petrol and then sweat him, but we need to find the van. If he says it's been nicked, or he's sold it, then we've got nothing. He could be another Cogan.'

Charlie told him their theory about the altered plates, and how he was waiting on a match for the year and model of the van in the Sarah Howlett case.

'What do you want to do?' the DCI asked.

'Hold off this time. Eyes on, covert entry soon as we can. Pivot peripheral surveillance. Amory's got a twelve-man crew; we use them. Once we find the van, we put a lump on it, track him on GPS. He'll lead us to Evie or Sarah. Hopefully both.'

The DCI looked back at the printouts. 'No convictions for sexual violence.'

'He is due to appear in court next month for an alleged assault on a twenty-one-year-old female outside Stockwell Tube station.'

A long-drawn-out sigh. The DCI was probably thinking about early retirement and improving his golf handicap. Anything but this. 'All right. We'll do it your way.'

'Thank you, sir. If it is him, all we need is twenty-four hours. He's gone to all the trouble of grabbing these two women; he won't just leave them tied up somewhere. He'll want his bit of fun.'

The DCI made a face, like he'd bitten down on a lemon. 'Fun is not what I'd call it. All right, but no mistakes, Charlie. If it goes bad, it's on all our heads.'

Well, mainly mine, Charlie thought. I'm at the bottom of the food chain here. I'm the one who's going to wear the dunce's hat in the morning.

'The super's breathing down my neck on this one. Miss Myers and Mrs Howlett are all over the media. We have to stay on top of this.' The DCI pushed the printouts back across the desk. 'The super wants to convene a Gold Group meeting for first thing in the morning, 0700. That's all the time you've got.'

Charlie took that to mean: *after that, the case is out of your hands.*

His reputation, his career; in the scheme of things, they weren't that important, he thought as he came back down in the lift. What was important was finding Evie and Sarah. He wondered where they were right this minute: in some darkened room, perhaps, trussed up, terrified. But with any luck, still alive.

CHAPTER FIFTEEN

There was a woman in a Rasta beanie pushing a Tesco trolley along the road with her shopping in it; no way that wasn't going to end up dumped down the church car park. Workmen in high-vis jackets were eating sausage rolls and smoking and staring at a hole their mechanical digger had made like it was the eighth wonder of the world.

Markham's house was on the other side of the junction, a narrow terrace with an overgrown front garden and a pram rusting in the middle of it.

Charlie tried the bell, but it didn't work. He hadn't really thought it would. He banged with his fist. He could hear someone moving about inside. After the third knock, the door inched open on the chain and a woman peered out.

He flipped his warrant card. 'Sorry to trouble you. I'm DI George and this is DS Grey. We're making house-to-house enquiries along your street; we're looking for some assistance. Can we speak with you for a minute?'

'What about?'

'I can't really talk to you through the door, now, can I?'

The chain came off, but the woman kept the door just ajar between them. She could have been any age, except young. She had thin permed hair and thick glasses. Her coarse woollen jumper was entrail purple and smelled vaguely of mothballs.

'Can you tell me if you've seen this vehicle?'

He showed her a still from the CCTV footage from the petrol station. She brought the picture up to her nose. 'It's a van.'

'Do you recognise it? The registration starts with OF58. We believe the passenger-side wing mirror is missing.'

He tried to get a good look into the house over the top of her head. There was a long, dark passageway and a kitchen at the end of it. Some nasty stains on the wallpaper – rising damp, he supposed – and a few tatty bits of carpet on the linoleum. He couldn't hear anything over the daytime soap opera playing on the television, which was turned up way too loud.

'Sorry,' she said and handed back the photograph.

'You haven't seen it parked anywhere up or down the street?'

'Lots of white vans park in the street. Why, what do you want it for?'

'Is there anyone else in the house we can speak to?'

Another shake of the head.

'Live alone, do you?'

'My son lives with me. He's out.'

Well, that's a flat-out lie, dear, Charlie thought. Surveillance have been watching your place all afternoon; he came in here just after three o'clock and he's not left.

'Working, then, is he?'

'Good boy, he is. Never been any trouble.'

'Right. Well, thanks for your help. Have a nice afternoon.'

The door shut again before he'd even finished speaking.

As they walked away, Grey said: 'Should we get a search warrant?'

'We could. But if Sarah and Evie aren't in there, then what?'

'His old lady was lying.'

'Of course she was, she's his mother. Not going to shop him, is she? They all do that, no matter how big a scrote their kid is.'

They saw a van as they crossed the street; it had *Thames Plumbing* written on the side, with a picture of a leaky tap. There was a two-man surveillance team in the back, and they were recording everything.

They turned the corner into the next street. A white Sierra was parked behind a skip. They got in to wait for James and Singh.

Charlie heard the familiar strains of Wagner and reached into his pocket for his iPhone. He didn't recognise the number.

'It's me,' a voice said.

'Who's that?'

'Forgotten about me already?'

Charlie turned to Grey. 'Go and get some coffees, will you? There's a Costa in the high street. I'll have a flat white; make sure they give me an extra shot.'

Grey got out and started to walk back towards the station. Charlie watched him in the rear-view mirror. 'Will, where are you?'

'I'm at your place. Ben just dropped me off. Have you got any sugar?'

Christ, that was quick. Ben must have rung him while he was on his way to Heathrow to collect Will. Cheeky bastard.

'What?' he said.

'You've no sugar for the coffee. I can't drink coffee without sugar.'

'I don't use sugar.'

'Who doesn't have sugar?'

'Me. I don't.'

'What am I supposed to do, then?'

'Go down the shop. There's a Tesco in the high street.'

'Fine welcome that is.'

He saw James and Singh heading towards the car. 'Will, I'll be back soon as I can. But I can't talk right now. Make yourself at home.' He hung up.

'Anything?' he said as they got in.

James shook his head.

'Went up and down the whole street,' Singh said. 'Only about half of them were in, and those that are look at you like you're from another planet. Aliens could land in the Tesco car park and no one round here would notice; they're too busy watching porn and playing FIFA 18 on their laptops.'

'How about you, guv?' James said.

'We eyeballed Markham's mother. Tried to get a look inside. It's your standard two-up, two-down. Can't see how he's hiding them in there.'

'What about her?' Singh said.

'Three monkeys.'

'So what now?' James said.

'You wait here to make the arrest. But nothing happens until I give the word.' Charlie saw Grey on the way back with the coffee. James and Singh got out. Their car was parked in the next street.

Best thing now was to get back to the nick. He still had to call Jack about the crime-scene report and see Parm about the intel from Sarah Howlett's laptop and her phone, as well as write up the policy book.

He had a bad feeling about this. He had always been taught – and knew from bitter experience – that an SIO shouldn't take the investigation down one path too soon. But because of the lack of quality leads, he had somehow been corralled into making some bloke who'd blagged fifty quid's worth of petrol their main suspect.

He hoped to God he wasn't wrong.

CHAPTER SIXTEEN

She heard someone moving about outside the van.

Her crotch was stinging. She'd wet herself, God alone knew how long ago. There was a smell, a horrible smell; she realised it was her. What was happening?

She was thirsty, and everything hurt, her shoulders, her wrists. Where was she? She couldn't remember. She felt sick from heat and hunger and thirst.

She wriggled upright against the side of the van. Someone climbed into the front. Did she know them? It was like peering through a mist. They took a bottle out of their pocket and took a long gulp of it.

'Please . . . it hurts.'

They didn't answer. She felt so weak. She slid back down the side of the van and lay on her back on the floor.

She did what she always did when she was scared, she got outside of her body, left it behind. She saw herself twisted on the floor of the van, helpless and wriggling, like a worm, a little white worm.

'Water.'

Perhaps they couldn't hear her. She took a deep breath, tried to say it louder.

'Please . . . *water.*'

Still nothing.

'Please!' She kicked the back of the seat.

She heard someone coming round the side of the van. The side door slid open and they climbed in, grabbed her by the hair, held the water bottle to her lips. Sarah gulped at it, started to choke. It was burning her throat! But they wouldn't let her go. She twisted her head from side to side in panic. Finally they slammed her head onto the floor and left her there, gasping, trying to rake air into her lungs, her knees pulled up to her chest.

She didn't remember anything much after that.

Danny peered through the curtains. The TV crews looked to have given up and gone home. He checked his iPhone. Jesus. Twenty-seven missed calls and a couple of dozen text messages he didn't want to look at. Half of them were from Taj. Nothing he could do until he could get back into the office, hack into the holding account and sort out these trades.

He took a deep breath and called Taj's number.

'Christ, Danny. What the hell's going on?'

'You saw the news?'

'Are you joking?'

'Got a bit of a problem here, mate.'

'What's happening?'

'I know as much as you do.'

'It's all anyone in the building can talk about. What are we going to do about these trades?'

'I can't come into the office today, can I? How's that going to look?'

'We are in serious fucking trouble here. We dropped another five on this morning's market.'

'I'll sort it, all right? I'll get into the office as soon as I can.'

'I still don't get why you did this. It wasn't what we agreed.'

'I said I'll fix it.'

'We were quids in!'

'Take a fucking chill pill, Taj.' He hung up.

Taj worried him. Last thing Danny needed was him going to pieces.

He took the burner phone out of the drawer, tapped a number on the keypad. 'Where are you?' he said.

He held the phone away from his ear.

'Why do you think? I had the police on my doorstep at three o'clock this morning.' He picked up the *caganer* sitting next to his laptop, Donald Trump crouching to take a crap. He'd bought it at a Christmas market in Barcelona . . . how long ago was it, six months, seven? Seemed like a lifetime. Back when some things in life were still funny. 'What do you mean, you didn't do it?'

He jumped to his feet. Fuck's sake, this couldn't be happening.

'Is she dead?' He made a face. 'Well, what do you expect me to do about that?'

He parted the curtains. Still a few of the neighbours standing about in the street, gossiping. This had made their week.

'Where's the van now?' He snapped the top back on the pen, threw it across the room. 'Wait a minute. What are you telling me? You left it *where*? Jesus Christ!'

He heard Ines yelling downstairs. She sounded panicked. For God's sake, now what?

'Is she still *alive*?'

Ines was calling him. Not now, Ines, not now.

'Jesus. You've got to move the van!'

'Señor Howlett!'

'If they find it there, with her in the back, they'll know I had something to do with it.' He dropped the phone on the desk, went to the door. What the hell was going on down there? 'Ines, I'm coming!'

He went back to the phone. 'I'll be there tonight. I'll fix this. All right? And then you have to stay out of the way.'

He hung up, put the burner in his pocket and ran down the stairs. Ines was kneeling in the middle of the living room, Oliver in her arms. He was covered in blood.

'What the hell happened?'

'He fell, in the kitchen, on the tile, Señor Howlett.'

'You're supposed to be watching him. You know he's no good on his feet.'

90

'*Lo siento, señor, lo siento*. I don't know how this happen.'

Danny picked the boy up and carried him into the downstairs bathroom. 'Get me some paper towels,' he said. Stupid girl, she was supposed to be looking after him; wasn't that her *job*? He ran the tap, grabbed the towels from her, washed the blood off Oliver's face. Where was it all coming from? Oh for God's sake, there was a gash in his scalp three inches long.

'We must take him to hospital,' Ines said.

No, Danny thought. No, no, no.

But there wasn't any choice, was there? Unless he wanted that cop asking him why his son was in a coma and he didn't give a toss. Don't sweat it, he thought. Quick trip to A&E, a few stitches, might work in his favour. If they kept Ollie in overnight for observation, that would be even better.

'I will come with you,' Ines said.

Danny loaded Ollie into the back of his X5. Christ, the kid was getting blood on the leather seats. He had Ines hold a cloth to his scalp. She put her arms around him, started cooing to him. Ollie seemed suspiciously quiet.

I can still be back in time, Danny thought. I can still do this. No need to panic.

CHAPTER SEVENTEEN

Charlie rang DC Khan, the family liaison officer for Evie Myers'
case. He told him about Markham, and what they were planning to do.

'Shall I tell them?' Khan said.

'Not yet. I don't want their hopes dashed if I'm wrong. How
are they holding up?'

'The doctor was here this afternoon; he's keeping Mrs Myers
sedated. Her father, he says he's okay, but his hands are shaking,
and he spends most of the time out the back, smoking cigarettes.'

'I'll call you as soon as I know something.'

'Guv,' Khan said, and hung up.

Charlie had just thrown the phone back on the desk when
it buzzed to life again. It was the duty sergeant at Shepherd's
Bush, Connelly. Charlie knew him from his days in uniform;
they'd gone through cadet school together. He was a Gooner
like him, poor sod, and they sometimes caught up for a drink
after a game.

'Charlie,' he said.

'Seamus, what can I do for you, old son?'

'Not a social call, sorry. You at work?'

'Well, it's before midnight and it's not Christmas Day, so yes.'

'Only we've got a noise complaint here and it looks like it's
your gaff. You got someone staying?'

Charlie remembered about Will. 'Jesus. Sorry about this,
Shay. What kind of noise complaint?'

'Loud music. The neighbour who rang up said she'd asked

the person responsible to turn it down and she'd been abused and physically threatened.'

Charlie imagined that was Mrs Dorsey from downstairs; she'd set herself up as unofficial caretaker for the whole street. 'I'll sort it.'

'They've already sent a car round. Thought you should know.'

'Appreciate it.'

Charlie swore under his breath. He found his car keys and shouted to the skipper that he was off out, told him to ring if there was any movement. When he got in the lift, he thumped the flat of his hand against the steel side. 'Will, you little tosser,' he said.

He could hear the music as soon as he drove into the close, reckoned they could hear it in Wembley. Lovely. He parked his car and ran up the steps. He could almost feel the walls shaking. What was Will playing? Sounded like hip hop. There were two uniforms on the doorstep, looked like they were fresh out of cadet school. His little brother was giving them the full drama.

'Go on, arrest me!' Will turned around and put his hands behind his back. 'Take me down the cells and waterboard me for playing tunes!'

'Sir, we just need you to turn down the volume on your music, please.'

'England's turned into a police state. It's worse here than Russia or even the bloody United States!'

To their credit, the two lads were not rising to the bait. Not yet, anyway. One of them recognised Charlie walking up the steps; he didn't need to get his warrant card out. Andrew, that was his name. Charlie remembered him from a shooting in Holland Park; he'd been one of the first responders.

'Andy, isn't it?' he said. 'DI George.'

'Yes, sir. I remember.'

'What's the problem here, then?'

'We're responding to a noise complaint, sir. I've asked this gentleman to turn down the volume a bit.'

'Brought in the big guns, have they?' Will said. 'Big Brother's brought in big brother.'

'It's all right, this is my gaff. My brother's probably just had a few too many. I'll take it from here.'

Andy looked relieved. 'Right, guv, thanks. I'll leave you with it.'

'Kiss my arse!' Will shouted at the cop's back as he retreated down the steps. Charlie grabbed him by the collar and dragged him inside.

'Go on, hit me,' Will said, pointing to his chin. 'You know you want to.'

How long since he'd seen him? Must be a couple of years, at least. They'd never been close; well, they had been once, when Charlie still had to help him brush his hair in the mornings before school. Hadn't had much to do with each other since.

The state of him. Charlie tried not to look shocked. There was a look in his little brother's eyes, a quick flash of something: was it guilt or was it resentment? The music was all about gangstas and motherfuckers. That's original, Charlie thought. I don't know how they think it up. He looked up at the Spotify on his TV. Geto Boys. Seriously? He picked up the remote and switched it off.

'Have you done?' he said.

'Well, look at you. That suit must have set you back.'

Charlie gave him a hug. It made his eyes water; Will was pretty rank. That stale sweat smell on him, someone would have loved sitting next to that on British Airways all the way from Sydney.

'Good to see you again, Will. You've lost weight.'

'It's all the triathlons I've been running.'

Charlie glanced around. Already the place looked like it had been ransacked by ice addicts. Will had emptied the contents of his backpack all over the living-room floor; there was crap everywhere. He was using one of Charlie's beer glasses as an ashtray, but most of it had spilled on the carpet. Looked like he was smoking rollies these days.

'Did you get some sugar?'

'Got no money, have I? I could nick some, but then they'd have to get you to come and arrest me.'

'Not me, not unless you murdered the manager at Sainsbury's. Did Ben show you where everything is? You must be gagging for a shower.' He fetched a couple of towels from the airing cupboard and tossed them at him, but Will didn't seem in any hurry.

'Is this where you live now? Thought you were living with some tart in Finsbury Park.'

'Nicole. And she isn't a tart. She's a very nice woman who couldn't hack the hours I work.'

'Not much, is it? This place. For all the overtime you put in.'

'When did you become such an expert on my working life?'

'Oh, come on, some things never change.'

Charlie picked up one of the cigarette stubs and sniffed it.

'It's only a joint,' Will said. 'Don't get your knickers in a twist. It's why I couldn't let the filth in. I was doing you a favour.'

'Seriously?'

'Okay. Sorry. I just needed the one, chill me out a bit. You ever done the flight from Oz? It's like spending twenty-four hours in a toilet roll tube.'

Charlie took the leavings and flushed them down the toilet. When he came out again, Will was halfway through one of his Lagunitas.

'How have you been?' Charlie said.

'All right.'

'How's Australia treating you?'

'Great. I go surfing every day and play cricket on the weekends. It's the life. Want to go out and get a pint?'

'I can't. I have to get back to work, I've got a serious flap on. You be all right?'

'Sure. Don't worry about me. You're an important man now.

So is Ben. And Michael too, of course, at least in God's eyes. Let's see, who does that leave? Oh right – me.'

Charlie wanted to say, *and whose fault is that?*

'I was supposed to have this week off, Will. It didn't work out that way.'

'Off you go. I don't need babysitting.'

'I'll be home later. I'll bring some beers.'

'If you want. I may be asleep.'

'Just keep the music down and don't burn a hole in the sofa with your cancer sticks.' Charlie took out his wallet and dropped a couple of fifties on the coffee table. 'That should be enough for sugar.'

'Should be, unless inflation's got right out of control since I've been gone.'

'No, you're thinking of *after* Brexit. You can get in some more beers while you're at it.'

Charlie headed for the door. He had a thought, turned back and put the remote in his pocket, just to make sure he didn't get another noise complaint at three in the morning while they were taking down Christopher Markham.

'Don't work too hard, sweetheart,' Will said.

'I'll see you when I see you,' Charlie said.

He walked back to his car. As soon as he got in, he checked in with the skipper. Nothing yet.

He took a moment to settle himself before he started the engine. Why was it that whenever he had a run-in with his family, he always felt like he was the one who should feel guilty? How did that work? He gave his little brother the run of his flat and his Spotify and his beers and a hundred-pound bonus and he was still the bad guy.

Hell with it.

On his way back to the nick, he rang Lovejoy on his hands-free. He didn't know what made him do it; perhaps he thought she could make him feel better about things. She sort of had the knack.

'Guv,' she said, sounding surprised.

'How are you feeling, Lovejoy? How's the foot?'

'Not good news. I'm checked into the hospital tomorrow. Another op.'

'What's the story?'

'Exploratory surgery, they're calling it. It's pretty bad this time. My leg looks like one of those sausages you see hanging up in an Italian grocer.'

There was a long pause on the other end of the line. He thought she might be tearing up, but Lovejoy never cried.

'They say I could lose it, guv.'

He nearly drove into the back of a road sweeper, swerved at the last second and almost collected a taxi. That was smart. The taxi driver jammed his fist on his horn and gave him an east London salute.

'Don't know what to say,' he managed finally.

'I guess there's nothing to say.'

'This is my fault.'

'Not everything that goes wrong in the world is your fault.'

'Which hospital are you going to?'

'It's a private clinic, in the Shard.'

No NHS for Lovejoy, Charlie thought. He sometimes forgot her old man was quids in. 'Look, I'm flat out right now, but I'll come and see you first chance.'

'I'm not going anywhere.'

'I'll bring some grapes.'

'I don't like grapes.'

'I do, they're for me. Take it easy.'

'Can't do anything else. Thanks for the call.'

She hung up. Charlie punched the steering wheel. No matter what she said, it *was* his fault. He nearly ran a red light. Concentrate, Charlie. Then the Nokia started buzzing on the passenger seat. He picked it up. It was the skipper.

'It's on,' he said.

***

When he walked in, Grey and the rest of his team were standing in a semicircle behind Dawson. There was a dedicated Nokia for surveillance; it sat in the middle of the skipper's desk like a live snake. They were all staring at it.

'What happened?' Charlie said.

'Amory rang about fifteen minutes ago,' the skipper said. 'They've lost him, the tatty wankers.'

'How?'

'They had eyes on him when he left his house at ten past eight, then he dodged down a ginnel and disappeared.'

Grey looked at Charlie. 'What's a ginnel?'

'It's like a snicket,' Dawson said.

Charlie put him out of his misery. 'An alley.' He turned back to the skipper. 'Did he know he was being followed?'

'Must of.'

'These blokes are professionals. How did this happen?'

'What are we going to do?' Grey said.

'Let's hope they pick him up again.'

'If they've lost him, we're for it,' the skipper said.

'Not *we*, just me, Skipper. I made the call.'

'Don't care who said what, guv. But there's two young women out there relying on us to get this right.'

Charlie willed the surveillance phone to ring. Come on, Amory. For God's sake, tell us you found him again. Don't cock this up.

'I'm going to the canteen to get a cup of coffee,' he said.

He went down the corridor to the elevators. He felt numb with fatigue, with the tension of it. You could stick pins in me right now, he thought, and I wouldn't feel a thing.

He pressed the call button, stared at the ceiling, counting the acoustic tiles. There was a ping as the lift doors opened. He got in. Just as the doors were closing, Dawson ran in after him and blocked them. He was holding the surveillance phone.

'They've got him again.'

Charlie grabbed the phone from him.

'Your boy just went to the chippie,' Amory said. 'It wasn't avoidance, it was a shortcut. He's got himself two cod and chips, a kebab and a large Coke and now he's headed back home.'

'Stay on him. Don't lose him again.'

'We won't,' Amory said, with more confidence than Charlie felt was warranted.

Charlie went back to his goldfish bowl in the corner of the office, stared at the copy of the arrest warrant sitting there on his desk.

It had to be tonight.

He imagined Evie and Sarah in a warehouse on some industrial estate, or a farmhouse miles from anywhere. It wasn't far to drive before you were in the green belt. But they would never find them without Markham's help, voluntary or otherwise.

He tried to catch up on his paperwork. Jack had sent him the crime-scene photographs from this morning; their media officer, Catlin, had copied him in on the latest press release; one of his mates at MIT 17 had forwarded an invitation to a murder mystery night. Very bloody funny.

It was no good. He couldn't think about anything but what might be happening in Brixton. He knew the stats: six hours from abduction to murder was usual. If either of the women had been abandoned alive, the window for saving them was seventy-two hours. That meant Evie was done, right about now, dead from dehydration or exposure.

But there was still a chance for Sarah.

He jumped up, grabbed his car keys. He couldn't stand the waiting any more. He had to be there when this went down, whatever happened.

CHAPTER EIGHTEEN

Danny looked up at the clock on the wall.

Other people were coming in and out of A&E and they were still sitting here. His whole life was ticking away, second by second, and there was nothing he could do to stop it.

Oliver was still cuddled on Ines's lap, eerily subdued. Normally he would be running around tripping everyone up, screaming at the top of his voice. Danny looked around the waiting room at the usual dregs: a mother with a sick baby and three screaming brats; a nasty piece of work in a Harrington with a bleeding hand – wouldn't be surprised if he got that sticking it through a jeweller's window; and a man on his own, sitting at the back. Danny didn't even remember him going up to the triage desk to report in.

Perhaps he's waiting for someone, he thought. He spared another quick glance; the guy looked a bit like a cop. It occurred to him that the police might be keeping him under surveillance.

The triage nurse was sitting at a desk behind what he supposed was bulletproof glass. Her attitude, she needed it to be. He got up and went over.

'Excuse me,' he said to her. 'How much longer will we have to wait?'

'Take a seat, sir, we'll call you as soon as a doctor is ready to see you.'

'I *cannot* sit here all night.' He wasn't racist, never had been, but there was something about a younger woman of West

Indian extraction telling him what to do that rubbed him up the wrong way. 'My son is bleeding to death over there.'

'He has been assessed. It's not a critical injury. We had a three-car motor vehicle accident earlier tonight and we are extremely busy. You will have to wait until you are called.'

He leaned in, lowered his voice. 'Look, have you seen the news today?' He made a motion with his right hand, drawing an imaginary screen around his face. 'I've been all over it. My wife is missing. They think she's been kidnapped.'

The nurse shook her head. She thinks it's an act, Danny thought, that I'm making it all up. One time I'm being absolutely straight with someone and they don't believe me. How's that for irony? He should have listened to that cop, the one who wanted to give him some sort of escort. That might have paid off about now.

'It's nearly eight o'clock. We've been here almost three *fucking* hours.'

'Please do not swear at me, sir. If you become aggressive, I will have to call security.'

He looked around. The Neanderthal with the bleeding hand was smirking at him. Must stay calm. One thing at a time, remember. You didn't lose your cool during the financial crisis; you can't lose it now.

He sat back down next to Inès. The burner phone kept buzzing in his pocket. He took it out, powered it down.

'Hold Oliver, *por favor*,' Ines said to him. 'I must go to bathroom.' She put Oliver on his lap.

Just one thing to go right, that was all he needed. Wasn't too much to ask, was it? Oliver was slapping the pages of the book Ines had brought with her from home.

'You want me to read to you, do you?' he said to him. 'What's this? Peppa Pig. Looks like the triage nurse, doesn't he?'

The nurse looked up from her computer screen at the front desk. He wondered if she'd heard him. Didn't care either way; she'd already ruined his life.

He smiled at her. She didn't smile back.

Charlie found James's Sierra at the end of Markham's street, where it had been all afternoon. James and Singh both grunted 'Guv,' as he got in the back. Nice night for muggers and gang-bangers, Charlie thought; no moon, half the street lights not working, the only light the eerie blue flicker of TV screens on net curtains up and down the street.

There was an arrest team from Stockwell nick somewhere close by, two ambulances in the high street on standby.

'Came over my radio on the way down,' Charlie said. 'I heard he was on the move.'

'Nah, he just went down Sainsbury's to get a packet of smokes.'

The radio crackled to life. It was Amory. Markham had ditched something out of his pocket on the way back to his house.

'What was it?' Charlie said.

'Handful of tissues, my lads reckon.'

'They bagged it?'

'Affirmative. Christ knows what's in it.'

'Hope they wore hazmat suits. Out.'

'I need coffee, man,' James said.

'You can go get one if you want.'

'Nah, I don't want to miss anything, guv. Not after all this.'

'It might not be him,' Singh said, and got a shake of the head from James. Singh glanced at Charlie. He knew he shouldn't have said that.

But he was right. All they had was James playing around with letters and numbers, like it was the *Times* cryptic cross-word. What would they try next? Call in a psychic?

And if it *was* Markham, what were they doing sitting around outside his house all night? If they busted his door in right now, he might just burst into tears and tell them where Evie and Sarah were and it would be all over.

102

Or what if he was strangling one of them at this very minute, while they sat here debating who was going to get the caramel cortados from Costa?

It was his call. It would be down to him if this went tits-up.

He'd worked on one of these cases before, when he was a DS. He still remembered the missing girl's name: Stevie Price, fifteen she was, disappeared on her way home from a party at a friend's house. Underage drinking and all that. She deserved to get grounded, she didn't deserve to get grabbed.

His guv'nor at the time, Tilbury, he'd banged up this bloke, Dennis Storey. The geezer had form. Tilbury knew it was him, but he didn't have enough to charge him. He decided to haul him in anyway, thought he could sweat the truth out of him. But Storey asked for a brief and then sat there in the interview suite for the full ninety-six hours saying 'no comment' over and over, like a broken record.

When they let him go, they put him under surveillance. What good it did. The next day his mother went round his gaff and found him hanging in the garage. No great loss to the world, but that wasn't the kicker. They didn't find Stevie Price, or what was left of her, until six months later, in a shed on a run-down farm in Essex.

It belonged to Storey's brother.

What tore everyone in the squad to bits was that the pathologist couldn't tell them how long she'd been there. There was no way of knowing if she was still alive when they arrested Storey. If they'd held off, been a touch more patient, would it have made a difference?

His guv'nor never got over that one; he retired a year later, still eight years short of his pension. Started driving buses.

That could be me next week, Charlie thought. The 168 to Hampstead Heath.

'There's a shed in his back yard,' James said, pointing to his phone. 'You can see it here on Google Maps, satellite view.'

'Maybe he's got her in there,' Singh said.

'What we need is a drone,' James said. 'The army's got them, why can't we?'

'Because the Taliban don't have privacy laws. Now turn your bloody phone off, everyone in the street can see you.'

'Sorry, guv.'

He kept thinking about Evie Myers' mother, when he had interviewed her after her daughter was abducted. That was what always got to him most, the grief. Dead bodies, even when they were mutilated or decomposed, they were just part of a giant puzzle. It was the husbands and wives and families that unnerved him. Seeing mothers wail over tiny coffins, grown men collapsing when he told them their wives or daughters were gone.

His mind kept coming back to the CCTV. What was on the rag Sarah Howlett's abductor had put over her face? The skipper was right, chloroform would take a few minutes to work.

'Do you think he knows we're on to him?' Singh said.

'Markham? Let's hope not.'

'I mean, does he seriously think we'd do a door knock over a few quid of petrol?'

'According to his file, he has previous for receiving. There may be other activities he's covering up. The door-to-door was to make him nervous, panic him into doing something.'

'You don't reckon his mother knows about all this, that they've got some weirdness going on, like that Fred and Rose West?'

'Who knows?'

Charlie couldn't stop tapping his foot. Nerves. He put his hand on his knee to stop himself. Once you've made your decision, live with it, Charlie my son. No point in trying to second-guess him, or yourself.

He wished it was tomorrow and this was all over, done and dusted one way or the other. He'd survived all sorts of cock-ups this last twelve months, but this was a career killer if ever he saw one. No way the DCI would protect him if he was wrong.

If only he knew what was going on behind those net curtains.

His iPhone rang. He stared at the screen ID. It was Will.

'When are you coming home?'

'Do what?'

'What's the story, do I just sit here all night on my jack? Welcome back, Will. Good to see you again, Will.'

'I'm still at work. Call Ben.'

'You ever tried getting hold of Ben? He never picks up.'

'Will, this is very bad timing.'

'What am I supposed to do? Jules is in freaking Brighton, God's Chosen is in Liverpool, you and Ben are the only ones in London I can talk to.'

'Go and see Mum. Catch the Piccadilly line to Gloucester Road, then the 49 bus.'

'All these years since I've seen you, you'd think you could spare an hour or two.'

'Will, I'm sorry. I'll make it up to you. But right now, I've got to go.'

He powered down the phone. He caught Wes looking at him in the rear-view mirror, but he didn't say anything.

There was a single light on in the house at the end of the street.

'What the hell's going on in there?' James said.

Danny told Ines he was going outside for some fresh air. An ambulance pulled into the emergency bay, lights flashing. He watched the paramedics push some poor sod into A&E. As the glass doors closed behind them, he saw this wild-eyed desperado staring at him. Christ, it's me, Danny thought. That's what I look like. He walked over to the car park, pulled out the burner phone, powered it up.

He pressed 1 on the speed dial.

'It's me,' he said.

He saw the man from the waiting room standing outside the glass doors smoking a cigarette. There was something about him, he was certain now. Had to be a cop.

Christ.

'Something's come up,' he said into the phone. 'Oliver's hurt. He's in hospital.'

He watched another ambulance pull into the emergency entrance. All these bloody sick people clogging up the system, pushing him further back in the queue.

'Have you checked her pulse?' he said.

He tried to think. His options kept narrowing down. If you don't sort this, Danny boy, you're looking at serious prison time. This is conspiracy to murder.

'You have to stay close to the van. I'll be there as soon as I can.'

He hung up, walked back into A&E. Stay calm, Danny boy. That's your strength. Don't let this rattle you. One step at a time. He went back to the waiting room, sat Oliver back on his knee and read him Peppa Pig again.

It was after nine when they finally called Oliver's name. Danny took Ines in with him to help keep the boy calm. The nurse wanted Oliver to lie on an examination table, and that was when the fun started. He went berserk, started screaming the one word he could say: '*Mama!*'

Ines broke down sobbing. A nurse asked them to wait outside, said they were making it worse. How could he be making it worse? Danny thought. Ollie was his son, wasn't he?

Eventually they called them back in. It was quite a bad gash, they said. They'd had to suture it. They wanted to know how it had happened. One of the nurses was looking at him in a way he didn't like; must have thought it was child abuse. Thank God he had brought Ines. She took full responsibility, explained everything.

'Did he lose consciousness?' the doctor asked her.

'No,' Ines said. 'He just scream and scream.'

'Will you be admitting him?' Danny asked.

The doctor shook his head. 'There's no need for that. All his neurological signs are normal. You can keep an eye on him tonight, wake him up every couple of hours.'

'Every couple of hours?'

'If he vomits or you have trouble rousing him, you should bring him back in. But I'm sure he'll be fine now.'

'I still think he should be admitted,' Danny said.

'No, he can go home,' the doctor said, and left.

CHAPTER NINETEEN

The radio crackled. It was Amory. 'Target is on the move. Everyone sit tight. I have eyes on him.'

Charlie saw Markham heading towards them down the other side of the road. He had his hood up, but they could see him clearly as he walked under the street light: a sparse beard and a face like a bag of spanners.

There was a bloke in a parka headed the other way, walking a dog. Nice touch, the dog. He moved his head slightly to call it in as they passed each other. There would be another one of Amory's team waiting at the end of the street to take over.

A minute later, Amory was back on the radio. 'He's turned east, on Kitchener Street.' Then another voice broke in: 'I have the eye.'

'Come on, come on,' Charlie said.

'He's turned down a laneway by the betting shop.'

'Can you see what he's doing?' Amory said.

'Target has stopped. There's a row of garages. Subject has keys. He's unlocking one of the doors.'

'Instructions?' Amory said.

'Keep your eyes on,' Charlie said.

They waited. James started tapping his fingertips on the dashboard. Singh stared at him and he stopped.

'Come on,' James muttered. 'What's going on?'

'Do you have vehicles ready to follow if necessary?' Charlie asked.

'Affirmative,' Amory said.

Singh gave Charlie a look: What are we waiting for?

'It could be just where he keeps the van,' Charlie said. 'Evie and Sarah might be elsewhere.'

The radio crackled. A voice said: 'Target has entered the garage and pulled down the roller door.'

'Is his van in there?'

'Can't get that close or he'll see me.'

'Roger that,' Charlie said.

'Instructions?' Amory repeated.

'Wait,' Charlie said. He wiped the palm of his right hand on his trousers. Two choices, he thought. The van's in there and he's doing running repairs; or two, he's there to rape one of the women.

Or murder them.

'How long's he been inside?' James said.

Singh looked at his watch, touched the digital display. 'Two minutes,' he said.

In situations like this, Charlie thought, some cops said they followed their instincts. But instinct was bloody unreliable, in his experience. In the end, you had to go with the odds, and with logic, and hope for the best.

He pressed the transmit button on the Airwave radio. 'That's it. Go in. Arrest target. Now.'

James started the engine. The tyres squealed as he made the U-turn and headed back up towards Kitchener Street. Charlie could hear sirens; the lads would be giving it the full drama, taking a crowbar to the roller door, running in with their Hecklers and body armour, *Armed police, down on the floor.*

Please let Sarah and Evie be in that garage, and alive.

There were four patrol cars skewed across the street, more uniforms running into the alley. Charlie got out and followed them. One of the pandas had its headlights pointed at the garage; there were torches going this way and that, coppers shouting orders, another voice, terrified, swearing and squealing.

'Lie down, *lie down*, do not move!'

Charlie felt suddenly calm. Remember your dignity, son. Right or wrong, it's done now. He put his hands in his pockets. The scrote in the hoody was face down on the bitumen under a scrum of beefy constables.

A sergeant was reading him his rights, one knee in his back, the other reaching behind him for his speed cuffs. 'You do not have to say anything, but if you do – keep still, you little bastard – say anything it may be taken down and used in evidence – fucking stay still – against you. It may harm your defence if you do not mention anything on which you later come to rely in court.'

Charlie nodded to the two constables with him and they dragged Markham back to his feet.

Charlie got straight in his face. 'Where are they?' he said.

Markham looked right through him. Could just be shock, Charlie thought.

Then he heard one of the uniforms shout: 'She's in here!' He turned away from Markham and went in.

The van took up most of the space. Charlie clocked it quickly, to make sure it was the same one. He swore under his breath. There was something wrong here. The van that had been used in the Howlett abduction had a broken wing mirror and a dent in the front right bumper.

He heard a woman's voice, something like a moan and a sob. He had never heard a sound quite like it. She was tied to a metal chair, hysterical, shaking, half dressed. 'Get her a blanket, for Christ's sake,' Charlie said. 'Where's the paramedics?'

Two of them rushed past him. The uniforms stood back, let the medics tend to her. One of them peeled a slick of grey tape off her mouth as gently as she could. Her partner started cutting the gaffer tape off her ankles and wrists.

The girl's knickers were in the corner, on a filthy mattress. There was blood on them.

Somebody found the light switch; there was a bare bulb on

the end of a piece of frayed flex. Charlie clocked a plastic bin in the corner, a pack of cable ties, some empty baked bean tins. Half a dozen Philips cartons were stacked against one wall. Wes gave him a look: just when you thought you'd seen it all.

Singh tore open one of the cartons. 'Plasma TV,' he said.

'Blagged,' Charlie said. 'Looks like kidnapping was a sideline.'

He did a full three-sixty, looking for somewhere that might contain a body. The obvious place was the back of the van. 'She must be in there,' Rupe said.

Charlie took a deep breath and threw open the rear doors.

He was prepared for anything. He was hoping she'd be there, trussed up, gagged, but somehow alive. He had also braced himself for a dead body. What he saw, he wasn't prepared for at all.

The van was empty.

'Where's the other girl?' James said.

CHAPTER TWENTY

A WPC crouched down next to the girl on the chair. 'Can you tell us your name?' she said.

She was too hysterical to make any sense. He recognised her from her photograph: it was Evie Myers. So where was Sarah?

The paramedics had Evie on her feet, supported on each side, and helped her out to the stretcher they had set up outside the garage. 'This is a crime scene,' Charlie said. 'Sergeant, put up a cordon, everyone out.'

'Sir.'

He stood outside with James and Singh. 'Get the CS team down here as soon as.' James nodded and pulled out his phone. 'Rupe, when he's done that, get back to Markham's gaff, effect the search warrant. I'll send Lube and Mac to help you. Bring his mother back to the nick with you; we'll talk to her as well. And get on to the skipper, tell him to find out who owns this place.'

He looked back at the garage. Where was she? Did Markham have a second hidey-hole?

Evie was still wailing as they loaded her into the back of the ambulance; it was more like a howl, sent shivers up him, the kind of sound that made him want to get the bloke that had done this to her and screw off his nuts with a monkey wrench.

Now, now, Charlie. Remember PACE.

There were lights going on up and down the street. Every man and his dog would be here soon. He found the sergeant. 'You'd better get another cordon down the end there,' he said. 'We're going to pull a bigger crowd than Beyoncé.'

Charlie got into the back of the patrol car where Christopher Markham was sitting, hunched over, his head almost between his knees. Charlie pulled his hood back. He had a buzz cut, scabs where the razor had nicked his scalp. He had a sort of beard, but it was just bum fluff. It amazed him sometimes when you came face to face with a villain how ordinary some of them looked, like they'd never done anything more gangsta than run out of Sainsbury's without paying for a packet of cheese and onion crisps.

'Hello, Chris. I'm Detective Inspector George. Where's Sarah Howlett?'

'What?'

'The other girl you abducted. Where is she?'

'The fuck you talking about?'

Back in the day, before civil liberties and bleeding hearts got into bed with the crooks, you could smack these scrotes about a bit, teach them some manners. But all that was before his time.

'If we find both of the girls alive, it's going to go a lot better for you.'

'I've no idea what you're fucking talking about.'

'Look, Chris, we have you bang to rights for this. No point being coy about it. Tell us where she is and let's get this over with.'

'I want a solicitor.'

'Well, you can have one, soon as we get you back to the station, but it will go a lot easier for you if we can send both these young ladies back to their families tonight.'

Markham gave him a look and shook his head. He had some sort of religious symbol tattooed on the side of his neck. It looked like a crucifix.

'Nice tatt,' Charlie said.

'Like it, do you?'

'You should get another one, just above your jacksie, something like "Wait Your Turn". Come in handy, that, when you're in Belmarsh.'

113

'You're a right comedian, aren't ya? Regular Ricky Ger-face.'

'Actually, I'm serious. Good-looking bloke like you won't last five minutes.'

'Go fuck yourself, copper.'

'That's original, I never heard that one before. I'm curious, Chris: what was your genius plan here? What were you going to do with Evie when you got bored with her? Say goodbye and promise to write? That's her name, by the way. Evie. She has a name.'

'I wasn't going to hurt her, was I?'

'I don't know. She didn't seem to me like she was having a lot of fun here. I could hear her sobbing through the ambulance doors.'

'It just happened. I never thought it all through, like.'

'Really? I'm amazed. This entire episode smacks of meticulous planning. Now I'll ask you one more time. Where is Sarah Howlett?'

'I dunno what you're talking about, all right?'

'If Sarah was ever in that van, we'll know. Doesn't matter how you think you've cleaned it up, we'll find a trace.'

'Be my guest, Sherlock. I told ya, I dunno what you're talking about. I'm not saying anything else till I talk to my brief. I know my rights.'

Charlie got out of the car. One of the surveillance crew was leaning against the wall at the end of the alley, having a cheeky puff on a cigarette. What he wouldn't give for a gasper right now. Should be a law.

See, the thing he'd realised about cigarettes, it wasn't the nicotine. What smoking did was help you inhale all the uncomfortable feelings before they could claw their way out. It was a way of swallowing your own emotions before they could cause trouble.

He turned away. A black Merc pulled up at the end of the alley and the DCI got out. He looked proper chipper, hair perfect, a new tie, all ready to talk to the media. He had a sixth sense for glory, did FONC. He won't be so chirpy when he finds out Sarah Howlett isn't here.

'Charlie! We've got him then.'

'Yes, sir, he's in the car. The team did a good job.'

'The two young women are safe?'

'Sir, are you a glass-half-empty or a glass-half-full type of person?'

'Talk English, Charlie.'

'We've got Evie Myers; she's alive, if not fabulously well. Trouble is, we don't have Sarah. Markham claims he knows nothing about her.'

'He's lying.'

'Possibly. But if she's been here or in the van, or in his old lady's house, we'll soon know.'

'There's definitely no sign of her?'

Charlie didn't bother to dignify the question with a response. He assumed his boss was being rhetorical.

'What am I going to tell those people?' the DCI said, nodding towards the media huddle already forming outside the cordon.

'More importantly, sir, what are we going to tell Mr Howlett and Sarah's father? We should let them know about this before they see it on the news.'

The DCI stood there opening and closing his hands into fists at his sides. He didn't mind failure – he could always blame that on someone – but this was different, this was confusion. Two women taken in two days in the same way by two different people.

How the hell could that happen?

'I told you, Charlie,' he said. 'You shouldn't have made Sarah Howlett part of Operation Loxley.' And he walked away.

CHAPTER TWENTY-ONE

The DCI was in his shirtsleeves. Charlie tried not to look shocked. He hardly ever saw him without his jacket.

'Sit down, sit down,' he said, pointing to the chair on the other side of his desk.

Charlie sat.

'Well, it's all over the morning news. The papers are going to eat this up. There's a right flap on upstairs. We told the press there was one bloke, and now we have to tell them, oh sorry, there's another one.'

Not my fault, Charlie thought. Wasn't my call. He looked over the DCI's shoulder at the view, sun just coming up, nice. He could see the Emirates from here, another place where disasters were always only a heartbeat away.

'How's the girl, is she going to be all right?'

'I don't know, sir. I'm not a shrink. Personally, I don't see how someone could ever be all right again after what she's been through. But she's alive at least. No permanent physical injury.'

The DCI pretended to read the file Charlie had brought him on Markham. 'This is the bloke, is it?'

'He's strictly low-level, well, has been up until now. Even his old mum didn't know what he was about. He rented this garage a few months ago, it's about ten minutes from where he lives; used it for storage, stuff him and his mates nicked or were fencing.'

'He has nothing to do with the disappearance of Sarah Howlett?'

'His brief gave us a prepared statement. He's bang to rights on Evie Myers but he's sticking with his story about Sarah. We won't be getting any more out of him. End of, far as he's concerned.'

'You think he's telling the truth?'

'Personally, I don't think he's anywhere smart enough to make up a lie this big. But we'll have to wait for forensics.'

'So, we could be looking at a copycat?'

'Or a very remarkable coincidence,' Charlie said.

'I don't believe in coincidence.'

'Our main suspect is still the husband. I hope it's him. If it's some random nutter, then we've really got our work cut out.'

'If it is Daniel Howlett, what's his motivation?'

'She's his wife. I think blokes rubbing out their spouses has happened a couple of times before.'

'No need for sarcasm, Charlie.'

'My intel has checked him out.' Charlie threw another file on the DCI's desk. 'No criminal dealings, apart from the fact that he works in the City. He has a couple of convictions for speeding, but that's about it. I asked him to surrender his phone and his laptop. He's let us download the data on his phone, but he point-blank refused to hand over his computer. Says there's too much sensitive information on it regarding his work.'

'That is suspicious.'

'Or it could be he has other things to hide that have nothing to do with the investigation.'

'Does he have an alibi for the night she went missing?'

'The whole street provided an alibi; seems like half of Clapham heard the shouting and screaming when she drove off. They all saw him go back inside the house. His phone records indicate he called her from home two minutes before the abduction.'

'What about the vehicle?'

'The plates were reported stolen Monday afternoon from an address in South Croydon.'

'ANPR?'

Charlie laid a printout on the desk. It was a map of the streets around Clapham Common, and the confirmed CCTV and ANPR grabs had been time-stamped and highlighted.

'The traffic team provided us with all the possible access and egress points. The plates only showed up here, on this side of the common.'

'You think he swapped plates?'

'The vehicle had certain irregularities; we were able to trace it on CCTV for a short distance, but lost it the other side of Tooting Bec. It suggests that the driver knew where cameras were located and had a route planned to avoid them. It wasn't a crime of opportunity. This was premeditated.'

'So if the husband is involved, he has an accomplice.'

'Yes, sir.'

'Do you have anything else?'

'If Mr Howlett is even half as smart as he thinks he is, he'll be using a burner phone. He would have arranged for someone else to do his dirty work; money wouldn't be a problem. Parm tells me Sarah Howlett is carrying half a million pounds in life insurance. If Mr Howlett has financial problems, he might have thought about cashing in early.'

'Where does that leave us?'

'I'd like to put him under close surveillance for at least the next forty-eight hours.'

The DCI turned his chair around and looked out of the window. Charlie's gaze was drawn back to the silhouette of the Emirates stadium. He felt a pang, thrill and pain all mixed together, like looking at the photograph of a lover who kept doing him wrong.

Still, he'd love to be there right now. Some academic he had read about reckoned that football was the common man's way of escaping from his life, that it was the preferred opioid of the blue-collar worker. There had certainly been times when the Arsenal had left him in a bit of a drugged stupor. But right now, he would have been proper happy to be sitting there in the sunshine with Ben, along with a load of podgy blokes with their shirts off, watching Arsenal grind out a 0–0 draw.

The DCI was quiet for a long time. He must be feeling a bit chastened, Charlie thought; he clearly couldn't blame anyone else for this mess.

'I blame you for this, Charlie,' he said finally. 'You were the SIO, after all.'

'Sir, if you recall, it was me that said Sarah Howlett's disappearance should not be part of Operation Loxley.'

'Well, let's not get into the blame game. What you have to work out now is what to do to save the situation. Report back to me at 1700 latest. We have to find this woman alive, or there's going to be hell to pay.'

He gave Charlie the kind of reassuring smile that said: and you're the one who's going to be doing the paying.

The team, thirty-five detectives and civilian staff, sat around the incident room in a rough horseshoe, Charlie and Grey in the middle. Charlie needed to get them all to refocus. It had been a rough night; the elation of finding Evie had quickly turned to frustration when they realised their job was only half done.

Dawson had made a start on a new whiteboard, taken down the crime-scene shots of Evie Myers and her car; there was just the map of Clapham up there now, together with some ANPR and CCTV stills.

Charlie let Parm open the meeting. While he and the lads had been living the dream in the back alleys of Brixton, she had been doing some hard yards in front of her monitor screen. The telephony confirmed that Daniel Howlett's last call to his wife was at 1.12 a.m. on the morning she disappeared, and that Sarah had not picked up.

'Her GPS showed frequent trips to Chelmsford, where her father lives, and a wildlife park about five miles away. She had also driven to the location where she was abducted on two previous occasions in the past ten days.'

119

'What about Facebook?'

'Just the usual, selfies with her kid, holiday photographs. If you didn't know better, you'd think she had the perfect life.'

'Dead giveaway, that,' Charlie said. 'The more miserable someone is, the more photos they put on their social media. Anything else? What about her financials?'

Parm had found two red flags: two weeks before she disappeared, Sarah had withdrawn fifteen hundred pounds from her savings account, cash. There had been another large withdrawal the week before, again in cash, of one thousand pounds.

'We'll have to ask Mr Howlett if he knows anything about that. Anything interesting in her emails, her WhatsApp?'

'Not much. I made a list.'

Charlie nodded for her to hand it to the skipper.

'Anything else?'

'The GPS on her car. The day before she disappeared, she drove to South Croydon railway station. It doesn't fit her pattern.'

'What would she be doing in Croydon?'

'That's what I wondered.'

Charlie turned to Lubanski, who was standing at the back eating a sausage roll. 'How did you and Mac get on yesterday?'

She checked her notebook, went through their canvass of the houses overlooking the Howlett crime scene; who they'd talked to, what they'd said, spelling out names and numbers. They'd grabbed CCTV for every conceivable route the van might have taken after kidnapping Sarah. The results had been on the printout Charlie had given the DCI.

Meanwhile, James and Singh had talked to the Howletts' neighbours.

'One of them said she saw women coming and going some evenings.'

'What sort of women?'

'Just women.'

'How many? All at once, one at a time, what?'

120

'One at a time. She was pretty vague. She said lots of women; when I tried to pin her down, it sounded like three or four over the last six months.'

'Well, it's something we should ask him about. How did you go at Dillon and Rowe?'

'Didn't get anything. All his colleagues say they're shocked, can't believe what's happened, the usual thing. What's London coming to, you know. A couple of them said that on the quiet he was a bit of a lad, but there wasn't any hot and heavy affair going on, not that any of them knew about. Consensus was, he had the perfect life. You could get jealous just reading the statements.'

'Did you speak to his bosses?'

'They think the sun shines out of his fundamental orifice. Apparently he's in charge of the currency trading division; it made them profits in the region of upwards of six hundred million quid last year.'

'I had my doubts about one bloke,' Singh said.

'Go on.'

He took his notebook out of his shirt pocket and checked the name. 'Reeves. Taj Reeves. He works in the compliance section.'

'What's that, then?'

'They're the ones who are supposed to make sure the rest of the bankers are behaving honestly.'

'He must put in a lot of overtime. What was wrong with him?'

'I don't know. He just seemed jumpy.'

'Too much nose beer, maybe.'

They had some trace on the van. Wes's contact at Ford had identified the make and model. 'It's a 1998 Ford Transit VG,' Wes said, putting down his muffin. 'I've run it through the PNC to see how many there are registered in the local postcodes.'

'And?'

'Quite a few. Over five hundred.'

There was a groan around the room. Getting the list was

easy, viewing them all not so much. As it was a commercial van, most of them would be garaged miles away from where they were registered. The process could take hours, weeks, and they still might not get them all. And what if it had been brought over from the Continent?

'Like looking for a polar bear in a haystack,' McCullough said.

'Snowstorm,' Charlie said.

'Looking for a snowstorm in a haystack? That doesn't make sense.'

'McCullough, what are you on?'

'Sorry, guv. Bit foggy. Haven't had much sleep.'

'None of us have. Try and keep up with the programme.' He looked at Dawson. 'Action that when we're finished, Skipper. Anything else?'

'How did the Lexus break down?' Singh said.

'Forensics say that it hit the kerb at speed, twice, punctured the tyre and damaged a tie rod. It would have made the car impossible to drive.'

'How did she do that, then?'

'She was upset, I suppose. According to Mr Howlett, she had also been drinking.' Charlie checked his notes. 'All right, that's it then. There's going to be another public appeal, TV, press, with CCTV pictures of the van. Meanwhile we need to talk to everyone on Parm's list, find out what we can about Sarah Howlett. We also need to interview the nanny. Skipper, set up appointments with all Howlett's work colleagues, family and known associates, run them all through the system. Then action the jobs. I don't think I need to remind you all that we're in a race against time. Let's crack on.'

Charlie went back to his office. He had three missed calls from Sanderson. He had been up in the wilds of Essex since last night with Sarah's father. Charlie called him back.

'Brett. How are you, all right?'

'Not brilliant, guv.'

'How did Mr Jones react to the news from this morning?'

'Not good. Came right undone, he did. Got in his car and said he was driving down to see you. Couldn't stop him. Sorry, guv.'

'When did he leave?'

'About an hour ago. That's why I've been calling you.'

'I was in meetings. Not to worry. I can deal with him. Did you get anything more out of him?'

'Not really. To be honest, he gives me the creeps a bit.'

'How do you mean?'

'There are photos of Sarah everywhere. He still has a room made up for her, like a little kid's room. He said it was just as she left it, but if that's true she must have been like ten years old when she left home to get married. Teddy bears everywhere, pink frilly curtains. Crazy.'

I was right about him first time, Charlie thought.

Never trust anyone who looks like Nigel Farage.

CHAPTER TWENTY-TWO

Tony Jones looked like he'd been pumped full of high-grade amphetamines. One of the staffers had put him in an interview room, got him a cup of tea and a biscuit. He hadn't touched them. He was doing laps of the room when Charlie walked in. He'd lit up, even though there was a sign right in front of his face: no mobile phones, no smoking. He'd been using his mug of tea as an ashtray.

Well, there's grateful for you.

'Have you heard anything?' he said to Charlie – shouted it really – as soon as he walked into the room. His eyes were red-rimmed, sunk into hollows; it hurt to look at him.

'Not yet, Mr Jones. How about you take the weight off?' Charlie held out a chair.

'That other cop, Samson . . .'

'DC Sanderson.'

'Him. He said if you found the first girl, you'd find my Sarah.'

'No, I don't think so. He's been trained not to make statements like that. He might have suggested it as a possible line of enquiry. We now believe your daughter's abduction was a separate incident wholly unrelated to the first.'

'He said you'd arrested someone. What are you people playing at?'

'Can you sit down, please, Mr Jones, my head's doing a three-sixty here. That's it. Now, a few deep breaths. Good. Okay, to answer your question, we're not playing at anything, I assure you. We have arrested someone for the kidnapping of

124

Evie Myers, but he has denied all involvement in the abduction of your daughter.'

'You leave me alone with this bloke for five minutes, I'll soon get it out of him where my Sar is.'

'Perhaps I'm not making myself crystal. We now have absolutely no reason to believe this person had any role in your daughter's disappearance.'

'Fuck,' Tony said, and slammed his fist on the desk, spilling the tea. He stood up again and did another circuit of the room. 'When I heard you'd arrested this bloke, I got my hopes up, I did, I was sure you'd found my little girl.' He started crying.

Oh for God's sake, Charlie thought, reaching for the tissues.

'Mr Jones, please sit down again. Getting yourself into a state isn't going to help Sarah right now.'

It was like someone had suddenly let all the air out. Jones slumped into his chair and hung his head between his knees. 'I can't stand it. Thinking of some bloke doing stuff to her. She's out there somewhere all alone, and no one to help her. She just wants her old dad. If anything happens to her, I don't know what I'll do. I'd be lost without my little girl. Promise me, promise me you'll find her.'

Cardinal rule number one, Charlie thought. Never make any promise you can't keep. 'We are working around the clock on your daughter's case, Mr Jones. All our resources are focused on finding the person who has taken her.'

'Do you have anything to go on? Any leads at all? You must have a registration number or a witness or something? She can't just disappear, right in the middle of London.'

'We're hoping we might get some help from the general public on this one.'

'Are you? If you're relying on the public in London, then you're up shit creek without a paddle.'

'What we would like you to do is go on television for us, make a public appeal for information. Perhaps side by side with Mr Howlett. Do you think you could do that for us?'

'I wouldn't get on a life raft with that bastard. I blame him for all this. What was he doing letting her roam the streets at one in the morning? You know about him, don't you, what he does?'

'What should we know about him?'

'He wants everyone to think he's this big City banker. What he is is a lowlife. He gambles, he does drugs. He's a deviant.'

Great, Charlie thought. Three new lines of enquiry. He wondered if any of them had anything to do with the case in hand.

'What sort of drugs?'

'I don't know. He's into everything, him. And he makes her do stuff.'

'What sort of stuff?'

'I don't know, she won't tell me. But I know there's something funny going on, I'm not stupid.'

Charlie mulled it over. It wasn't unusual for in-laws not to like each other, so he wondered how much substance there was to all this. He needed something a bit more substantial than a bit of name-calling.

'You told me yesterday that you thought your son-in-law had a hand in your daughter's disappearance.'

'Well, I wouldn't put it past him.'

'That's not really hard evidence, though, is it?'

Tony shook his head and reached for his cup of tea. Charlie put out his hand and stopped him, pointed to the cigarette butt floating in it. 'I need to get back to work, Mr Jones. I'll get someone to fetch you another cup of tea, and then our media officer will be down to talk to you about doing the appeal. Is that all right?'

Tony let out a sob and nodded his head.

When Charlie walked into the incident room, the skipper was eating watermelon out of a Tupperware container. He had juice on his chin. 'Now then,' he said when he saw Charlie.

'You got bits of fruit on you, old son,' Charlie said. The

126

skipper wiped it off with his hand and then stared at his fingers, like: *What do I do now?*

Wes leaned over and threw him a napkin out of his Pret croissant packet.

The skipper wiped his hands and chucked the napkin in the bin.

'You're welcome,' Wes said.

'Anything on the hotline?' Charlie said.

'Usual twonks and mentals. Nothing so far.'

'The DCI has authorised a televised media appeal. We're going to use Sarah's father.'

'What about her husband?'

'He's not been that helpful. We're going to see him now. Matt, get the car keys. We'd better have another chat with Mr Howlett. I don't think we have had anything like full disclosure yet.'

CHAPTER TWENTY-THREE

Ania woke with a start. She sat up, couldn't remember where she was. It was light, and already warm. She didn't remember falling asleep; she had lain awake most of the night, going through things in her mind. Her head ached, her neck hurt, her back and legs were cramped and stiff.

Sarah.

She looked into the back of the van. Sarah lay like a bundle of rags against the bench seat. Her skin was grey, like a dead person. Ania picked up her arm, felt for a pulse on her wrist. She couldn't find one. But she was too warm for dead. She felt at her throat, thought she detected something, put her cheek down, close to her mouth. She was still breathing, not much, a little bit. She was still alive.

She checked the phone. Nothing. Danny hadn't called. No messages.

What if he didn't come?

She tried to shake Sarah awake, but she didn't move. When she comes around, Ania thought, I will talk to her: okay, Sarah, let's do a deal. You don't tell my name to the police, I will let you go. No hard feeling. You tell the police Danny did this, this farm belong to a friend of his, okay. Did you know that?

I will go back to Poland, but you don't tell anyone about me.

Oh sure, she will say, yes, okay, and we wave goodbye at the train station, blow kisses. This is not going to happen.

Anyway, nothing for me in Białystok. No choice. Must go through with this, come too far to go back now.

128

She saw something in the wing mirror. There was a vehicle coming along the road at the end of the track. It slowed down. It was a work van; there was a name written on the side.

Please don't stop. Don't be Good Samaritan, whatever.

The van sped up again and headed off down the lane.

'That's it,' Ania said aloud. 'Nothing to see here.'

She watched it in her side mirror until it was almost out of sight. As she let out her breath, she saw the brake lights flash.

'No. Mind your own business.'

She saw the glow of the reversing lights as the driver started to back up.

There was a noise behind her. She looked over the bench seat. Sarah's eyes were open. Ania tried to grab her, but Sarah squirmed away, across the floor of the van, kicked both her feet against the side door. She was making grunting noises, her mouth opening and closing like a beached fish.

'No, Sarah, don't,' Ania said. 'It's all right, I'm going to let you go. Please don't make noise.'

Kick-kick-kick. The van started to rock.

Ania clambered over the back seat, grabbed Sarah, tried to pull her away from the door. 'Shut up! Just shut up!' Sarah was wriggling and moaning. Ania tried to find something to stuff in her mouth. She put her hand over her face. Sarah bit her, then raised her hips and kicked out. Her heel caught Ania in the mouth, sent her reeling back.

Ania looked for something, anything to use to subdue her. She saw a wrench lying under the bench seat. She grabbed it and hit Sarah with it, not hard, just enough to scare her maybe, keep her quiet. The blow caught her on the shoulder; her eyes went wide and she screamed. The noise panicked Ania and she hit her again, but Sarah twisted away and the blow landed on her back.

She hit her once more. Sarah stopped kicking and yelling and lay still. A torrent of blood pulsed out of her hair and down her neck.

She dropped the wrench and scrambled back over the seat.

The van was coming up the private road, the tyres crunching on the gravel. It stopped and the driver got out. He looked young; he had long hair and a donkey jacket. What does he want? Ania wondered. Maybe he thinks I've broken down, or he just wants to know what I'm doing here. I hope he isn't one of those creeps who sees a woman on her own, thinks he can do what he wants.

She grabbed the phone off the dashboard as she got out, held it to her ear so he would think he had caught her mid conversation.

'Yes, honey, yes, love you too.'

'Got a problem?' the man said, smiling. He was mid twenties, she supposed, long-limbed, nice smile. He had left his van door open; that was a good sign, it didn't look as if he was about to try anything.

She held up her hand to let him know that she was talking to someone on the phone.

'No, a man has stopped in a van, it says "Reid Auto Body Repairs" on the side. No, I'll wait for you, sweetheart. Bye.'

That should stall him, she thought, if he is thinking of trying anything with me. She put the phone back in her pocket, felt for the wrench, remembered she had left it in the van.

'Broken down?' he said.

'Yes, but it's all right, my boyfriend's coming, he knows all about cars. He's not far away.'

'Where are you headed?'

Ania tried to remember the road signs she had seen last night. 'Hastings. But I got tired last night and came up here, wanted somewhere quiet to sleep, you know? Now the van, she won't start.'

'I can take a look for you,' he said. 'I've got some tools in the back. They're pretty basic, these old vans. No computers to fiddle with.'

'No, please, it's okay. Anyway, my boyfriend, he is on his way.'

130

'Okay, well, if you're sure you're going to be all right . . .'

'Yes, fine. Thanks for stopping.'

He shrugged and got back in his van. 'Hope your friend gets here soon,' he said.

She stood in the middle of the lane as Reid Auto Body Repairs reversed down to the road. She watched until he was out of sight, then went back to the van and opened the doors. Dear God, what had she done? Sarah lay still, blood all over her head and her face.

Ania's legs gave way and she slumped to her knees. She retched in the bushes, over and over, until her stomach hurt.

CHAPTER TWENTY-FOUR

They drove over Blackfriars Bridge. When he was a kid, Charlie had never imagined they'd need anti-terror bollards up here to stop a bunch of religious nutjobs running down the tourists. Made you wonder what kind of God they imagined in their diseased brains, some monstrous old man who would nod along approvingly while they were doing it, cheering them on, like: *Yeah, way to go, boys, that's worth a few virgins, one more and you can have my sister as well.*

He was glad the Oxo Tower was still there, hadn't been tipped over to make way for some glass needle with a funny nickname. Used to love Oxo cubes when he was a kid; take them out of their wrapper and suck them all the way to school on a cold day.

'Nice suit, guv,' Grey said.

'Thanks. It's Ted Baker overcheck.'

'Regent Street?'

'Stoke Newington. There's a Sally Army shop. Fifty quid. Nice lady in there gave me a discount when she found out I was a copper.'

'Fifty quid?'

'Well, they didn't know Ted Baker from a hole in the ground.'

'How did a Ted Baker end up in Stoke Newington?'

'Dunno. Maybe a really intense mugging. Look out for the old lady.'

'She's crossing on a red light.'

'She probably can't see the red light. Give her a break, Sergeant.'

Grey did as he was told and slowed down. He glanced over. 'What's that you keep checking on your phone, guv?'

'The Arsenal website. I don't know why I do it; season's still a couple of weeks away.'

'Arsenal?'

'I'm a Gooner.'

'A what?'

'That's someone who's passionate about the Arsenal. It's not brilliant if you like winning, but it's a great way of learning to deal with the disappointments of life. Who do you follow?'

'No one really. I'm more of a rugby man.'

'Rugby, right.' Well, that killed that conversation. Charlie turned off his phone and stared at the grey ribbon of river. 'Did you know,' he said, 'there's so much cocaine in the Thames, it's making the eels hyperactive and threatening their survival.'

Grey looked blank.

'People in London are ingesting too much Bolivian marching powder and then pissing it into the sewage system. End result, the poor old eels are getting coked out of their nuts. They're swimming to France and back every day.'

'I've never touched cocaine.'

'No, me neither,' Charlie said. 'But I've stopped eating jellied eels before a shift. What do you do for fun, then?'

'I'm married, guv.'

'Does that mean you've stopped having fun?'

'No, I do, but I mean, it's like built in. We have two kids now and they keep us pretty busy.'

'Nice. How old are you, Sergeant?'

'Twenty-nine. I'll be thirty in a few months.'

'And you've already got a wife and two kids? You're a man on a mission. Get on, do you, you and your missus?'

'We've known each other since school. She's my best friend, I suppose.'

Jesus, Charlie thought. What am I doing wrong?

'Are you married, guv?'

133

'No, still single, me.'

'Girlfriend?'

Charlie shook his head. 'Who'd have me? Face like a Chernobyl fireman.'

'Don't think that's quite true. Lubanski reckons you clean up good. Actually, "bangable" was the word she used.'

'Lube? Get away.'

'True. I overheard her talking to one of the staffers.'

'Well, that's very nice of her.'

'Not your type?'

'She's one of my detectives, so that makes her definitely not my type. All squad members are strictly off limits. Anyway, I'm taking a break. It hasn't been a good year, romantically speaking. Turn left here.'

'I thought we were going to Clapham.'

'I want to look in on DC Lovejoy. She's having another op.'

'Right. I heard what happened.'

'Yeah, I think everyone in Great Britain has.'

The clinic was on the fifth floor. He found Lovejoy propped up in bed. She had her own private room, a plasma TV on the wall, no one coughing up a lifetime of Benson & Hedges in the next bed.

'Nice,' Charlie said. 'Lovely view, if you like railways. Look at that, there's even a bit of Tower Bridge. Amazing what you get on the NHS these days.'

'Dad paid for all this.'

'Yeah, I know. I was being ironic.'

She picked up the remote and turned down the sound on the television, then rearranged her hospital gown.

'First time I've seen you in a dress,' Charlie said.

'You should see it from the back. It's quite a statement. What are you doing here, guv?'

'Come to cheer you up.'

'Go on, then.'

'All right. What's sweet and eats people?'

134

'Don't know. What is sweet and eats people?'

'Hannibal Nectar.'

'That's crap, guv.'

'Sorry. It's all I've got. How's the foot?'

'Still there. For the moment.'

'I forgot to bring the grapes.'

'A giant Toblerone would do. You look like shite, guv.'

'Thanks.'

'I've been watching the news. Thought you'd be too busy to waste your time in here. You're the last person I expected to see.'

'Funny expression, that. The last person would be like Vladimir Putin or Donald Trump, wouldn't it? Anyway, I was just passing.'

Beside the bed she had a picture of Charlie the spaniel with a toy Union Jack bone in his mouth. Charlie was her rescue dog; he'd done the rescuing himself, which was how the dog had got its name.

'Dad brought the photo in,' she said. 'He thought I'd be missing him.'

'Are you?'

'Suppose.'

She'd seemed all right at first, but now that he'd got closer, he could see she'd been crying. She had that hollow-eyed look people get when they're desperate.

'How they treating you in here?'

'Proper nice. The food's amazing. Three times a day. I even get vegetables.'

'What are vegetables?' Charlie said.

A male nurse came in. He looked a bit like Chris Hemsworth, Charlie thought. He stood back while the guy did Lovejoy's obs. He saw the way she looked at him, or he thought he did, and he felt a twinge of something. What was that? Not jealousy, Charlie, surely?

After the nurse had left, she said, 'I keep thinking about

135

what I'm going to do with one leg. Do you know many murder squad detectives with a prosthetic foot?'

'Not in Serious Crime, but every other bloke in the Flying Squad's got a prosthesis. You'd be surprised. Go to Scotland Yard, ask the senior detectives to roll up their trousers. Hardly a complete set of socks anywhere.'

That almost got a smile out of her, but not quite. 'Might have to start again, I suppose. Not easy, when you're over thirty, just when you think you've got everything sorted.'

'So, are you one of those people that likes to have everything mapped out?'

'Not really. I suppose it was more like one thing leading to another, and then one day here I am, lying in a hospital bed, no house, no life and a doctor saying, sorry, might have to chop your foot off.'

Charlie was going to say, *it could be worse*, but that was easy to say when you had all the bits you were born with. So he didn't say anything.

'I liked being a cop. I felt like I'd finally found something I was good at. Know what I mean?'

'I've never wanted to do anything else, so I don't know, really.' He sat down on the edge of the bed, then stood up again. That might be considered too familiar. 'How did you end up in the Met anyway?'

'I was a journalist with the *Echo*. They sent me to cover a murder case at Chelmsford Crown Court, this homeless bloke who'd been set on fire by some low-lifes in Clacton. And these two detectives were up there giving evidence, and it struck me they were the only ones who cared about this poor sod. They made sure he got justice in the end, and I thought, well that's what I want to do. It's something worthwhile to do with your life.'

'Impressive,' Charlie said. He looked at the view across the Thames. 'Me, I joined up because I wanted to get in the Drug Squad and take bribes.'

She grinned. 'And here you are, on the side of the angels after all. Life is unkind.' She gave him a look that he could have interpreted as tender, so he glanced away. 'You should ask one of the nurses to turn a bed down for you, guv. Don't mind me saying, you look proper stuffed.'

'Don't remember the last time I slept.'

'You're no closer?'

'To finding Sarah Howlett? No. We've had to start again from square one. We should be celebrating right now. We got a result: Evie Myers is alive and back with her family, happy days. You should have seen her father when I told him, thought he was going to kiss me. After that, I should have been down the boozer with the skip and the rest of the team, then maybe even twelve hours' shut-eye. Instead I'm still hard at it. This is the case that never ends.'

'Any leads?'

'Unless forensics says otherwise, we have to discount Markham. We've also got the husband under surveillance. FONC isn't happy about it; I've already blown out his budget for this year. But I've had a funny feeling about the bloke right from the off.'

'Is he your main suspect?'

'At this stage, yes. You should see him, thinks he's the dog's bollocks. When I went round there yesterday morning, when his missus first disappeared, he was like, *meh, that's inconvenient, I'll have to cancel my meeting.* Still, if he'd been in floods, I'd have been suspicious too. He volunteered that they'd had a huge fight the night before. He's clearly not in love with her.'

'I saw the DCI on the TV, going public. Looked good in his uniform.'

'Yeah, he loves all that. Puts on his BBC announcer voice for the cameras.'

'Any joy?'

'Lots of calls from women pointing the finger at their former or current partners. It's pretty depressing when you realise the number of women who genuinely think their boyfriends are undiagnosed psychopaths.'

'Wish I was there to help out.'

'No, you don't. You'd be staring at CCTV and wandering around London asking people if they've seen a white van. How's your dad, by the way?'

'Worried sick about me. He doesn't really understand what's happened. Tried to explain it to him, but he doesn't get it.'

'What about my namesake?'

'Dad reckons he just sits by the window waiting for me to come home. Howls whenever a white car goes by.'

'Must be nice having someone to howl when you're not there.'

'You could have someone to howl if you wanted.'

'Not like I haven't tried.'

'Doesn't have to be a person. You could get a dog. You could have kept Charlie.'

'No, poor bugger would have been on his own all day, wouldn't be fair. Still, I wouldn't mind someone to come home to.'

She was still looking at him funny. He wondered what had made him say something so, well, sentimental. He was here out of professional concern for a member of his team, that was all. He didn't want her getting the wrong idea.

'How's your new outside DS?' she said.

'DS Matthew Grey. Happily married, likes rugby and doesn't appear to have any vices.'

'A fish out of water, then.'

'In this squad? I'd say so.' Charlie looked at his watch. 'Better be getting back. When's your op?'

'Tomorrow afternoon.'

'I'll try and look in tomorrow night, then.'

'Do me a favour?'

'What's that, then?'

'Can you check on Dad? If you get a minute. Which you

138

probably won't. I worry about him being left on his own. He'll forget to eat.'

'I'll make time, Lovejoy.'

'Try and smuggle some stuff out while you're there.'

'Do my best.'

There was an awkward moment. He didn't know whether to kiss her on the cheek, shake hands or wave goodbye from the door. In the end, he did none of these things; he kept his hands in his pockets and mumbled something, and when Chris Hemsworth came in to take her pulse again, he sidled out.

He couldn't wait to get away. He hated hospitals. Made him think about his Uncle Pat, shriven and forgiven, dirty bastard that he was, with his brother Michael singing hymns and sitting vigil; his old man, just a skeleton, still foul-mouthed and cursing till his last breath.

The main thing now was to find the copycat who'd taken Sarah Howlett. She was out there somewhere and there was a chance she was alive. It was all down to him and his team now, if they were smart enough to work out the pieces of the puzzle.

CHAPTER TWENTY-FIVE

It was a different Daniel Howlett this morning. Hard to believe this was the same man Charlie had spoken to just twenty-four hours before. He couldn't stop moving, checking his pockets, scratching his ear, rubbing his nose, his hands constantly in motion. Ben had this mate who was a professional poker player. He had told Charlie once that the classic way to play was to have no tics of any kind; but there was another way, which was to have so many that you not only unsettled your opponent but totally confused the other players with your non-verbal clues.

He sat in his living room under a Damien Hirst, crossing and recrossing his legs. It almost constituted aerobic exercise.

'I don't fully understand what you're telling me,' he said.

Charlie went through it again: the successful locating of Evie Myers, the arrest of Christopher Markham, how they now believed Sarah's abduction was a copycat crime.

'A copycat crime?' Daniel said.

'Yes, sir.'

'So what happens now?'

'We are continuing the search for your wife, Mr Howlett. There are over thirty detectives and at least twice that many uniformed police now involved in this case.'

'Right. You could have told me this on the phone.'

'We need to ask you a few more questions.'

'Hasn't this gone far enough? I believe some of you people went to my office yesterday and started quizzing my employers and colleagues about my private life.'

'We had to confirm your whereabouts in the hours before your wife disappeared. It's routine.'

'You people always say something is routine when it's exactly the opposite.'

Charlie checked his iPad. 'Your wife's banking records indicate that she took out the sum of fifteen hundred pounds sterling two weeks before she disappeared. The week before that, she took out one thousand. That's quite a large amount of money, isn't it, to carry around in cash?'

'For a policeman. Not for my wife.'

'Do you know what she intended to do with it?'

'Are you accessing my wife's private financial records?'

'It's normal procedure.'

'I don't understand why you're wasting your time on this. Some monster has snatched her off the street and you're checking to see if she's late making the payments on her car.'

'You'll have to trust that we know what we're doing, Mr Howlett. Now, do you know why she would have taken a not insignificant amount of cash out of her bank account on that date?'

'No, of course I don't. I'm not her keeper. It's her money; she can do what she likes with it. As you have clearly been pawing through her private life, you'll know that Daddy pays large sums into her account every month. I suppose it's his way of making himself feel needed. And undermining me, of course. What she does with that money is her affair. I never see it, I know that. She puts all the large expenses on our joint credit card for me to pay.'

'Your neighbours say that over the last six months you have had several female visitors in the evenings.'

'For God's sake, I don't believe you people. What has that to do with anything?'

'We are trying to establish if there are other circumstances that may have contributed to your wife's abduction.'

'Such as what?'

'You tell us.'

'The only thing you need to know is that someone saw my wife standing alone and vulnerable on a dark street and took her. I know you people like to play Agatha Christie, but does it get any simpler than that?'

'You have had no communication from anyone about her?'

'You think she's being held hostage? If she was, surely I would tell you about it.'

'Not necessarily. Kidnappers asking for a ransom usually tell people not to involve the police.'

'I assure you, if I was to receive a threatening phone call, I would inform you immediately. Besides, anyone who had Sarah for over twenty-four hours would be calling to offer *me* money to take her back.' A tight smile. 'Now, is there anything else?'

'I understand you're under a great deal of stress, but we both want the same thing. To get Sarah back safe and well.'

'Look, I have a four-year-old son, who – to be un-PC about it – is handicapped. The press is camped outside as if they're waiting for Wills and Kate to step out through the front door. I cannot get to work, and my bosses pretend they're sympathetic, but to be honest, the only thing they care about is turning a profit. They're ringing me every half an hour. You cannot *possibly* want this over with as much as I do.'

'We'll be in touch.'

Charlie and Grey got up to leave.

'By the way, Inspector. Am I under surveillance?'

'For your own protection, Mr Howlett. We cannot be sure that whoever targeted your wife might not also be watching you.'

'I thought you said, when this first happened, that it was a crime of opportunity.'

'I said it appeared to be. But we can't discount any possibility.'

'A question for you, Inspector. Am I under suspicion myself?'

'Should you be?'

'That's a cute answer. I suppose what I'm asking is should I have a solicitor present at our next conversation?'

'It is your right to engage legal advice at any stage.'

'I see.' Another tight smile. 'Just find my wife.'

'We're doing everything we can.'

Charlie and Grey walked back to their car. There was hardly anywhere to park, the TV vans nudging for any empty spaces; they crossed the road to avoid a dog walker with half a dozen dogs, all shapes and sizes, yapping and straining. Charlie didn't see the point of a dog if you got someone else to walk it. Did you get charged per stick throw?

'You reckon it's him?' Grey said as they climbed back in the car.

'That's where the smart money is,' Charlie said. He looked in the wing mirror and wondered if the surveillance team was in the plumber's Hilux on the other side of the street or the unmarked builder's van parked next door.

'If it *is* him, he's pretty sure of himself.'

'No argument there,' Charlie said. 'But I'll tell you what, Sergeant, he's not half as smart as he thinks he is.'

After they'd gone, Danny paced the study, trying to think the way a copper would. He'd worked out a schedule; it would be tight, but if everything went to plan, he would be back here before morning and the precautions he was taking would all be unnecessary. But experience had taught him that things seldom went to plan. You had to be prepared for Sod's First Law: if anything can go wrong, it will.

It was all about quantifying risk.

As soon as they'd figured out that he was gone, that cop would get a warrant and they'd be over the house like flies over a carcass.

Her diary.

He'd seen her once, scribbling away at something; she'd tried to hide it from him, and he'd pretended like he hadn't seen anything. He'd been looking for it ever since. It was possible she'd taken it with her, but he didn't think so. It would have been too bulky, and all she'd left with that night was her clutch bag.

He had to find it. There would be too much stuff in there that he didn't need the cops to know about.

If it was still in the house, she would have put it somewhere he wouldn't think to look. There was no point in going through the bedroom; it wouldn't be with any of her stuff, that was too obvious. His best guess was that it would be in Ollie's room somewhere.

He went in, stood there for a long time, did a complete three-sixty, trying to think what he would do if he was Sarah.

He felt around under Ollie's bed, pulled out all the drawers in the dresser, even checked the bottom of his toy box. He looked behind the framed Spider-Man picture, under the rug, felt all the pillows. Getting crazy now.

His eyes settled on the clutch of teddy bears at the foot of Ollie's bed. There were a dozen of the freaking things. Hardly a day went by she didn't come home with some kind of toy bear; she was obsessed.

He picked up the large brown one she'd bought about a year ago from that wildlife park she was always going to, near her dad's place in Essex. The stupid thing was almost as big as Oliver, but not as fluffy as the others. He ran his hand along the seam at the back, smiled when his fingers found the Velcro fastening. Now that was new; someone had unpicked the stitches and sewn it on afterwards.

He pulled the Velcro apart and ran his hand through the polyester stuffing inside. There it was. He pulled it out. It was expensive, with a soft leather cover; her father had bought it for her last Christmas. She had told Danny she never kept a diary.

Lying bitch.

He flicked through the pages, reading entries at random.

He doesn't care about anyone or anything but himself.

Lovely. Thanks, sweetheart.

He's just like Dad. I always thought he was different.

He tried to think when it was that he'd found Ania on the swingers site. April, May? He flicked back through the pages. Nothing about Ania. At least Sarah wasn't that stupid. Whatever deal the two of them had made, she had had the sense not to write it down.

I need to get out of here. Today I sat in the park, with Ollie, looking at the bears, thinking how it would be to start again, without a past, without a family, without a husband. Just me.

It was fascinating stuff, but he didn't have time right now. He went into their bedroom and stuffed the diary in his day-pack. Must have a good read of it later, before it ended up in a bonfire, or a large, deep body of water.

He looked around the room, thinking about what to take. He might be in transit for a while. When he'd done, he paced the floor, taking deep breaths. Stay calm, Danny, stay focused. They couldn't pin the murder on him; they already knew he was in the house when Ania grabbed her near the common. Perhaps conspiracy to murder, but that was her word against his. Besides, he hadn't had a hand in any of it: it was Sarah who'd organised it, given Ania the dosh to buy the van, bought the burner phones. All he'd done was suggest to Ania that there was another way of playing it.

No one had ever seen them together. He'd put the roofies in Sarah's drink the night they planned it. Sarah didn't remember anything about it. She'd thought she had a hangover from the wine.

Still, Ania wouldn't go quietly; she'd take him down with her. The van was on Geoffrey's property, and he was the only one who knew the place was empty.

He told me to drive the van to the farm, he said he would do the rest.

That was what she'd say; ask for a reduced sentence if she cooperated. You didn't have to be Einstein to see how this would play.

He had to get down there and sort it. The challenge was to

get out of the house, get down to Westbridge and then home again, all without the cops seeing him.

He went into the dressing room, pulled up the carpet and opened the floor safe. There was a laptop case in there with his emergency cash. He had hoped he'd never need it.

The case was empty.

Fuck.

The dirty bitch.

He rocked back on his heels and slumped against the wall. For a while he felt too numb even to think. There had been a hundred thousand pounds in there, in twenties. It was clean, his biggest ever win at the casino.

Jesus.

He went downstairs. Ines had strapped Oliver into his push-chair and was getting ready to take him for his walk, as she always did before lunch. She saw the look on his face and lowered her eyes.

I hope she didn't tell that cop about Sarah and Ania, he thought. How far can I trust her?

'Nice day,' he said. 'Going to the common?'

'Oliver, he likes the ducks.'

'Got some bread?' She looked like she was in a rush. Perhaps I make her nervous. He lowered his voice. 'Ines. Did my wife talk to you much? You know, about our personal life?'

Her cheeks flushed bronze. She knew what he was talking about. She nodded.

'What did she say?'

'She say . . . she is not happy.'

'Did she go into details?'

'No, *señor*.'

'Good. Well. Every couple has their problems.'

He helped her down the steps with the pushchair, watched her head off down the street, then went back inside. He turned on his laptop and pulled up Google Maps. He had a lot to organise before dinner.

CHAPTER TWENTY-SIX

Charlie felt beat. He tried to work out how many hours he'd been on his feet. Hardly slept since Evie Myers had been taken. How long ago was that?

'I need a coffee,' he said.

'There's a Starbucks,' Grey said.

'I'll forget you said that.'

'What's wrong with Starbucks?'

'See, the thing you have to understand is that some people take their caffeine addiction very seriously. When I say I need coffee, I do not mean flavoured milk. I don't want pumpkin spice latte or caramel cold foam nitro. I want caffeine. I want strong. I want bitter. I don't want desserts.'

'Right. Sorry, guv.'

'Good lad. Now we've got that out of the way, stop here. And watch where you're driving. Mind the pigeon. Pigeons are people too.'

Charlie had seen a place he thought looked likely. It was called Gusto, a bar-restaurant, mainly tapas. He had a quick look at the menu in the window; the prices were eye-watering. He'd buy lunch later at Pret. He ordered a flat white with an extra shot. While he waited, his attention wandered to the plasma screen mounted on the wall behind the barista. It was perfect timing: the news was on.

Tony Jones was reading out the statement that the media people had prepared for him, sitting in the conference room at Essex Road between Catlin and the DCI. Halfway through, he broke down and couldn't finish, so the DCI took over, looking suitably grave and heroic, and loving every minute of it. The hotline numbers and Twitter handles scrolled across the bottom of the screen.

Charlie got his coffee and was about to leave, turned back to watch some mobile footage of a nutjob jumping into a polar bear enclosure in Frankfurt. There wasn't much to see – the part where the bear grabbed him had been pixelated out – but there was a lot of screaming going on. The newsreader said the man had received serious injuries to his legs and lower torso.

'Hope he's going to be all right,' the barista said.

'Never mind him,' Charlie said. 'What about the bear?'

'The bear?'

'Hope they didn't shoot it. Trouble with the world, people worry about the cause of the problem and forget about the innocent parties.'

'They have to protect human life, though, don't they?'

'Do they? If you jump in a bear pit and things go pear-shaped, don't blame the bear. Life comes down to the decisions we make, mate. The problem isn't the bear or the husband or the past, it's the choice to jump in there with it.'

'Right,' the barista said.

Thinks I'm a nutter, Charlie thought. Perhaps I am. Trying to save a young mother's life on three hours' sleep can turn anyone into a gibbering wreck.

148

CHAPTER TWENTY-SEVEN

It was getting dark. Ania peered into the back of the van. I should check, make sure she is really dead, she thought. But she couldn't work up the courage to do it. Make someone disappear, that was one thing; bash their head in, be violent with someone, it frightened her. She never thought she could do something like that.

She saw movement in her wing mirror, a car coming down the road from Sevenoaks. She recognised the logo on the side and jerked upright in her seat. It was the same van that had stopped this morning.

No, please.

'Don't stop,' she murmured, 'don't stop, don't stop.'

The van went past. She realised she had been holding her breath. She let it out slowly.

Then the brake lights blinked, and she saw the reversing lights come on. It was that young man from this morning; he was coming back. Couldn't mind his own business.

He turned up the farm road, stopped about twenty yards behind her. I must talk to him, Ania thought, find some excuse for why I am still here, make him go away. Without thinking, she reached around and scrabbled on the floor of the van behind her, found the wrench. The handle was sticky with Sarah's blood, but the weight of it in her hand was reassuring. She put it in her pocket and got out of the cab.

The man wound down his window. 'Your boyfriend didn't show up, then?' he said.

'Something come up for him. He will be here soon.'

'You've been here all day?' She didn't know what to say to that, and her moment's hesitation was enough. He got out of his van. 'Let me take a look. It may be something really simple.' He walked towards her. 'Tell me what happened.'

Maybe he can fix it after all, Ania thought. As long as he doesn't try and get in the cab, doesn't see in the back, perhaps he can help me, and everything will be all right. 'I cannot change the gear,' she said. 'Just hear this crunch, crunch, and she will not go.'

'Open up the bonnet for me,' he said.

She reached into the cab and pulled the lever. The boot clicked open and he pulled it up. 'Have you got a rag?'

Ania reached over the bench seat and found the rag she had stuffed in Sarah's mouth. As she looked down, she saw that Sarah's eyes were open.

She threw the rag to him.

'My name's John, by the way.'

'Ania.'

'Where are you from?'

'Poland. Białystok.'

He gave her a winning smile. 'Never been. Is that near Vladivostok?'

'No, Vladivostok is Russia.'

'Never was much good at geography. Went to Prague once. A mate's stag weekend. Furthest I've ever been.' He held a dipstick up to the light and frowned. 'Looks like there's no transmission fluid.'

'Is that bad?'

He smiled and shrugged. 'It's not good. It's an old van, you get a crack in the line or a broken seal, you can pretty much lose all the fluid. That's why you can't change the gears. Did you smell burning when it happened?'

'Yes, it was real stinky.'

He shook his head.

'Can you fix it?'

'Reckon you'll have to get her towed to a garage. Can't really get an accurate reading while the engine's cold. Let's turn her over for a few minutes, see if there's any fluid left at all.' He wiped his hands with the rag. 'Start her up.'

'No, please. Everything will be all right. You already help me too much.'

'Won't take long. Go ahead.'

She hesitated, but she had no choice. She got behind the wheel, turned the engine over.

'I could go into Westbridge for you, see if I can find some transmission fluid at one of the garages. But if you've run her dry, you'll need a tow truck. How much is this crate worth?'

'I do not know. I borrow it.'

'Well, the owner won't be too happy, I'm afraid. Is it your boyfriend's?'

Ania nodded, one lie as good as another now.

'Hop out, let me try the gears.'

'No, is okay.'

He grinned. 'Come on. I'll save your fella a trip.' His smile vanished. 'What's that?' He pointed behind the seat.

Ania looked down. It was blood. He could see Sarah, see the top of her head, slumped against the side of the van.

'Don't,' she said.

He walked around and slid open the door. She followed him, close enough to see the shock register on his face. She felt in her pocket for the wrench and hit him on the back of the head.

He made a grunting sound and his legs gave way. He turned towards her; the look in his eyes, it terrified her, so she hit him again, as hard as she could. He slid to the ground.

Danny took the map out of the printer and folded it carefully. It was a satellite image of his house and the surrounding streets. He checked his daypack: torch, water bottle, an Ordnance Survey map of Westbridge, a printout of Southeastern train times from

151

Charing Cross. In a separate zip pocket, he had a pair of pliers to cut the phone line at the farm and disable the alarm to the security company. He had wire strippers and a Phillips head screwdriver for hot-wiring Geoffrey's jeep in the garage. He'd use that to push the van into the dam. Afterwards, he and Ania could drive back into London. He would have to park the jeep somewhere and be back in the house before dawn. He would get it back to the farm later, when all the attention had died down.

He unplugged the laptop and put it under his arm.

Now all he had to do was get in and out without being seen by whatever goon squad the cops had parked outside. But if he wasn't smarter than your average copper, then he didn't deserve to get away with it. His main problem was Ania. He had to keep her out of the way after all this was done. The woman was mad; he should never have got involved.

How could the police link her to him? Ines had never seen Ania, and Sarah wouldn't have mentioned her by name. The only other way was if they found her profile and messages on the swingers site. But why would they go looking there? Everything was on his laptop, and they weren't getting their grubby little hands on that.

That just left the van. Was it in Ania's name, or Sarah's? He would have to find out. It wouldn't be a problem unless the police found it, and that was the whole point of putting it at the bottom of Geoffrey's dam.

Poor Geoffrey. He didn't even know him that well.

The burner phone vibrated in his pocket. That bloody woman again. If he was that way inclined, he'd put her in there too.

'Ania. Sit tight, I'm getting ready to leave, all right?'

She sounded hysterical. Christ, what now?

'Ania? What is it?'

She started talking, but he couldn't make sense of any of it.

'Slow down, take a breath. What are you saying, what's the problem?'

He blinked.

'Who's dead? What are you talking about?'

More crying. She was trying to gasp the words out, but it was all just gibberish.

'Look, don't worry. I'll fix it.' He closed his eyes. This couldn't be happening. 'I said, I'll fix it. Keep calm. I'll be there.'

He hung up, took a deep breath. This should have all been so simple. What the hell had she done now? He could hear Ollie yelling in the bedroom. He was awake. He called out to Ines, but she couldn't hear him.

He stopped at the top of the stairs. He had to keep himself together. One thing at a time. He couldn't do anything about Ania right now.

He went downstairs. Ines was making dinner for him, *fabada asturiana*, one of his favourites. She gave him an uncertain smile.

'I think Ollie's awake,' Danny said. 'He needs changing.'

She had been crying. She tried not to look at him so he wouldn't see her eyes, but it was obvious anyway. 'Sorry if I've been short with you the last couple of days. I'm under a bit of strain.'

'*De nada*. This is very bad for you.'

'You've been wonderful through all this. I appreciate it isn't easy for you either.'

She sniffed and blew her nose in a paper tissue.

'Are you all right?'

'This. Is all so sad.'

'Yes.' Oliver was still yelling upstairs. 'I think Oliver needs you,' Danny repeated, as gently as he could.

She nodded, took off her apron and went upstairs. He bent over the range, lifted the lid on the saucepan. Smelled amazing. One of the things he'd miss if he didn't make it back tonight, her stews. She wasn't much to look at, but God, she could cook.

She came back down the stairs holding Ollie. The doctors had shaved his skull so they could suture the gash. They said it looked much worse than it was.

153

'What time do you have to leave?' Danny asked her.

'At six o'clock, *señor*, the usual time.'

'I don't suppose I could get you to stay on a little bit later?'

'*Lo siento*, I have a boy, I say I will go with him tonight. I cannot change.'

He saw the look on her face. Was there a boyfriend? Probably not. She was such a bad liar; that detective must have seen right through her. But he supposed he didn't blame her, not wanting to stay around any longer than she had to.

'Of course, I understand.'

He went out the back to the workshop, put the laptop on the bench and took a hammer from the rack. Destroy the hard drive, only way, couldn't have the cops nosing around in it. He hesitated; what was he thinking? If he did make it back tonight, this would be a big mistake.

He put the hammer back, found a Phillips screwdriver and removed the back of the laptop. He took out the hard drive and slipped it in his pocket. Worst comes to worst, he thought, I can throw it in the river. But I might need it if I want to start trading privately later.

He went back into the house. Ines was putting on her coat, getting ready to leave. 'I will see you tomorrow, Señor Howlett. The *fabada* is finish. Maybe ten minutes, to make hot.'

'Thank you, Ines. Watch out for the gentlemen of the press as you leave.'

He walked with her to the door, saw her run to her car. Still a handful of journalists out there. God's sake, what were they hoping to see?

Oliver was in his booster seat at the end of the kitchen table. Ines had given him a bowl with some apple, cut up into pieces. Danny went to ruffle his hair, then remembered the stitches. 'Good boy,' he said. He fetched the daypack from the workshop, took out the map of Marlowe Road, checked it again. He knew the houses with dogs, or he thought he did. That was the only variable as far as he could make out.

The house next door, he could get over their side gate, here at the back. They were away in Spain somewhere for their summer holidays, so no problem there. Then over three more fences and over the back here, then up this side path.

The old lady at number 46, she wouldn't know if a bomb went off. The ones next to her he wasn't sure about; he would have to be careful, check first. The one at the back that faced onto Kidd Avenue, that was foreign territory. It looked all right on the map, had easy access along the side -- it was why he'd chosen it -- but he might have to improvise.

He poured himself a single malt, the Springbank 1992 that he'd been saving for a special occasion. Pity to leave it behind, but he couldn't afford to have more than one; he'd need his wits about him tonight.

Nothing to do now but eat his dinner and wait for it to get dark. Ollie had finished the apple and was running around the living room, shouting and banging into things. Well, never mind. He'd give him some Phenergan later.

CHAPTER TWENTY-EIGHT

Ben was in his City uniform, a Tom Ford navy blue suit, open-necked Hugo Boss shirt and brown Oxfords. Charlie saw a few of his blokes look up and give him an appraising look as he walked in. They all got around in sale items from TK Maxx, bought their suits in the high street. I wonder what they see when they look at him, Charlie thought. But to me he's just little Ben, has been all my life.

He was carrying a plastic bag with a six-pack of Punk IPA and a packet of cheese and onion crisps.

'That your dinner?' Charlie said as he guided him through the incident room to his office.

'Thought I'd get you something to help you relax after work.'

'After work for me is about three o'clock tomorrow morning.'

Ben ran his finger along the slats of the blind on the window and made a face. 'They really look after you, don't they?'

'Have a seat.'

'Is there a chair in here? Christ, Charlie, this looks like your bedroom when you were fifteen. How do you get any work done?' He sat down and took out the beers. 'Want one?' He cracked a can and offered it to him.

'I'm working, you do get that? I'm not making it up.'

Ben shrugged. 'Tough gig, this.' He looked back through to the incident room. Most of the team were still there, tapping keyboards, staring hollow-eyed at CCTV footage and making excuses to their wives on their phones. A trainee DC scrolled through black-and-white stills with vehicle number plates showing in yellow and black at the foot of the screen.

'Always wondered what your office looked like,' Ben said.

'You never been here before?'

'You know I haven't. So, this is what you do, is it? Sit around playing video games on your laptops until you get a lead on the hotline?'

'It's CCTV, and stop winding me up.'

'Thought you'd all be out cracking heads, not sitting around staring at computers.'

'First we've got to find the heads to crack, and anyway, they don't let us do that any more.'

'So, what's the flap? Someone take an Uzi to a bunch of gangbangers down one of the estates?'

'I wish. What we have is a missing wife, a dodgy banker who's threatened us with lawyers, a very handy life insurance policy, and a van that's managed to miraculously vanish off every camera in London.'

'I'm sure you'll crack it, Sherlock, you always do. Who's the banker? Would I know him?'

'Don't you read the news?'

'Only interested in the currency rates and the sports pages.'

'His name's Daniel Howlett.'

'That wanker. Dillon and Rowe, isn't it?'

'You know him?'

'Only by reputation.'

'And what is his reputation?'

'If I had a spare hundred thou, I'd put it on a horse before I gave it to him. Left his last job under a bit of a cloud.'

'What sort of cloud?'

'One of those little dark ones where a bit of dosh goes missing and no one can quite prove where it's gone. So next time there's a performance review, the suspects are told they're surplus to requirements.'

Charlie made a note in his book. 'I take it all back,' he said. 'You are good for something.'

Ben twisted around in his chair. 'Any talent in the squad?'

'All my squad are talented at what they do, or they wouldn't be here.'

'You know what I mean.'

'This isn't the world of international finance and weekend skiing. We don't mix business with pleasure in here.'

'When was the last time you had any pleasure, Charlie? You should get on Tinder.'

'I don't have time.'

'What happened to that other copper, the one who stepped on the nail?'

'It wasn't a nail, it was a booby trap, and she's in hospital. We don't know when she'll be back.'

'You fancied her, didn't you?'

'She's a work colleague.'

'You always got that daft look on your face when you talked about her. I've known you a long time, Charlie, don't try and snow me. What was her name? Lovelace?'

'Lovejoy.'

'I worry about you, know what I mean? They're going to find you in here one day slumped over your desk. I can see the headline in the *Metro*: *Dead: the notorious virgin copper who never slept.*'

'Not everyone's got a job like yours, work from eleven to half past then knock off for an early lunch. Some of us actually have to keep the wheels turning.'

'You're too good for this world, Charlie. Sometimes I look at you and get pangs of conscience.'

'Do they last?'

'Not for very long.'

'What are you doing here anyway? You should be out with Will, take him to see Mum or something.'

'He's next on the list. I shall be making my way out to the wilds of Acton Park right after this. My car will get keyed and I'll get mugged for my watch. How's he settling in?'

'Apparently the accommodation is not up to requirements.'

'Well, it is Acton Park, Charlie. Even homeless druggies have standards. Hope he has a shower before he gets in my car.'

'Should you be drinking and driving?'

'I'm only having one. The rest were for you.'

'Leave them in the fridge at my gaff. Will will have them for breakfast. Thanks for dumping him at my place, by the way.'

'Not a problem.' Ben's Adam's apple bobbed in his throat as he took a long swallow of beer.

'Did you talk to him on the way back from the airport?'

'Tried to, but he wasn't making much sense. Speaking in tongues. God knows how many he'd had on the plane, can't believe they didn't stop serving him. All I got was this long diatribe about Brexit and Donald Trump and the ice caps melting. He stank, too.'

'I noticed that. My gaff smells like an underpass in Charing Cross. And what's that bloody beard for? He looks like a proper tramp.'

'Well, we're stuck with him for a bit.'

'No, I am.'

'It'll be all right, he just needs time to settle in again. I thought we could all get together, the three of us, on Saturday. Watch the game.'

'What's on Saturday?'

'That International Champions Cup thing. In Singapore. The Arsenal are playing PSG. It's on at lunchtime.'

'International Champions Cup is not a thing, Ben. It's a holiday. They take their boots with them for a kick-around after they've been drinking all day and lying round the pool.'

'That's a very cynical viewpoint. Charlie, it's the Arsenal. We have to watch it. It's a moral obligation.'

'That depends on work. What are you telling me for, anyway?'

'I thought we could watch it at your place. You know, the three of us. Be like the old days.'

'The old days. Will has never been to a game in his life, and neither had you until a couple of years ago. You never even went to the old Highbury; you were always out fleecing the punters down Walthamstow market. Anyway, why do you want to watch the game at mine? Why don't we go to your place? I've been to cinemas with screens smaller than the one you've got in your living room.'

'It's a bit awkward at the moment.'

'Awkward how?'

'I told you, I've moved a friend in. Anyway, Will's already at yours. Does it matter where we watch it? We can get a few beers, order a pizza. Three Musketeers. Bit of brotherly bonding.'

'Like I said, Ben, it depends how we go with this case. Is that what you came in to talk about, the football?'

'Not really,' Ben said, and suddenly got a furtive look about him.

Right, Charlie thought. Now I've got it. 'If it's about the old girl's birthday party, I told you already, I'll do my best to be there. Michael isn't planning any extras, is he?'

Ben looked evasive.

'Is he?'

'A short Mass.'

'A short what?'

'Out in the garden. If it's nice.'

'If it's nice. Yeah, he wouldn't want to get his wafers soggy. Can't have a waterlogged body of Christ. You're going to let him get away with that?'

'It's to celebrate Ma's life.'

'What is there to celebrate? She did her best, got knocked around for her trouble, then got Alzheimer's. Thank you, God.'

'Charlie, that's blasphemy.'

'What do you care, you're a futures trader. What did you say to Michael when he suggested this?'

'You know what he's like. I said it wouldn't hurt. She'll probably like it.'

160

'Like it? She doesn't know what's going on most of the time. He could give her a bar mitzvah and she wouldn't know the difference.'

'No, I think she knows the Mass, if nothing else.'

Charlie conceded the point. Ben was right, she probably would like it. 'Bloody young to have Alzheimer's, innit?' he said. 'She's only seventy. I know ninety-year-olds in better nick than she is.'

'It's all the knockings-about he gave her, I reckon. Like what happened to Muhammad Ali.'

'At least Muhammad Ali won most of his fights,' Charlie said. 'She lost all of hers.'

'Well, it was a featherweight up against a heavyweight, with no rules.'

'A lot of the time she took the punches that were meant for us.'

Ben took a long pull at his beer. 'You know, she told me once she had this plan to run away. But she didn't want to leave Will behind. Said she was just waiting until he was old enough, then she was going to go.'

'She never told me that,' Charlie said. His ma never told him a lot of things.

'Well, it was all talk. She never did go, did she? Even when Will was old enough to look out for himself.'

'He still isn't old enough to look out for himself.'

'I suppose she didn't run because she knew what would happen. There's no getting away from blokes like our old man.'

Charlie nodded. 'Suppose you're right. What a way to live your life.'

'It's funny, isn't it? She wouldn't leave because of Will, but first chance he got, he took off, got as far away as he could.'

'Didn't exactly escape the booze and the squalor though, did he?'

'Ever felt like you wanted to do that?' Ben said. 'Run away?'

'Me? No. I love London, I love what I do. I only wish I had some time to myself now and then.'

161

'No, you don't, Charlie.'

'Do what?'

'It's not work that's the problem ⸻ ⸻ me you can't get right. That's why ⸻ ⸻ to go home.'

'What are you, Dr Phil ⸻'

Ben stood up. 'Sorry, none ⸻ business. ⸻ I?' He picked up the beers. 'I'll ⸻'

'No, tell him to keep the noise ⸻ in the house.'

'See you Saturday,' Ben said, and ⸻

CHAPTER TWENTY-NINE

How long had she been here?

She couldn't work it out. Ania must have given her something. Could be just hours, might be days, even weeks. She had lost all track. Every small movement made her retch. It was like the worst hangover she had ever had. Times a hundred.

At least the fog in her head was starting to clear.

Her wrists were tied behind her. Could hardly feel anything in her hands any more.

It was quiet inside the van, just the whine of a summer mosquito. She moved her fingers. There was a metal runner under the bench seat; it had a jagged edge. She worked the nylon rope over it, felt it catch. If only she could get leverage, she might be able to cut through it, a strand at a time.

She didn't know if she could do it, but she had to try.

Danny stood on the landing dressed in black jeans, a black hoody, black trainers. He checked the daypack again, felt for his credit cards in the side zip pocket. He would max them out at an ATM. He also had a change of clothes so he could switch his identity when he got to Charing Cross. He felt for the burner. He would turn it on again when he got to the station.

He stared at Ollie asleep in his bed. The Phenergan had done its job; he was dead to the world. It should keep him out of it until morning, unless he had one of those bloody night terrors again.

He might never see him again. He waited to feel something; if he was a proper father, he should feel at least a little bit torn, but the fact of it was, he didn't. It was just a bloody enormous relief. No point trying to fool himself.

Anyway, he might be back here again in a few hours and all this fuss would be for nothing.

He went down to the kitchen, found the baggie he had kept hidden in the coffee jar and tore it open. He took a credit card from his daypack and cut the powder into two lines on the worktop. A strong smell came off it, a bit like petrol. He always wondered if that was the drug or whatever it was cut with. He snorted one line, then the other, held on to the worktop as he rode that first buzz.

The back of his nose and throat felt numb. He licked his finger and swiped up the residue, then rubbed it on his gums. He wiped the counter clean. He supposed the police forensic people would find some atom that he had missed, but that didn't matter any more.

He reckoned it was dark enough now. He went straight out of the back door, locked it behind him. Better get moving; the high would only last ten to fifteen minutes and then he'd want another one. Use the buzz while he could; it should get him as far as the Tube at least.

He was in pretty good shape; the gym membership wasn't a complete waste of money. He shinned over the fence, landed on his feet on the lawn on the other side. The Finches were still away, so the house was dark. He sprinted across the lawn. Just had to think of it as an obstacle course, that was all it was. Over the next timber fence, dead easy. He saw the blue glow of a television through some French windows, no one at the kitchen window, all clear.

Up and over the trellis; the bloody thing near collapsed – why didn't people look after their properties? That left just one more. The third house at the back was in darkness; that was the one he was heading for.

He heard yapping – shit, it was a dog, but he had no idea what sort of animal he was dealing with. As he ran towards the back fence, he felt something latch on to his leg. It had teeth like needles, and found the gap between his jeans and his running socks. He gasped and tried to kick it off as he hauled himself up the fence.

Little fucker wouldn't let go. He looked down. It was some terrier thing. Another kick and it fell back onto the lawn and he launched himself over and fell heavily into a flower bed on the other side. He lay there, stunned. Please God I haven't broken any bones. If I have, it's all bloody over for me.

He got to his feet. No, all good. He limped to the side gate. There was a latch and no lock – people just weren't careful enough. He leaped over the front wall and ran down the street. The coke helped, it helped with a lot of things; if anyone saw him, they'd think he was just some mad jogger, training for the fire brigade or the army.

He didn't stop running until he got to the high street, went to an ATM and maxed out his cards. He crossed the road to the Tube station, put his foot up on one of the bike racks behind the bus stop. He pulled up his trouser leg. That shit of a dog had broken the skin; there was blood everywhere. Well, nothing he could do about it now.

He went into the station, decided to exaggerate the limp as he went through the barrier. He would drop it after he left the station at the other end. It would help the disguise when he changed into his other set of clothes. There was CCTV everywhere on the platform, he was sort of counting on that. He kept his hoody up; it was what they'd be looking for later.

The train pulled in and he jumped into the first carriage. It was empty except for a couple of fuelled-up goths dry-humping each other at the far end. He wondered how they managed, all that metal. It must sound like a 1963 Peugeot when they were screwing each other.

His leg was agony. He inched up his trouser leg; his sock was saturated with blood. That was going to get infected, wasn't it? Something else he'd have to take care of later.

By the time the train reached Charing Cross, his whole leg was throbbing and he realised that shrugging off the limp wasn't going to be that easy. At first he hoped he could walk it off, but every step made him wince. He limped out of the station, jumped into a cab in the forecourt. 'King's Cross station,' he said to the cabbie.

He stretched out his leg. Jesus. That fucking dog.

'Looks like we're going to get a bit of rain,' the cabbie said.

'What?'

'I said, looks like we're in for a bit of rain.'

His accent, cockney, like his father-in-law's. It made his teeth ache.

'Summer in England, eh? Can't wait to get away, me. Going on holiday in a couple of weeks.' He peered in the mirror, made sure Danny was listening. 'I said, can't wait to get away, me.'

A talker, just what he needed. In a minute, he'd have the man's whole life story and the complete itinerary for his seven days and six nights in the Algarve.

'Where are you headed tonight, then? Train to catch?'

'Going up north for a couple of days.'

They were stopped at the lights outside Zimbabwe House. The cabbie started on a description of his family weekend in the Yorkshire Dales the year before.

'Changed my mind, I'll jump out here,' Danny said and threw a tenner at him.

He exaggerated his limp, in case the cabbie was watching, and headed towards Covent Garden. He went up Agar Street, waited for a bit, then doubled back and ran across the Strand to the Coal Hole.

The place was packed, he'd thought it might be, and he had to shove his way through the crowd to the toilets. He went inside one of the cubicles, put down the seat, opened his daypack. He put on the baggy silver track pants he'd found in the bottom of one of his drawers. He'd bought them for a fancy-dress party a couple of years ago, he'd gone as a rapper. He took off his hoody

166

and swapped it for the lime-green rain jacket his mother had bought for him one Christmas, back when Jesus was a boy. He had one of Sarah's beanies, a black one, the reading glasses his father had left behind the last time he came to stay. He couldn't see a thing in them. He would have to put them way down his nose and peer over the top.

He tore off half a roll of toilet paper and wrapped it round his leg. That would have to do until he could get a proper first-aid kit. He would have to walk through the pain.

He pushed his way back out through the crowd, mostly tourists and theatregoers. He thought he'd get looks, but no. To them he was just some bloke in a beanie and inappropriate track pants. That was the great thing about London, he thought, it was full of weirdos, no one looked twice unless you were naked and bleeding through the eyes.

He shuffled back towards the station, pretending to look at his phone. He caught a glimpse of himself in the window of Superdrug. He looked nothing like the bloke in the sharp jeans who'd got on the Tube at Clapham Common. They'd have to be pretty sharp to pick him up on the CCTV.

Try not to favour your leg, he thought as he made his way across the station concourse. You're on *Candid Camera*. He paid cash for a ticket, checked his watch. How long since he had left the house? An hour and nine minutes. He was four minutes behind schedule.

CHAPTER THIRTY

Sarah saw a torch flickering outside in the dark. Someone was coming. She was almost out of time. She worked frantically on the rope.

She heard Ania say, 'Who is it?'

'Who do you think?'

'Thank God you've come.'

'What the fuck have you done?' There was the crunch of footsteps on the gravel, close to the van. 'Jesus Christ Almighty.' Danny's voice.

'He saw her. I had no choice.'

'Is he dead?'

'I don't know.'

'What's wrong with the van?'

'The man, he said something about transmission. Is empty.'

'What? Where did you get it?'

'I borrow it.'

'You *what*? Oh, fuck. Beautiful.'

Sarah heard him stamp around the side of the van. He's right outside, she thought, just a few feet away, on the other side of that door. Any minute now, he'll open it and see me.

'Who is he?'

'Don't know.'

'Is that his van back there?'

She heard Danny walk away, heard a door slam as he checked inside the dead man's van. She didn't have long. Hurry, *hurry.*

'What are we going to do?'

'I'm going up to the shed, Geoff keeps an old jeep in there. We'll use it to tow the van up to the dam.'

'What about the man?'

'Put him in the van and that can go in the dam as well.'

She could barely move her arms. Still no give in the rope.

She had run out of time.

Charlie picked up some Indian takeaway, headed to Lovejoy's place in Belsize Park. No one answered when he knocked, but then he saw Charlie the spaniel stick his head through the curtains, wagging his tail and barking for England. He went around the side; the gate was unlatched and the back door was wide open.

Lovejoy's dad, Howard, was sitting in his red leather armchair in the middle of all his junk with his head lolling back. For a minute Charlie thought he was dead, but he was just passed out. There was a spliff in the ashtray the size of a hot dog. The smoke was thick and sweet; you could get high from the fug, he reckoned. It was amazing the dog could still stand upright, never mind bark.

Charlie shook Howard awake. His eyes opened halfway, red as plums, and he tried to focus. 'Oh, it's you.'

'Anyone ever warn you about locking your doors?'

'What?'

'Your door. It's wide open. Anyone could come in.'

'Not worried about that.'

'This is London. You should be.'

'Bloke broke in here a few weeks ago, said he wanted money. I said put your gun down, I'll help you look.'

'Don't come the poor old pensioner with me, Howard. Your daughter's told me all about you and your hidden millions.'

Howard offered to relight the spliff for him.

'No, thanks. You do remember I'm a cop, don't you?'

Charlie the spaniel brought him a tennis ball, dropped it at his feet then just stared at it, like he was daring it to move.

'He wants you to throw it for him.'

'I know what he wants, I'm not stupid.'

'That's not yet a proven fact. Go on, throw it.'

Charlie threw it, wished the dog good luck with retrieving it. He didn't know how anyone found anything in this place.

'I brought you some takeaway.'

'That was nice of you.'

'It was your daughter's idea.'

'Thought so. Never expect charity from a copper. She does look after me, that one. Well, put it in the kitchen, I'll have it later.'

'I bought enough for two, thought I'd share it with you.'

'Oh well, if that was your plan, I suppose I can't stop you.'

The spaniel was jumping up at his leg. 'Where's the ball?' Charlie said.

'It's not fetch, it's hide-and-seek.'

'How am I supposed to find it in here?' He looked around at the piles of newspapers, the teetering stacks of cardboard boxes.

'Call yourself a detective? Remind me never to get murdered.'

'You're in a high-risk category,' Charlie said, 'if you don't mind me saying.'

He looked around. Lovejoy had warned him, try and get some stuff out of the place while he's not looking, else there won't be room for me when I get home. It could have been a nice enough place if they could shovel out all this . . . rubbish.

It was like Howard could read his mind. 'Don't you go moving things,' he said. 'I know where everything is.'

Charlie clocked the photos on the wall. Some of them looked like Lovejoy, only with long hair. He realised they couldn't be her; not those clothes, that car. It must be her mother. There were quite a few of her with some hippy-looking bloke and an awkward-looking teenager with a long fringe.

'Is that you?'

'Of course it's me,' Howard said. 'I haven't changed that much.'

Only like Justin Bieber turning into Iggy Pop, Charlie thought, but he kept that thought to himself.

'Is that Lovejoy?'

'Her name's Lesley, and yes, it is. She must have been about thirteen in that one. Taken down in Brighton, on the beach. We all got on that day. I remember, because we never really got on most of the time. Lovely kid, she was, always laughing. Never thought she'd grow up to be one of the enemy.'

'The police?'

'No, listening to reggae. Shite, that is. Mind, joining the police was a bit of a surprise as well. I always thought she was going to be a musician like me, but I suppose she wanted regular money and a regular life.'

'Hardly a regular life,' Charlie said.

'She hasn't had much luck in love either. She's like me there. All the blokes she's been out with have been complete losers or bell ends. Like that Romanian bloke she was seeing. Not that I've got anything against Romanians. He was just a proper tosser. Treated her like shite, he did. I told her, I'll kick him in the balls for you, but she wasn't having it.'

'How long did she go out with him?'

'She was living with him off and on for about five years. A proper lazy bastard. Never did a stroke of work. Reading between the lines, I reckon he was cheating on the side as well. I don't know why she put up with it. Then there was that last one. A right bitch.'

'Bitch?'

'Her name was Tanya. She was a woman. Anything wrong with that?'

'No. Nothing. Should there be?'

'The look on your face.'

'I was surprised, that's all.'

'You have to take love where you can find it. Only it weren't love in the end. Just another scrag-end bleeding her dry. Fancy her yourself, do you?'

'What?'

'You sleeping with my daughter?'

'No, absolutely not. She's my work colleague.'

'I used to sleep with people I worked with all the time.'

'Yeah, but you worked in a rock band; that's part of the job description.'

'Only the way she talks about you sometimes, I wondered.'

'How do you mean?'

'Always Charlie this, Charlie that, isn't that Charlie wonderful? Can't see it myself, but she's got a better nature than me.'

'Really? I hadn't noticed.'

'But that's her, isn't it? Always liking blokes that are completely wrong for her. I blame myself.'

'Because you and your missus split up?'

Howard looked at him as if he was mad. 'No, because she was born under the wrong star. If me and her mum had only waited a bit, she'd have been born a Capricorn. Capricorns are luckier in love.'

'The scientific approach.'

'She's in hospital because of you, you know. If you'd done your job properly, it would never have happened.'

'Did she tell you that?'

'No, like I said, according to her, the sun shines out of your jacksie. But if they take her foot off, no bloke's going to be looking at her twice.'

'A person is more than just their foot, Howard.'

'A bloke, maybe. But women are judged different.'

'She's very attractive. Lovely face. Nice figure. And she's a genuinely nice person. Brave. Loyal. She's got it all going on. No bloke worth his salt is going to care about one little foot.'

'One little foot? She's got feet like a LEGO man. Listen to you. Knew you fancied her. Well, are you going to take Charlie for a walk or what? Look at him. Poor bugger's going off his nut.'

Charlie looked around. The spaniel was curled up in his bed, with a pillow that said *RESERVED*. His eyes were half closed, and he had a teddy bear in his mouth.

'He looks like he's falling asleep to me.'

'It's all an act. Take him down the park at the bottom of the road. He likes it there, lots of nice smells. Their sense of smell is ten thousand times better than ours, did you know that? I read about a sniffer dog that found a plastic container with thirty-five pounds of marijuana submerged in diesel *inside* a petrol tank.'

'Wasn't yours, was it?'

'Was it my dog?'

'Was it your stash?'

'Not on this occasion. Anyway, stop faffing, his lead's over there. And don't kick him soon as you leave the house.'

'I would never kick any animal. I was the one that rescued the poor little bugger in the first place.'

'Well, that's what you say. I'll warm up the curry. You want a joint with your jalfrezi?'

Charlie the spaniel had found something to roll in. Howard might be right about their sense of smell, but a dog's idea of personal fragrance was a lot different as well. Charlie dragged him away and the spaniel looked up at him, like: *What are you, the fun police?*

He threw the tennis ball, to distract him.

Sarah Howlett had been missing for forty-four hours. Time was running out.

There was nothing on intel. Parm had come up blank on telephony, nothing significant from either the helpline or *Crimewatch*, just the usual nutters and time-wasters. They'd interviewed the neighbours, both families, all her known associates, and not found a single worthwhile lead.

The van was key. He had instigated a search, every 1998 VG Transit van registered in a two-mile radius. It would take weeks to track down all the owners; more than half of them were registered to businesses, so there were multiple drivers that would have to be checked out.

He had thirty detectives working on it around the clock, but it was the clock that was working against them. Charlie was sure he had missed something, and if he had, a woman was going to die.

He knew in his water that Daniel Howlett had something to do with this. He had him under twenty-four-hour surveillance but there wasn't much else he could do. He didn't have enough evidence for a search warrant. If only he could get his hands on that hard drive . . .

'So what should I do, Charlie?'

The spaniel sat at his feet with the ball. He was a good listener was the spaniel; he didn't try to interrupt or give unnecessary advice, but Charlie wasn't sure he always had his full attention.

He threw the ball again.

So what now?

He'd chuck the ball a few more times, then go back to the house, shovel down a bit of curry and drive to the nick. Probably spend the rest of the night going back through witness statements, writing up overtime logs, making sure his policy book was up to date, all ready for the enquiry that would be coming later.

He'd probably sleep on the camp bed in his office, not because there was work to do early but because it would feel disloyal if he didn't. One o'clock in the morning, he would be sitting there, just him and the night shift, staring at Sarah Howlett's photograph on the whiteboard and murmuring under his breath:

Where are you, Sarah? What the hell have they done with you?

CHAPTER THIRTY-ONE

Sarah felt the van bumping over rough ground. Her head bounced on the floor. There were black spots in front of her eyes, and she fought to stay conscious. I won't die, she thought. I won't give up now.

The van bumped again, and she came down on the point of her shoulder. It didn't even hurt. She had been in pain for so many hours, she had started to feel almost euphoric, the agony morphing somehow into something else. She seemed to be coming in and out of her body.

I won't die.

The van lurched, and she slid across the floor, couldn't stop herself, landing up against the side door. She wriggled back to the bench seat. She didn't know how long she had now.

Come on. *Come on.*

She found the strip of jagged metal, kept working on the rope. It felt a little looser. She had to contort her whole body, ignoring her screaming joints. She felt it catch as the metal edge bit into the fibres. Just a little more. Her shoulders cramped up, she had to stop; her whole arm was numb.

She heard the roar of an engine; it sounded like they were bogged in the mud. Then Danny's voice again. 'You'll have to push.'

'Why I have to push?'

'Because it's stuck in the fucking mud. I can't tow it into the fucking dam, I have to reverse it and push it in. Just fucking do it, Ania!'

The jeep's engine roared back to life, the pitch rising to a scream as Danny gunned the motor. She heard Ania yelling things in Polish and then the back of the van was lit up by the jeep's headlights. He'd managed to get it free.

Please God please God please God. Don't let them win.

She could feel the rope loosening.

So close.

'Fuck you,' Ania said.

'You should thank me. You won't have to go to the gym this week.'

'Now what we do?'

'We'll take care of our little problem and drive back to London. And after that, you need to stay out of sight.'

Sarah felt the rope loosen around her wrists and pulled as hard as she could. One last wrench and the nylon split. Her hands came free.

'What about my money?' she heard Ania say.

'You'll get it, don't worry. You haven't left anything behind? Where's the burner phone?'

'I don't know.'

'For Christ's sake.'

Sarah heard Danny walking back to the van.

She couldn't move. The muscles in her shoulders were locked, her hands numb. She twisted her head, saw the wrench under the seat, still smeared with that man's blood.

She lay on her back, her arms held out in front of her, useless, fingers locked into claws. It had all been for nothing. Then, suddenly, the blood rushed back into her hands. It was pure agony, and she bit her lip to stop from crying out. She concentrated on her fingers, clenching them into fists, unclenching them again.

I won't let him win.

She managed a spastic movement of her arm to her face, winced as her hand touched the crust of blood over her eye. Her hands felt like they were on fire. She bit down on the collar of her track top. Mustn't make a sound.

176

She clutched the bench seat with her right hand, managed to lever herself upright. Her ankles weren't as tightly tied. She hooked a thumb under the rope, pulled as hard as she could. Her heel jerked loose and she was free.

Come on.

She had to rest. She felt faint, swallowed down a wave of nausea. She retched, but there was nothing but bile.

Must stay conscious.

Then without warning, the door opened and the cabin light went on.

CHAPTER THIRTY-TWO

Kevin Bailey reached for the cardboard cup in the console. He'd bought it from the service station a few minutes before and it was still too hot, but he was desperate for something to wake him up. It was just getting light; there was mist in the trees, a pink glow over the wood. The sun would be up in a minute.

As he turned off the motorway and made his way towards Westbridge, he thought he saw something out of the corner of his eye in the fields to his right. He glanced over, but no, he must have imagined it, it was gone.

He slowed down at the roundabout, though there wasn't much traffic about at this time of the morning, and went past the old pub. Some budget hotel chain had bought it and prettied it up; end result it wasn't half as good as it used to be.

She came out of nowhere, stumbled into the middle of the road like she was drunk. As he stood on the brake, she looked right at him. One side of her face was streaked with blood, and her track top was torn, one sleeve hanging half off. He wasn't going fast when he hit her, but she bounced off the bonnet with a thud and went down.

Oh Christ, I've killed her, Kevin thought, and leaped out of the cab.

She lay on her side in the middle of the road. She raised herself on one elbow and tried to get up.

'Stay there, stay there,' he said. 'I'll call an ambulance.'

She lay down again and mumbled something, but he couldn't make out what it was.

He saw headlights coming the other way and waved frantically. A car pulled over to the side of the road and he ran over.

'You all right, mate?' the driver said.

'It wasn't my fault. She walked straight out in front of me.'

'Calm down, mate. I'll get an ambulance.' The driver pulled out his mobile phone and rang 999. Kevin went back to the woman. She was trying to sit up again, saying over and over: 'They tried to kill me.'

Kevin put his jacket round her and the driver of the other car got his first-aid kit out of his boot, but he didn't really know what to do with it and just dropped Band-Aids all over the road.

'My husband,' the woman said to Kevin, 'my husband tried to kill me.' And then she went limp in his arms.

CHAPTER THIRTY-THREE

The CS team were swarming all over the place. The local uniforms had blocked off both ends of Marlowe Road because of the media scrum. Charlie and Grey had arranged to meet Jack outside number 38. Charlie didn't suit up, had no intention of going in.

Jack was standing on the front doorstep with a clipboard. He saw Charlie and raised a hand.

'Morning, Jack.'

'Charlie. Nice day for the race.'

'What race?' Grey said.

'The human race,' Jack said, delighted to find someone who hadn't heard that one before.

'Well, this is a gold-plated cock-up, isn't it?' Charlie said. 'How are we doing?'

'Nothing much so far. He left his laptop behind – we found it in the shed out back – but took the hard drive with him. Left the kid on his own; he was shut in his bedroom all night until the nanny got here at half past seven this morning. Can you believe it?'

'Been doing this job most of my life, Jack, nothing surprises me.'

'Anything?' Grey asked.

'Not yet. There's a floor safe in the main bedroom, but that's been emptied out, as has the jewellery box on the dresser. Found some rather imaginative sex toys.'

'Yeah, well, we'll be counting them up later, make sure

they're all there, so don't try sneaking any of them out. How did he get away?'

'We found footprints in the flower bed by the fence. Wouldn't be hard, would it, just to shin over. On a good day, even I could manage it.'

Charlie patted Jack's stomach. 'You flatter yourself, my son.'

'Kid's the one I feel sorry for. He just buggered off and left him.'

'Takes all sorts, Jack.'

'I'll give you a bell if we find anything.'

Charlie saw Amory from Surveillance leaning against one of the patrol cars, his hoody up, smoking a cigarette. He looked depressed. So he bloody well should, Charlie thought, though that was uncharitable. It wasn't Amory's fault, or his team's; they didn't have X-ray vision and drones with night scopes.

He saw Charlie and gave a bit of a shrug.

'Looks like he legged it over the back fence,' Charlie said.

Amory checked his notes. 'Lights went out at ten thirty. Jack reckons they were on a timer. Nothing to report after that.'

'Didn't your guys hear the kid screaming?'

'It's a watching brief, Charlie. Sitting in a car with the window up, halfway down the street, you can't hear a thing.'

In some ways it makes it simpler, Charlie thought. At least I know I was right about Howlett. Now we just have to find him.

'Here's your guv'nor,' Amory said.

'Happy days,' Charlie said.

'He don't half look mad.'

'He always looks like that.'

The DCI was clearly fed up with all these early mornings. The look on his face, like a hanging judge with indigestion.

'So much for "Let's watch him, see what he does".'

Right, no *Good morning, Charlie, looks like rain*. Straight to business then.

'It's unfortunate, sir.'

181

'That's the understatement of the bloody year. Neighbours didn't see anything?'

'We're doing the house-to-house now. But there was nothing called in last night; you'd think if someone saw anything, they would have reported it.'

'So what are we thinking, Charlie?'

'Well, unless he has a confederate with a car, we'll be able to track him. My team are on to it; they're collecting CCTV from the Tube station, bus companies. We're contacting all the cab firms in the area.'

'If we find him, we find Sarah.'

'Let's hope so.'

'What game's he playing here?'

'Not sure, sir.'

'He may try to skip the country. Put out an alert to border control.'

'I've done that, sir. But he may already be out of the country.'

'All right, Charlie. I want a full report, ten o'clock, my office.' The DCI went back to his car.

Ines was in the back of a patrol car, trying to settle the little boy. A sergeant told Charlie that social services were on their way.

Oliver was screaming and rolling around in the back seat. Charlie leaned in through the window. 'Ines, I'm Detective Inspector George – you remember me, we spoke on Tuesday?'

She nodded. Not going to get much out of her for the minute, Charlie thought, not with the little boy near hysterical. 'He is crying all night, I think.' She didn't look subservient any more, just angry. 'Cannot believe a man can leave his son this way.'

'Do you have any idea where Mr Howlett might have gone?'

'I do not know. I make him dinner last night, everything is usual.'

Oliver started throwing himself from one side of the car to the other. This was hopeless. It would have to wait till later. Charlie started to walk away.

'Inspector,' Ines called to him through the open window.

He turned back.

She got out of the car. 'Señor and Señora Howlett, they are not . . . usual.'

'Sorry?'

'Señor Howlett, he tell me not to say. I am afraid I will lose my job. Maybe now I think is important.'

'I'm listening,' Charlie said.

'Señora Howlett, sometimes she tell me about . . . things. She say he likes . . .' She held up three fingers. 'Two woman, one man.'

'He was into threesomes?'

A nod.

'How did Mrs Howlett feel about this?'

'She does not like.'

'Where did he find these other women?'

'Computer, I think.'

'This happened a lot?'

'Yes. I think. Once I find . . . What is the word?' She pointed to her own breasts.

'A brassiere.'

'Is not belong to Señora Howlett. Too big. Expensive, you know. I can tell.'

So that was what I was missing, Charlie thought. Would have been nice if she'd told me this on Tuesday morning. But what the hell did it have to do with Howlett's disappearance? 'Right. Well, thanks, Ines. Social services won't be long; they'll be taking the boy into care until we can organise for someone in his family to have him. When that's done, I'll need you to come down to Essex Road and make a proper statement.'

He walked back to the car, where Grey was waiting for him.

'Well,' Grey said, as he started the engine, 'we're going further down the rabbit hole here.'

'People,' Charlie said. 'They never cease to astonish.'

Everyone had some sort of secret, he thought. Like the

skipper. He was always going on about eating healthy and going to the gym, and nibbling carrot sticks in front of everyone in the incident room. He didn't know Charlie had seen him just last week coming out of the McDonald's in Upper Street with two Big Macs and a thick shake.

Perhaps he thought none of them had figured it out. If all he was eating every day was rabbit food, his gut wouldn't be hanging over his belt like a saddlebag, would it?

The Nokia rang. 'Speak of the devil,' Charlie murmured.

He listened, said, 'We'll be straight in,' and hung up the call.

'Guv?' Grey said.

'Well, there's a turn-up. They've found Sarah Howlett. She's alive.'

CHAPTER THIRTY-FOUR

The district police headquarters for Westbridge was at Linton Spa, about ten miles away from the town. Charlie and Grey left their Sierra in the car park and went into reception to announce themselves. The inspector in charge, Halpin, must have been waiting for them. They had barely sat down to wait when he burst through the door.

He was a big man, looked like he used to be a rugby player in his younger days. He was gone to seed a bit now, though he couldn't have been much older than Charlie.

Charlie shook his hand. 'My inside DS says you have someone we've been looking for.'

'I think we do.'

What Charlie had been expecting all along was a body; thought he'd have to be the one to tell Tony Jones that his daughter had been found dumped in a lane or tangled in some weeds in a reservoir somewhere. But against all expectations, she was alive. Not well, by all accounts, and in a bit of a mess, but alive.

Result.

Halpin led them into his office, got one of his staff to bring them coffee from the machine.

'You've made my day, you have,' Charlie said.

'That's what my wife said this morning,' Halpin said. 'Then I woke up.' He took out his iPad and brought up Google Maps. He zoomed in and passed it across his desk. 'She was found here,' he said. 'Walked right in front of a delivery van near the roundabout. Driver thought he'd killed her. Said she was in a right state, covered in blood and mumbling nonsense.'

'Where do you think she came from?'

'Well, she was barefoot and pretty knocked around, so we figured she couldn't have walked far.'

'Have you managed to get anything out of her?'

'She said she'd been held in some kind of warehouse, she thought it was on an estate. The nearest light industrial area is here, about a mile away, on the other side of the fields from the roundabout. I've concentrated my search there, brought in some extra uniforms. I'm waiting on a proper search team with sniffer dogs from headquarters.'

'Has she told you anything else?'

'Doctors wouldn't let us talk to her for long. My officers say she was delirious, could barely remember her own name. Just kept saying over and over about how her husband tried to kill her. He's the one you're looking for, yes?'

'Daniel Howlett.'

'Do you want to see her? I can take you down there.'

Halpin got his jacket and cap from the coat rack and picked up his coffee.

'When do the doctors reckon we can interview her properly?'

'Last I heard she was still in A&E, but they should be finished with her by now. She can't be too bad or they'd have her in ICU.'

'Did she say how she got away?'

Halpin shook his head. 'Like I said, she was delirious.'

It was a ten-minute drive to the hospital. Charlie was hoping Sarah would be more lucid by the time they got there. He had put out an alert to every airport, every ferry terminal in the country, but he supposed there was every chance Howlett was gone by now.

At least they had Sarah. Finally, they could get some answers.

Tony Jones seemed to have aged a hundred years since Charlie had last seen him, what was it, only forty-eight hours ago. He was sitting on a plastic chair in the hospital corridor, a litter of cardboard around his feet where he'd torn up his takeaway coffee cup. He looked like one of those Guy Fawkes figures kids used to make, waiting to be wheeled off somewhere.

He came to life when he saw them. He jumped to his feet, and by the look on his face, Charlie thought he was going to have a go at him.

'About time you got here,' he said. 'Have you seen what that bastard did to my little girl?'

Halpin positioned himself between them, clearly concerned that Tony was about to start swinging punches. Charlie was more worried about Tony's well-being than his own. If he'd wanted to, Halpin could have tucked him under his arm like a garden gnome and inserted him in the central flower arrangement in the foyer.

But Tony didn't want to fight. Instead, he pulled a hundred-year-old Kleenex out of his cardigan pocket and blew his nose. 'I knew it,' he sobbed. 'I knew that wet wipe was no good. I told you, didn't I? Doctor reckons he hit her with a hammer or something. He could have killed her.'

'Take a seat, Mr Jones,' Halpin said.

'Walked out of the house and left his little boy there on his own. Little Oliver! What kind of bloke does that? Bloody monster he is, needs locking away for good.'

'Here we are, Mr Jones, come and sit down.' Halpin guided him back to his chair. Tony put his head in his hands. His shoulders heaved.

'Hardly recognised her lying there in the hospital bed like that. My poor little girl.'

'She's alive,' Halpin said. 'That's the main thing. It could have been a lot worse.'

Tony looked up at Charlie. 'You should of listened to me!'

'I did listen to you, Mr Jones. We had Mr Howlett under round-the-clock surveillance. Unfortunately, he was able to evade the team that were sent to watch him.'

187

'How the fuck did he do that then?'

Charlie sat down next to him. 'We're not MI6.'

'You should of arrested him when I told you.'

'Suspicion and hearsay are not evidential. I needed something concrete for a warrant.'

'What, like him nearly killing my little girl? Is that enough for you now? What he's put her through.'

'Have you spoken to her, Tony?'

'She hardly said a word. Just kept mumbling about how Danny tried to kill her. Have you found him?'

'Not yet. He may have tried to leave the country.'

'So now what?'

'Once we find him, he'll be placed under arrest. There are extradition laws; even if he's fled overseas, we'll track him down. He will have to face justice eventually. He can't hide for ever.'

Well, he can, Charlie thought, but not very easily. Most people weren't cut out for it and it needed a lot of planning, a lot of discipline to do it successfully. If you really didn't want to be found, you couldn't contact your friends or your family ever again, couldn't use your credit cards either. You had to throw away your phone, avoid Facebook, and forget about checking your emails, even once.

In a way, it was like dying.

Tony must have been reading his mind. 'If I find him,' he said, 'I'll do for him myself. I swear to God.'

'You leave that side of things to us,' Halpin said and patted him on the shoulder. There was a box of tissues on the desk at the nurse's station. Grey got him a handful.

Charlie rang the skipper at Essex Road.

'Now then.'

'I'm down in Kent.'

'How is she?'

'Alive, just about. Not saying much, apparently. Send Wes and Rupe down here so they can take a proper statement as soon as she's compos.'

'Do we know when that will be?'

'God knows. They'd better bring their lunch money. Did you get the warrants for Daniel Howlett?'

'All sorted.'

'Get Parm on to his financials then, see if we can trace him through his cards or his phone.'

'Would he be that stupid?'

'Probably not, but we're the ones who'll look stupid if we don't do it. I'll see you back at the nick in an hour or so.'

He went to find Sarah's doctor. The name on her badge said Mukerjee. She looked overworked. You and me both, Charlie thought.

He showed her his warrant card.

'You can't talk to her for long,' she said.

'I only need a few minutes. It could be very important. How is she?'

'She has two broken ribs, and extensive bruising to her wrists as well as ligature wounds to her ankles. She also has concussion and severe dehydration. Her most significant injury is a scalp laceration that required eleven stitches. We'll keep her in overnight, and she should be able to go home in a couple of days. Her MRI shows no evidence of subarachnoid or subdural haematoma; however, there does appear to be some significant short-term memory loss.'

'Because of the blow to her head?'

'Possibly. It's not uncommon in certain types of head injury. Her loss of memory could also be psychological. That will probably be the most significant issue, long-term. I have asked for a psychiatric assessment.'

'She's conscious, though?'

'She is in what I would describe as a fugue state. Talking to her may not be of great benefit at the moment.'

'How long might that last?'

'It could be a few hours, it could be a few months. I saw this sort of presentation many times when I was in the army

189

in Afghanistan, at the onset of post-traumatic stress. If you do wish to talk to her, I'll have to insist that you make it brief.'

'Thanks,' Charlie said. Hold the bunting and the ticker parade then, he thought. This isn't over yet.

Charlie felt he knew Sarah from the photographs of her pinned to the whiteboard in the incident room, so it was a shock walking into the hospital room and realising he wouldn't have recognised her if it wasn't for her name in the slot above her bed. It was partly because of her injuries: one side of her face was grossly swollen, and the doctors had shaved off all the hair above one ear to suture her head wound.

But it was also something in her eyes. He had seen that look before, in the faces of people who had suffered extreme violence. 'The thousand-yard stare' they called it in the army.

The blinds were down to keep out the sun. Someone had brought her teddy bears instead of flowers; there were half a dozen of them scattered around the room. It looked like the entire stock from the shop in the hospital foyer.

Charlie sat down next to the bed. Sarah didn't turn her head to look at him; he wasn't even sure she knew he was there. She stared fixedly out of the window.

'Hello, Sarah. I'm Charlie, I'm a detective inspector with the Metropolitan Police. I was in charge of the investigation into your disappearance.'

A slow blink. Had she heard him?

'Can you hear me?' he said, but her face remained impassive. It's like she's in a coma with her eyes open, he thought.

'I need to ask you a few questions. Would that be all right?'

The slightest nod of her head.

'Can you talk, Sarah?'

He saw her lips move, but he couldn't hear what she said. He moved closer to the bed.

'Do you know where you are?'

She shook her head.

'You're in hospital. Someone tried to hurt you, but you're safe now. I know this is hard for you, but we really need to understand what has happened to you. Is there anything you can tell us?'

Another whispered response that he couldn't quite make out. The doctor was right, this was like pulling teeth.

'We need to know who it was that abducted you. Do you remember? Your car broke down and someone forced you into a van.'

'Don't remember,' she mouthed at him.

'Do you remember where they took you?'

Another shake of the head.

'We want to find the people who did this to you.'

'Danny,' she said. Well, he could make that out easily enough.

'Was it Danny that hurt you? Your husband?'

'Tried to . . . kill me.'

'Who helped him?'

Sarah started to cry, a small keening sound like a wounded bird. He patted her hand. For God's sake.

A nurse came in and started fussing. 'I think she needs to rest now,' she said. 'All these questions are upsetting her.'

All these questions? he thought. He'd barely asked her anything.

Well, he wasn't going to get very far with her today.

There was a uniform camped on a chair outside her door. He remembered having to do that once, back in the day: guarding a convicted murderer who had been taken to the ICU. It had been the most boring eight hours of his entire life. He would rather have watched Chelsea.

Halpin took Charlie and Grey back to the station to pick up the Sierra.

'Did you get anything out of her?' he asked.

'Nothing that helps.'

'God knows what the bastard did to her.'

'Well, she's alive. That's something.' Howlett had set it up,

191

that seemed clear, but Charlie wanted to know who had been driving the van. They didn't have it sorted just yet, but at least he'd be able to get to Ma's birthday party.

CHAPTER THIRTY-FIVE

There were cheers and handshakes all the way across the incident room to his office. This should feel like one of the best days of my life, Charlie thought. But it didn't. He felt like a fraud. He felt like he hadn't really done his job.

They didn't have the full story here. Everyone else in the squad seemed happy enough to take it, and he supposed he didn't blame them; they'd all put in hellish hours for the last week. The two young women were alive and safe, and that in itself defied the odds. You couldn't always tie up all the loose ends. A result was a result.

Dawson was the only other bloke in the squad with a frown on his face. Charlie knew he was thinking the same thing that he was; it was like getting an A in an exam knowing you cheated.

There was a message on his desk when he got back into the office. The DCI wanted to see him upstairs straight away. Well of course he did.

The DCI had on a new tie and his best suit. He looked reasonably happy for once. He was getting ready to soak up most of the credit. Charlie didn't feel robbed of his moment of glory, particularly. Sarah Howlett stumbling in front of a delivery van wasn't his idea of brilliant detective work.

'Have you seen the newspapers?' the DCI said, and pushed the *Mirror* and the *Telegraph* across the desk. Charlie glanced at them but kept his hands in his pockets. Rags like that, you didn't know who'd been touching them.

'You don't look very happy about things. You got the job done, Charlie. I knew you would.'

'I'm not sure we've got the whole story here, sir.'

'We've got her back, that's the main thing. Two out of two. I score that as a good week. Her father called me a little while ago. He wanted to thank me personally for helping to find his daughter.'

'That was nice of him,' Charlie said.

'I thought so.'

'He's a very warm and generous man.'

'Been through a lot this last week.'

'And handled it all with such grace.'

'It's distressing about the little boy.'

'Apparently Howlett walked out and left him in the house on his own. It's hard to imagine what was going through his head.'

'It's not the worst thing we've seen in this game. I'm told Sarah's father is going to be looking after him until she's well enough to come home. How is she?'

'Not great,' Charlie said.

'What does that mean exactly?'

'It means she's sitting up and taking solids and staring into space.'

'Not surprising, I suppose, after everything she's been through. She'll need trauma counselling. What about her injuries?'

'Looks like someone took to her with a blunt object. She has concussion and eleven stitches in a head wound. Couple of broken ribs. They've done an MRI but they can't find any serious damage. Lucky.'

'I had concussion once. Car accident. Almost a month before I could come back to work. Hopefully she'll be able to tell us more when she's fully recovered.'

'The one thing she does keep saying, over and over, is that her husband tried to kill her. I've sent Wes and Rupe down there; hopefully they can get a proper statement from her when she's feeling better.'

'But at this stage, she doesn't remember who abducted her, or where they took her?'

Charlie shook his head. 'There's a light industrial area not far from where she was found. The local police did a thorough search, but so far it hasn't yielded anything.'

'That's puzzling.'

'They've brought in sniffer dogs and a search team, but they've had some heavy rain down there the last few hours and that's made it difficult.'

'Well, I'm sure it will all come out in the wash.'

I could pull a muscle trying to share your confidence, Charlie thought. He edited his initial response carefully, and then said, 'Sir, I don't think we should be too hasty in closing the file on this. Howlett was not acting alone. We still don't know who his accomplice was.'

'We're not closing the file, Charlie. Airports and port authorities across the UK have been alerted, as have Interpol. Howlett will show up eventually.'

'Jimmy Hoffa didn't.'

'We will find him, and when we do, we'll get chapter and verse.'

'There are still so many questions, aren't there? If they wanted to kill her, why didn't they do it straight away?'

The DCI shrugged. Couldn't care less about the details.

'What I'd like is to do a trace-and-eliminate on all the Ford Transits caught on ANPR cameras in the Westbridge area in the last twenty-four hours.'

'Are you serious, Charlie? You realise how many man hours that will take?'

'We have a job to do.'

'Charlie, two words: budget cuts.'

'This just doesn't feel right.'

'If you ever want to sit in this chair – and let's face it, you don't want to be stuck as my DI all your life – then you have to start thinking like an administrator as well as a detective. Our victim has named her husband as the man who tried to murder her. We can safely assume he also arranged the kidnapping, with person or persons unknown. Yes, I would like to dot our i's and cross our t's, but we don't have the money or the time to do it. You have been working ungodly hours for the last week. Fortunately, I don't have to pay you for that. But most of your team have averaged about eighty hours each. That means the overtime budget has ballooned. From now on, all your DCs and sergeants will be limited to eleven hours' overtime a week.'

'That is hardly sufficient, sir.'

'It's policing in the twenty-first century.'

'I'm not happy about this.'

'You are not paid to be happy, Charlie. Just get on, all right? Howlett has most likely dumped the van somewhere and fled the country. He's not going to turn into a serial murderer overnight, nor is he an ongoing threat to the general public. Sooner or later, justice will be served. When he is finally apprehended, you can get all the fine details for your autobiography. Until then, you've still got a full workload. The CPS is waiting for paperwork on that stabbing in Bermondsey, and you need to finalise the pre-trial documentation for the shooting in Chigwell.'

'Yes, sir.'

'Why don't you finish up here, get home early and catch up on your sleep.'

'Thank you, sir. Though that's unlikely.'

'Why is that, Charlie?'

'I've got my brother staying with me.'

'I didn't know you had a brother.'

'I have four,' Charlie said. 'Three living.'

'You never told me that.'

'You never asked.'

'Where's your brother from?'

'The one who's staying with me? Australia. He's come over for my mum's birthday.'

Go on, he thought. Act surprised and say you didn't know I had a mother.

The door opened and the chief super, Brownlea, came in, followed by her PA and Catlin, the media officer. They were all in full fig, Charlie felt like he'd stumbled into an amateur production of *The Pirates of Penzance*.

The DCI leaped to his feet. There was a lot of hand-shaking. 'Well done, Fergus,' the superintendent said. 'You named the main suspect early, it was a good call.'

'Thank you, ma'am,' the DCI said. 'I was a bit nervous about it. I'm relieved I was proved right.'

'But he got away,' Charlie said.

Brownlea shook his hand. 'Pass on my congratulations to your team. Wonderful job.'

Charlie realised they were headed up to the fifth floor for a press briefing. 'Would you like to join us?' Catlin said to him. He saw the DCI's expression: *I'll kill you if you say yes.* No point, they'd make him sit on the end, out of camera view.

'I'd better get on,' Charlie said. 'Paperwork.' He gave the super his best smile. 'You can't just be a good detective, you have to be a good administrator as well.'

Dawson followed him into the office and shut the door. Charlie threw his policy book on the desk and his jacket at the coat hook; missed. That was his Corneliani, he shouldn't leave that lying on the floor. But he didn't have the energy to pick it up. He collapsed in his chair.

'Sit down, skip.'

'You all right?' Dawson said.

'I'm all in.'

'We're going out for a few jars tonight to celebrate. You coming?'

'I should get home to my little brother.'

'Come on, just one. We did get her back alive, after all.'

Charlie looked through the blinds, mentally checking off who was in the office. 'Where is everyone?'

'Parm's still working on the financials. Lube and Mac are grabbing CCTV from Charing Cross, talking to cab drivers. What did FONC say to you?'

'He wants me to close it down.'

Dawson shrugged. 'Hard to argue with that, guv. We're all pretty much exhausted.'

'I realise that,' Charlie said. 'I'm out on my feet too. But we still don't know who took her, or why, and what Howlett's role was. They're all congratulating us; they might as well congratulate the van driver who found her. Look at this.' He pulled the mouse towards him and opened a file on his screen. 'The night she was taken.'

They had all seen it a hundred times. 'Guv?'

'Nothing look funny to you about this?'

'Only that Lube said that if it was her, she'd have put up a bit more of a struggle.'

'If it was her, the attacker would have needed life-saving surgery to his testicles. But look here, this bloke comes at her, tries to drag her off. And what does she do? Just sort of melts.'

'Well, people get paralysed, don't they? Fear does that.'

'Maybe. But it doesn't make sense. Someone took her, but left it to her husband to find his way down to Kent to murder her. That's mad, that is.'

'Perhaps it wasn't part of the deal. Offing her.'

McCullough knocked on the door and put his head round. 'Guv, skip, think we've got something here.'

They followed him into the incident room. Lubanski was staring at the grainy CCTV on her laptop. Charlie pulled up one of the roller chairs and sat down next to her. McCullough and Dawson watched over his shoulder.

'This is the CCTV we picked up from Clapham Common Underground,' Lubanski said. 'Here we go. This is him, we reckon. We'll get a good look in a second.'

It wasn't the Daniel Howlett that Charlie remembered: this fella was wearing a black hoody, backpack and trainers. But then he turned around, looked up at the camera, and Lubanski paused the footage and zoomed in on his face. It was Howlett, no doubt about it.

'He wants us to see him,' Dawson said.

'He's planning something,' Charlie said.

Lubanski closed the file, scrolled down, clicked on another one.

They watched Howlett hurry out of the Underground at Charing Cross and round the corner to the exit onto the Strand. Lubanski opened another file, one of the exterior cameras, and they saw him get into a cab on the forecourt.

She enlarged the frame and pointed to the plates on the cab.

'Did you find the cabbie?' Charlie said.

'We did,' McCullough said. 'He remembered him. Said he was acting weird from the moment he got in the cab. Said he wanted to go to King's Cross, then jumped out halfway down the Strand and threw a tenner at him.'

'Did the cabbie see where he went?'

'Headed off towards Covent Garden, he reckoned.'

'No, he would have doubled back to Charing Cross station,' the skipper said.

'That's what I think too,' Charlie said, leaning back. 'He takes the train down to Kent, tries to kill his wife, makes a dog's breakfast of it and she gets away. Then what?'

'He takes off in the van with Mr X, gets the ferry or the train, disappears.'

'So that's it,' McCullough said. 'He's gone.'

'Not that easy to disappear,' Dawson said. 'For one thing, he'll need cash.'

'Unless,' Lubanski said, 'whoever he's with, he uses their money.'

Charlie shook his head. 'That means that whoever is helping him, they're not a professional, they're a friend. And we've looked and looked, and none of his known associates are missing.'

'So what's next, guv?' Dawson said.

'There is no next, Skipper. Word from On High. We have spent enough of the taxpayer's coin on this one. We've got a result, and now we leave it alone. When Mr Howlett next appears on the radar at Interpol or somewhere, we can continue with the prosecution, but for now we move on.'

'Time for a drink, then,' Dawson said.

'That's your answer to everything,' Lubanski said.

'And if it isn't, you aren't asking the right question. Coming?' Dawson glanced at Charlie.

'I should get home, got my brother staying from Australia.'

'One drink.'

'I'll think about it.'

Dawson looked across the office at Grey, who was busy writing up the policy book at his desk. 'Coming for a drink, Matthew? Celebrate your first win with the team?'

Grey looked up and shook his head. 'Thanks, but once I've finished up here, I should get home. Wife doesn't like me drinking.'

Dawson muttered under his breath, 'Not exactly fifty shades of Grey.'

'More like fifty shades of vanilla,' McCullough said.

'Leave him alone, he's all right,' Charlie said.

'He's not one of us,' McCullough said.

'No, he's not an alcoholic and he's happy.'

Charlie went down the corridor to intel. Parm was still at her desk, looking at data on her monitors. 'Anything on our Mr Howlett?'

'Phone's still switched off; last handshake was at Clapham. He made large cash withdrawals on his cards at the Barclays near the Tube station and at Charing Cross. Since then, nothing.'

'How are you doing with the financials?'

'He has five-figure sums going out every month to an online

200

poker site. The man has a gambling problem. There's also this.'
She pointed to her screen.

'What's that?'

'It's a holding company; they own ukswingers.co.uk.'

'So, he did have a kink in his chain. Tony Jones was right.'

'Looks like it.'

'I would love to explore that, but my hands are tied, figuratively speaking. Thanks, Parm.'

He saw Dawson heading for the lifts.

'Are you coming?' he said to Charlie.

'I'll grab my jacket and see you there.'

'Don't get caught up, guv'nor. First round's on you, and that includes a packet of cheese and onion crisps for me.'

'I'm good for it.'

Charlie went back to his office and got his jacket, powered down his computer. Enough. The DCI had told him to close down Operation Loxley, nothing else he could do about it. But he couldn't help himself, kept replaying the CCTV of the abduction in his head, the numbers ticking over in the top right-hand corner, the abandoned Lexus, the AA van pulling up a few minutes later, Michael Donnelly sprawled across the road, trying to get up.

The strangest thing, he thought, was that they had it all recorded so perfectly.

Almost as if that was what someone wanted.

Forget about it, Charlie. You've got both women back alive, you deserve a Lagunitas and some sleep. They're all waiting for you down the boozer. Let it go for now.

'Guv,' Grey said as he headed towards the lift. 'Something here you might want to take a look at.'

Charlie hesitated. Hadn't he had enough for one day? One look wouldn't hurt. He turned around and went back. 'What have you got, Sergeant?'

'The skipper asked me to chase up any Ford Transits stolen in the last couple of weeks. Didn't come up with anything interesting. Thought I'd make one last search. And there's this.'

Charlie leaned over his shoulder and stared at the screen. 'Why has he only just reported it?'

'He was out of the country. Thinks it was taken on Monday.'

'"*Distinguishing marks: broken passenger-side wing mirror, dent in front right bumper.*" When was this filed?'

'This morning, Croydon.'

'Got an address?'

'I thought we were closed down?'

'I can work as much overtime as I like. I don't get paid for it.'

'Does that apply to your DS as well?'

'I'm afraid so. You've used up your allowance for the week. From now on, you're on your own coin.'

Grey stood up and pulled his jacket off the back of the chair. 'An hour won't hurt.'

CHAPTER THIRTY-SIX

They pulled up outside a terraced house with pebble-dashed walls about a mile from East Croydon station. Not that salubrious, but then you didn't get much for your money in London; nothing much at all unless you were a Saudi prince. This place was typical short-of-a-quid London. There were rubbish bins all up the path, and an old mattress on the front lawn. Even the satellite dish on the roof looked shabby.

Someone had tried to pretty the place up; there was a green plastic hose down the front of the house, looped from a hole in the bathroom wall to the pot plant hanging next to the front door. The plant was dead now; whoever had had that bright idea must have given up.

Charlie knocked. A burly young man in a red and white Polish football shirt and baggy jeans answered the door. Charlie showed him his warrant card.

'I'm looking for a Mr Wojciech Przeworski.'

'You pronounce that pretty good.'

'I've had practice. We had a Polish goalkeeper at the Arsenal.'

'Szczęsny.'

'That's the one. We got rid of him for smoking too much.'

The young man flicked his cigarette butt into the garden. 'Good I don't play for your team then,' he said and grinned.

Better than good if you don't set fire to the mattress in your front garden, Charlie thought. 'I'm Detective Inspector Charlie George, this is DS Matthew Grey, we're from the Major Incident Team at Essex Road.'

'Is it about my van?'

'That's right.'

'Is not a major incident. It was a pretty rubbish van.'

'Can I come in?'

The man led the way into the front room. There were two young women sitting on the sofa in T-shirts and shorts watching a DVD in Polish. 'Zofia and Maja. They don't speak much English. You want to sit down?'

'That's all right, this shouldn't take long.' Charlie checked his notes. 'You filed a report of a stolen vehicle. A van. It had a missing wing mirror on the passenger side.'

'Sorry about that. I was going to get it fixed.'

'Yeah, I'm not from the MOT, Wojciech, don't worry about it. When was your van stolen?'

'Monday. Tomas and me, we went back to Poland – our kid brother got himself married. We decided to come back early, you know, make some money before your government has this Brexit bullshit. We got back last night, I look up and down the street, and hey, my van's gone. I need it for work.'

'What do you do?'

'I'm a builder. I do renovation.'

'And your van was stolen from the street?'

'No, I told the police, Ania took it.'

'Ania?'

'She rents a room here. The girls said Monday night, they saw her take the keys – they were over there, on the bookcase. She said she was going to borrow it for a few hours, that I wouldn't mind. I do fucking mind. Is the last time they saw her.'

Another man came into the room wearing only a towel. He worked out, by the looks of him; he could weight-lift for the Eastern Bloc. There were tattoos snaking up both arms and covering most of his chest.

'Who's this?' he said to Wojciech.

'Cops. They've come about the van.' He turned back to Charlie and Grey. 'This is Tomas. He's my older brother.'

'You found this fucking bitch?' Tomas said.

'Sorry, no. I didn't even know we were looking for her.' Charlie looked at Grey. 'We do now.'

'She is batshit crazy, I tell you.'

'Do you have any idea where she might be?' Grey said.

Tomas laughed and shook his head. 'You think if I knew, I would need you guys? Man, I get my hands on her, I am going to kill that bitch.' He mimed for Charlie the way he planned to do it; it seemed strangulation was his preferred method of execution.

'Yeah, Tomas, bit of a tip: probably best not to say that in front of a police officer, in case her body shows up somewhere in the next couple of days.'

'He's just joking,' Wojciech said.

'I'm not,' Charlie said. 'How do you know Ania?'

Wojciech shrugged. 'We advertise in the paper, you know? She called up, same day, she seemed okay. Pay a month in advance. Bitch. Not just she steal my van, she owes us rent, too. Three weeks.'

'How long has she been here?'

'Two months maybe.'

'Do you know where she works?'

'Some bullshit call centre in Paddington. Don't worry, man, Tomas and me, we already went up there, the guy says she hasn't been in all week, he don't know where she is.'

'Write down the name of her employer,' Charlie said, handing him his notebook and pen.

Tomas pointed to the television. The girls were sharing a box of tissues between them like it was popcorn. 'Do you get this show here in England?' he said. 'Is called 42. Is so sad. Poor guy loses his wife, his business, his friends, everything.'

'Even his mother,' Wojciech said.

'Yeah, even his mother,' Tomas agreed and leaned between the girls and helped himself to a handful of tissues.

'Which is Ania's room?' Charlie said.

205

Wojciech indicated a door along the hall. Charlie pushed it open and went in.

There was a bed and an ancient wardrobe. The room looked like it had been ransacked. There were clothes littered everywhere. A suitcase was upended in the corner, a toiletries bag lay open on top of the bed; some cheap cosmetics and a hairbrush had spilled out.

'If you are looking for passport, don't worry,' Tomas said, leaning on the door jamb. 'We already check.'

'I can see that. Do you know her surname? Where she was from?'

'She said something about Białystok,' Wojciech said.

'That's it?'

Tomas shrugged.

'Either of you sleeping with her?'

Wojciech looked shocked. 'No, man. That's our girlfriends out there. They wouldn't like it.'

'I guess not,' Charlie said. 'So, you basically know nothing about her.'

'We trusted her,' Tomas said, and Charlie immediately revised his impression of him. So refreshing to hear of people trusting each other, in London of all places. Even in the face of three weeks' loss of rent, he hoped Tomas didn't become cynical.

'Did she ever have any visitors?'

'She is hardly ever here,' Wojciech said. 'When she is, she just go to her room, spend all her time on her computer.'

'No sign of that, I suppose?'

Wojciech shook his head, no.

'I told the girls,' he said, 'they can have her clothes, anything that fits. The rest we throw in the trash. We got someone else to come look at the room next week.'

Grey held up a pair of jeans. 'Look at this. She's long. Windcheater and a jumper, that could have been her driving the van that night.'

'Which night?' Wojciech said.

'We're thinking aloud,' Charlie said. 'How tall would you say Ania is?'

'She says she plays basketball, in Poland.' He raised a hand a few inches above his own head. 'She is big, for woman.'

Charlie made a note.

'Hey, this is great, man,' Tomas said. 'We appreciate it. In Poland, the police wouldn't give fuck about one lousy van.'

Charlie shook his head. It seemed a shame to disillusion Tomas a second time.

'Actually, we believe the van was used to abduct someone.'

'What?'

'A woman was kidnapped near Clapham Common on Monday night. We suspect your van was used in the crime.'

'No way, man.'

'See,' Tomas said to his brother, 'I told you she was batshit crazy.'

'I'll need you both to come to the station and give a statement. I'd also like to get you to help us with an E-FIT picture of Ania.' Charlie handed Wojciech his card. 'And if she does get in touch, I want you to call me straight away.'

'She kidnap someone?' Wojciech said. '*Kurwa piekło!*'

'Matt, can you go out to the car and get us some evidence bags?' Grey nodded and went to fetch them. Charlie looked around. He was sure Wojciech and Tomas had been pretty thorough when they went through Ania's stuff, but he and Grey would have to do a proper search of the room themselves. They would definitely bag and tag her hairbrush.

As the DCI said, Howlett and the mysterious Ania would have to show up one day, and they would need evidence to tie her to the van and the case. She could change her name, she could change her hair colour, but she couldn't change her DNA.

***

'What now, guv?' Grey said when they got back to the car.

'Now nothing,' Charlie said. 'Officially, Operation Loxley is suspended.'

'So we're not going to look for this Ania woman?'

Charlie shook his head.

'Pity.'

More than a pity, Charlie thought. But the DCI had been quite clear about it: they had used up the budget on the investigation. Anyway, Howlett and his mystery woman were almost certainly out of the country by now. But he would have a quiet word with Parm, get some intel on Ania for the file before it started gathering dust on the shelf in Records.

He hoped Howlett did show up, or this was going to be one of those cases that would gnaw at him until the day he retired. So many unanswered questions. For instance, how did a Polish girl renting a room in Croydon hook up with a merchant banker with a seven-figure income?

'The threesome,' he said aloud.

'Guv?'

'That's how he met her. She must have gone on that swingers site, looking for a mark. That's how she met the Howletts.'

'All along, we thought it was a man that abducted Sarah.'

'We made an assumption, which is always mistake number one.'

'But how does she go from kinky sex to kidnapping?'

Charlie rubbed his thumb and fingers together. 'It's money what makes the world go round, Sergeant. Amazing what even the sweetest human being will do if you offer them enough dosh.'

'But how did she happen to be just driving past at exactly the moment that Sarah's car broke down?'

'She set it up.'

'Who?'

'Sarah Howlett. She orchestrated her own abduction, used Ania to make it look like someone had snatched her. She planned to disappear. Only this Ania woman must have double-crossed her and told Howlett his wife's plan. That way she gets money from both of them. The kidnapping is easy, because Sarah's in on it. She doesn't find out she's been royally set up until she's tied up in the back of the van. Beautiful.'

'Only something went wrong.'

'Yeah. But what?'

'So when do we arrest her?'

'Who?'

'Sarah Howlett.'

'What for? No law against trying to make yourself disappear, last time I checked. That would look brilliant in the papers, wouldn't it, charging her after she's been beaten black and blue and dumped in the middle of the next county. No, we're going to leave it alone, it's not our problem any more. I promised the skipper and the team I'd buy them all a drink. Sure you don't want to come?'

'Better not.'

They were halfway back to Essex Road when Dawson rang. Charlie supposed he was going to rubbish him for not buying the first round at the pub.

'Skip? I'm on my way.'

'I'm not in the boozer, I'm back in the office.'

'What's up?'

'Thought you'd like to know. Just got an urgent call from the City of London Police regarding our Mr Howlett.'

'What did they want?'

'They've arrested one of his colleagues, a Mr Taj Reeves. He's given them a statement implicating our Daniel in a fraud at his bank in excess of thirty million quid.'

CHAPTER THIRTY-SEVEN

When Charlie got out of bed, Will was standing in the kitchen in his underwear. He was staring into the refrigerator as if he'd never seen one before, and scratching his balls.

'That's a good look,' Charlie said. 'You been working out?'

'You trying to be funny?'

'Not at all. Waking up in the morning and seeing you in your off-white briefs, that's made my day, that has.'

'Is that a problem?'

'Well, some things you see, you can't unsee them. That's the trouble.'

'Couldn't you have got some beers in for your brother, made him feel like he's wanted?'

'I gave you a hundred quid the other day.'

'You talk like that's a lot of money. How long did you think it was going to last?'

'Want some coffee?'

'I don't drink coffee. It's an artificial stimulant.'

'Are you trying to wind me up?'

A smile, the first one he'd got from him since he'd been there. 'Too damned easy to wind you up, Charlie.'

Charlie put coffee in the *macchinetta* and put it on the stove.

'Sorry I was late last night. I had a lot of paperwork to catch up on.'

'Do they sell beer in paper cups now?'

'We got a result yesterday. I had to take the team out to celebrate.'

'Some celebration. You could hardly walk when you got in. Hope you didn't drive.'

'The car's still at work.'

'Good for you. Otherwise I'd have to make a citizen's arrest.'

'Did you go and see Ma?'

'Funny you should mention it. I don't have a car.'

'I gave you my Oyster card. It had ten quid on it.'

'I lost it.'

'Ben left me a message, said he called around and you weren't here.'

'I went to that pub down the road, the Half Nelson or whatever it is.'

'The Lord Nelson.'

'That's the one. Had a few beers. It all gets a bit vague after that.'

There was a San Miguel coaster lying on the coffee table in the living room. Charlie picked it up; there was a number scrawled on it in red biro.

'Whose number is this?'

'No idea. Could be a girl, could be a dealer. It's all a bit of a blur. I might ring later and find out.'

'If it's a dealer, don't invite them round here.'

'What if it's a girl?'

'Highly unlikely, but that's a negative as well.'

'You got something against sex as well as drugs?'

'No offence, but I wouldn't trust the sort of girl who goes in the Lord Nelson and gives a bloke like you her phone number.'

Funny, he seemed to remember Ben once telling him that Will was gay. Not that it mattered, but it showed how little he knew his own brother.

'Charlie, I appreciate you putting me up and everything. I do. But I can't wait to get back to Australia. Being here is like living in a Catholic boarding school.'

'Will, we do care about you, you know. We're your family.'

'Yeah, well, family is what I've been trying to get away from.'

211

'That's nice.'

'Nothing personal. But it's why I left in the first place. I wanted, you know, a fresh start.'

'And have you got one?'

'I'm working on it.'

A fresh start, Charlie thought: homelessness and at least one serious drug overdose. But what was the point of getting into that? It was like walking on broken glass talking to Will, and he didn't want another row.

Where was that little boy who used to believe in rain fairies?

'Have you ever wondered what it would have been like if we'd been born in another family?' Will said. 'Like those O'Shaughnessys across the road from us, remember? You never heard them rowing all the time; they didn't have a cop car outside their door every other week. The oldest, Tommy, he's a millionaire now, he's got an import–export business, lives in Essex in a country manor. He's your age and practically retired.'

'If the grass is greener on the other side,' Charlie said, 'it's probably artificial lawn.'

He knew all about Tommy O'Shaughnessy, or TJ as he was more commonly known. It was true he lived quite a glamorous life these days. He'd made his dosh laundering money for organised crime, some Romanian outfit. So crime did pay, but the cheques invariably bounced; the CPS were currently preparing a case against him. He was looking at serious time when his little house of cards came tumbling down. But he couldn't tell Will that and have him blabbing it to everyone down the Lord Nelson.

'Are you staying on after Ma's party?'

'Don't see the point, do you? I should be getting back.'

'What's waiting for you back there that's so urgent?'

'I thought you'd be pleased to be rid of me.'

'I don't want to get rid of you, Will. Look, I've got court next week, but I might be able to squeeze a few days off after that. We're not rostered on for another eight weeks now. You and me, we can spend a bit of time together.'

'What, you want to take me to the zoo?' Will fiddled with the plate he'd commandeered for an ashtray, scraping together the leavings of last night's joint. 'Funny, it's the one thing I remember from my glorious childhood, my big brother taking me to the zoo. Remember? You showed me the meek rats.'

He went into the kitchen, found a safety pin in one of the drawers and tore off a bit of tin foil. He brought the pin and the foil back to the table.

'Meerkats,' Charlie said.

'Are you sure?'

'I'm positive.'

'The meerkats, then. And the rain fairies.'

'I thought you'd forgotten about the rain fairies.'

Will crumbled the leavings into the tin foil and rolled the foil into a ball, then skewered it onto the end of the pin. 'Sure I remember. We were watching the rain splashing on the windowsill, and you told me it was fairies dancing. I still look for them when it's wet outside.'

He picked up his cigarette lighter and lit the silver paper, then put it up his nostril and inhaled. His face turned beet red and he exploded into a coughing fit. Tears streamed down his face.

'What are you doing?' Charlie said.

It took Will a long time to get his breath back enough that he could talk. He wiped his face with the back of his hand. 'It's called a snorter. Really gets me going in the mornings.'

'You can't wait for the coffee?'

'Not the same thing at all.'

'That's barbaric, that is.'

'Not at all. Like an espresso, but it burns off your nose hairs at the same time. Brilliant.'

'You know, Will, no matter what has happened in the past, sooner or later you have to put it down. You can't walk around for the rest of your life with an albatross tied round your neck.'

'Is that little sermon aimed at me?'

213

'Shouldn't it be?'

'The thing is, Charlie, you don't get it. You weren't like the rest of us back then. None of it seemed to bother you. The old man thought the sun shone out of you. A chip off the old block, you. Sorry, but I'm just being honest.'

Weird thing, Charlie had noticed, whenever people said *I'm just being honest*, what they meant was *I've just made up an excuse for being cruel*.

'I suppose we all see things a different way,' he said, and there was a pain in his gut and he knew he had to get out of the house before Will landed any more blows. He made the coffee and went upstairs to get dressed for work.

When he came down again, Will was sitting in front of the TV watching the morning news. 'I'll see you later,' Charlie said as he went out.

Will waved a languid hand in his direction. 'Back to work?'

'Have to get my car, and a bit of paperwork to tidy up.'

'Don't worry about me, I'll be fine. I don't want to stand in the way of law and order.'

On the way to the station, Charlie thought about something a psychologist had once told him: *When someone's damaged, they're damaged, and if you think you can change it, you'll only end up getting hurt yourself.*

Will was Will and he should stop expecting some sort of an epiphany. He couldn't spend the rest of his life looking for the lost chord. He'd helped save the lives of two strangers this week. Wasn't that enough?

Parm came in and shut the door. 'There's nothing,' she said.

'Thought that's what you'd say,' Charlie said.

'The name she gave the call centre in Paddington – Ania Katarzyna Milik – there's no record anywhere. The documents she provided were forgeries, and not very good ones either. She must have entered the country illegally.'

'So we basically have no idea who she is?'

214

'Sorry, guv.'

'Thanks for trying.'

As she was leaving, the skipper put his head round the door. Howlett's sister was waiting to see him downstairs, he said.

Charlie took the lift down to Interview Room 3. He already knew a little about her; she was Daniel's senior by two years, had married a Russian IT millionaire called Piotr Voronin and lived in Cheshire, in a mansion not far from where Gary Neville was going to build his Teletubby house. Worse, Piotr was actually a season ticket holder at Old Trafford. Charlie hoped he would never have to meet him.

Kate Voronin was an attractive woman, or she probably had been before she got addicted to Botox. The tattooed eyebrows were a total distraction, made him feel like he was talking to an avatar. She was fully accessorised, Gucci and Chanel, and was wearing way too much perfume; it gave him a headache before he even sat down.

'Thanks for coming in,' he said, and shook hands. He laid a thick brown file on the table between them. It was full of waste paper, but he found it always helped in interviews, made people think you knew far more about them than you did.

'I'm Detective Inspector George,' he said. 'I was in charge of the investigation into your sister-in-law's disappearance. I imagine this must all be a bit of a shock to you.'

Kate fidgeted with the gold jewellery on her wrist; there was probably enough there to bankroll a small African republic. 'It doesn't seem real, Inspector. You see these things on the television; you never think they're going to happen to you.'

'You haven't heard from your brother?'

'The last time we spoke was Tuesday, after Sarah disappeared.'

'He rang you?'

'I rang him. I offered to come down, be with him. I thought he'd want someone, you know. Family.'

'And what did he say?'

'He was quite abrupt. He said he'd rather deal with it on his own.'

'Did that surprise you?'

'Not really. He's like that. Doesn't like to be fussed over.'

'Were you surprised when Sarah went missing?'

'Of course. What happened was terrible. For *her*. Not for us, of course.' And then, almost as an afterthought: 'Is she all right?'

'She claims Daniel tried to kill her.'

'You don't believe her, do you?'

'He's not exactly helping his cause. Leaving his house in the middle of the night, jumping over fences, abandoning his four-year-old son – these are not the actions of a man with nothing to hide.'

'I can't believe he would . . .' she said, and stopped. Charlie could see her thinking about the things her brother might or might not do. 'This is just unbelievable.'

'Did you know he was having financial problems?'

'Daniel? Financial problems? He gets a seven-figure bonus from the bank every year.'

'We believe he may have considerable debts accrued from online gambling. He was also a frequent visitor to the casinos in Park Lane.'

Kate looked shocked, or at least as shocked as her cosmetic surgery would allow.

'There's something else . . .'

'Oh my God. That sounds ominous.'

'We have just been informed by our colleagues in the City of London that one of Daniel's associates at Dillon and Rowe has been arrested for fraudulent activities concerning unlawful currency trading. A separate warrant has been issued for Daniel.'

Kate looked even more startled. If she could have raised her eyebrows, she would have done. 'Fraud? You're not serious? This will *destroy* my mother and father. Daniel has always been the golden boy. Are you sure?'

216

'This is not something my guv'nor lets me joke about.'

'You think he's absconded with the money?'

'There is no money to abscond with. Daniel and his colleague are accused of incurring losses in excess of thirty million pounds.'

She stared at him. Finally: 'I don't know what to say.'

'I am sure you will be interviewed separately about this. Our investigation only concerns the abduction and assault on Mrs Howlett.'

'Daniel couldn't have abducted her.'

'No, that's correct. He was at home when she was taken; we have his phone records, and he called her from Marlowe Road seven minutes before she was abducted.'

'Well. That's one good thing.'

'Not really. We believe he was part of a conspiracy.'

'This is all so much to take in. I just can't believe . . . Look, I know Daniel has always been . . . confident. Overconfident. He likes to make his own rules . . .'

'That's just a nice way of saying that he breaks the law, which is why the City of London Police have issued an arrest warrant.'

'Yes, but that's just money. I can't believe he would ever do something . . . violent.'

'You've never seen him lose his temper?'

'We all do, don't we? But he wouldn't physically hurt anyone.'

'How do the two of you get on?'

'He's my brother. I know he can be a real shit, but you know, blood is thicker than water and all that.'

'Would you say you were close?'

A shrug. 'Not really, I suppose.'

'When was the last time you saw him?'

'My husband and I came down to London a couple of months ago. We all went out to dinner, the whole family.'

'Did you speak with him then?'

'Yes, but it was quite superficial. It always is with Danny.'

'He never confided in you?'

'He always seems so ... I don't know, self-contained. I suppose I never know quite what he's thinking. I mean, his marriage was a mess, but that's not something you can hide very easily. At least Sarah didn't try to hide it. She was always so bloody miserable.'

'Do you know if he was having an affair?'

Kate didn't even blink at that. 'I assume so,' she said.

'You assume so?'

'Well, nothing serious, I don't expect. Being married wouldn't have stopped Daniel doing what he wanted. That's why he didn't want to give her a divorce.'

'So you knew she wanted to leave him?'

'The whole family did. I didn't blame her, you know. I wouldn't have married him myself. But it cut both ways. He only married *her* because she was pregnant.'

Charlie made a note. 'Do you have any idea at all where he might have gone?'

'I'm afraid not.' She put her face in her hands, but it came off as theatrical rather than desperate. 'I keep thinking what would have happened if I had just followed my instinct on this. I should have come down, shouldn't have listened when he told me not to.'

'I doubt it would have made any difference, if that's any consolation.'

'Poor, poor Daniel. What on earth has he got himself into?'

Charlie rose to his feet. 'If your brother does happen to contact you, please let us know.' He handed her his card.

'It's funny,' she said. 'He's my brother, so I've known him all my life, obviously. I can't believe he'd do this.'

'But did you?' Charlie said.

'Did I?'

'Know him. Really.'

She stared at Charlie's card. 'I suppose you have a point.'

'Thanks again for coming in,' Charlie said and showed her out. 'We'll be in touch if there's any news.'

218

CHAPTER THIRTY-EIGHT

Lovejoy was sitting in a wheelchair in the back garden when Charlie brought the spaniel back from his walk. She had one leg up in a moon boot. She didn't see him straight away; it seemed he'd caught her in an unguarded moment.

She looked lonely and sad.

As soon as the spaniel saw her, he almost throttled himself on the lead trying to get to her. Charlie let him go, and the dog launched himself at her, jumping up and down on the spot, trying to spring into her lap.

Lovejoy let the spaniel lick her face, and when he'd finished, Charlie said, 'You know he was licking his bits for ten minutes before we got here.'

'Thanks.'

'Didn't know you were coming home today. Just popped round to check on your dad, like you asked me to. Said I'd take Charlie for a walk while I was here.'

'I was let out early for good behaviour. Got a cab home; it had special wheelchair access at the back. Has he been a good boy?'

'Charlie, or your dad?'

She smiled.

'He lives like a prince, does Charlie. Your old man feeds him bits of his bacon every morning. I told him to stop, it's no good for his cholesterol. You can't give a dog everything it wants. He keeps that up, Charlie's going to look like a furry hippopotamus come Christmas.'

He watched Lovejoy talking to the little dog like it was a toddler. He wondered what the squad would think if they saw her, especially the ones who called her an ice queen behind her back.

The spaniel got so excited he squatted down between them and took a dump.

'You are not serious,' Charlie said, and Lovejoy gave him a look: *Well, nothing I can do about that, I'm in a wheelchair.*

'Tell me you brought bags with you. You can't take a dog out for a walk if you haven't got poo bags.'

Charlie reached into his pocket and found one. He hesitated.

'I'll never understand this about you,' she said. 'You can roll a week-old corpse, talk about blood splatter while eating a sausage roll, but one dog poo and you look like you're going to faint. You'll be one of those fathers who can't change a nappy.'

He gave her a look. It seemed weird to him that anyone could ever imagine him as a father.

As he cleaned up, he could feel the spaniel watching: *There, look, you missed a bit, human.* When he got back from the wheelie bin, he said, 'Makes you wonder who's the master and who's the servant. I mean, we're supposed to be the boss of the dog, but we're the ones that run around after them cleaning up the mess.'

'They don't see it that way. In their view, you've taken charge of all the smells, and smell is everything to a dog, so that makes you even more of a boss. What you did is actually a sign of dominance.'

'I never thought of it that way. I suppose nothing is ever quite how we think it is.'

'Are we still talking about dogs?'

'No, I'm probably still thinking about my little brother, but let's not get into that now.'

The spaniel curled up on Lovejoy's lap and settled in for a nap. Charlie pulled up one of the garden chairs and sat down.

'So how did the operation go? Good news, I hope.'

'They can save the foot, but they say they'll have to amputate the rest of me.' She grinned. 'Your face. Come on, Charlie, it was a joke. When they were passing out the guilt ration, you must have come back for seconds.'

'It was all down to me.'

'No, it wasn't. Could have been you just as easy. Anyway, I'm fine. They found something in there they missed first time round; they reckon that was the cause of all the problems. I'll be running the hundred-metre hurdles in no time.'

'So, the upside, the doctors can save your foot?'

'I won't even have a limp.'

'That's good, because the downside is Charlie's chewed up all your shoes.'

'That's all right, I love shopping for shoes. Hope you're still saving a seat for me in the incident room.'

'No, we threw all your stuff out. You've seen my office, I hate needless clutter.'

'What's happening with the Sarah Howlett case?'

'Did you watch it on the news?'

'They said her husband's done a runner.'

'I'm left with a mountain of paperwork. We've got Sarah and Evie Myers back alive and well, an arrest for one and a prime suspect for the other. It's all done bar the shouting.'

'But you're still upset about it.'

'Well, you know.'

'No, I don't, guv. Tell me.'

'None of us likes loose ends, and this case is frayed like an old jumper. It's how it goes, I suppose; you can't always tie everything up with a bow.'

'Sarah Howlett hasn't told you anything?'

'Not yet. She has short-term memory loss, her doctor says, perhaps because of the knock to her head, perhaps because of the emotional trauma.'

'Where do you think Howlett is?'

'Your guess is as good as mine. He could be driving around Greece right now in England's Most Wanted Campervan.' He looked at his watch. 'I'd better get going. Still got some things to finish up back at the nick.'

He tickled Charlie behind the ears. The dog opened one eye and wagged its tail twice. Then went back to sleep.

'Thanks for coming,' Lovejoy said. 'And thanks for looking out for my dad.'

'Take it easy, Lovejoy. No playing football until the doctors say so, all right?'

'Guv,' Lovejoy said, and she had a worried look on her face. 'Don't go getting into any scrapes without me, will you? And if you do, remember to wait for backup this time. Okay?'

'Of course I will,' Charlie said. 'I'd never do anything to put myself in harm's way. Would I?'

You got to see a bit of London in this job, Charlie thought: first Croydon, Belsize Park, now Mayfair. Life in all its glorious diversity.

Daniel's parents had come straight down to London when they heard the news of his disappearance. Charlie had spoken to them on the phone, but this was his first chance to interview them face to face.

When he and Grey arrived, the Howletts were already waiting for them in the foyer of their Mayfair hotel. Mrs Howlett ordered a pot of Earl Grey from a white-jacketed waiter. What is it with people and tea? Charlie thought. They keep giving it to me, I keep leaving it. What I need is a double espresso, the week I've had.

He looked around. Nice place to hang out: wood panelling, Jacobean fireplaces, ornate plaster ceilings, fashionable fabrics. A pianist in a monkey suit was tickling the ivories on a baby grand, tourists were eating finger sandwiches and scones with clotted cream in the tearoom. Grey seemed quite at home. He looked like the sort of bloke who'd scoffed a cucumber sandwich or two in his time.

Mrs Howlett was a formidable woman. Well preserved. She

was perched on the edge of her chair, eager to make sure her points were made. Mr Howlett sat back, let his wife do most of the talking. He was dressed like a country squire, in a tweed jacket with a silk cravat. Didn't see many of those these days, Charlie thought. He appreciated a good cravat.

Mr Howlett's left hand gripped his right wrist, to disguise a tremor.

'We don't come down to London much these days, do we, Andrew? Too loud. Too *brash*.'

Charlie was surprised to hear her say that; he thought her son was a caricature of brash.

'I can't believe this thing about Daniel being involved in financial shenanigans. It must be a mistake.'

'The charges brought against your son by the City of London Police are not related to our investigation, so I can't comment.'

'We shall fight this every step of the way. We have an appointment with our London solicitors in the morning. It's this Reeves fellow. He's the one to blame for all this.'

'Taj?'

'You know him?'

'Two of my officers interviewed him after Mrs Howlett went missing.'

'You think he's involved in that as well?'

'We have absolutely no evidence linking Mr Reeves to Sarah's abduction.'

She looked disappointed with that answer.

'Mrs Howlett, do you have any idea where your son might have gone?'

'Of course not. Inspector, he is a highly respected man in his profession. It is not in his nature to do something like this. Is it, darling?'

Mr Howlett looked like a backbencher who'd been asked to vouch personally for the prime minister's integrity. He shifted uncomfortably in his chair and gripped his right arm a little tighter. 'Course not,' he managed.

'He was a rugby blue at Oxford, you know.'

'Really?' Grey said. 'What position did he play?'

'He was a half back. A very good one.'

'I played on the wing for Durham.'

'You must have known Sam Watkins, then?'

Charlie leaned in before Grey could answer. Much more of this and he'd lose the will to live. 'We should come back to that later. Mrs Howlett, when was the last time you spoke with your son?'

'Monday, I think it was. I rang him at work; I'd arranged for him to come up to stay. My daughter Kate and her husband were coming as well.'

'Was Sarah invited?'

'She was invited. She wasn't welcome.'

'You didn't get on?'

She answered that with a raised eyebrow.

'She says that Daniel tried to murder her.'

'Well, that's just nonsense. She's making it all up.'

'It doesn't look that way. She is at present still in hospital with a serious head injury.'

'Daniel would not be involved in something so . . . sordid. It's her and that father of hers, they've cooked up this whole thing between them. I told Daniel not to marry her. He felt he had no choice, I suppose, after she got herself pregnant.'

'That's not quite possible,' Grey said. 'Getting yourself pregnant, I mean. You need help.'

'Unless your name's Mary,' Charlie said, before he could stop himself.

Mrs Howlett gave him a look that could have melted steel. 'You know she wanted a divorce? All she was after was his money. Just like her father. He won all his money on the pools and then he thinks he's as good as the rest of us.'

'Mrs Howlett, if your son is innocent of these charges, then it would be best for him to give himself up, so he can tell us his version of events.'

'What do you mean, *if* he's innocent?' She looked at her husband. 'Oh, for goodness' sake, Andrew, say something.'

'What do you want me to say? These fellows are only doing their job.'

The tea arrived, a full bone-china service. The waiter gave them a long explanation of where the tea was from and how it was harvested. After he had withdrawn, Mrs Howlett picked up the pot. 'Shall I be mother?' she said.

'Mrs Howlett,' Grey said. 'You do understand? Your daughter-in-law is in hospital with eleven stitches in a head wound, and suffering from severe post-traumatic shock. Daniel's employers are facing losses in excess of thirty million pounds. One of his colleagues looks like going to jail. These are all very serious matters.'

She reached into the handbag on her lap and dabbed at her eyes, even though they looked pretty dry to Charlie. 'Poor Daniel,' she said.

'Well, that was cosy,' Charlie said as they were driving back to Essex Road. 'Played on the wing for Durham. That's nice.'

'Just trying to establish a rapport.'

'I love talking about rugby, me.'

'Sorry, guv.'

'Careful! Did you see that Deliveroo bike? You run down one of those blokes in a Met vehicle, someone doesn't get their pizza, and we're filling out forms till Guy Fawkes Day. So, tell me about university.'

'What do you want to know?'

'What did you study?'

'I was reading law.'

'Did you graduate?'

'Honours. First class.'

'Impressive. Begs the question, what are you doing here, son?'

'It's a long story.'

225

'We've got time. Central London traffic at this time of day, plus the way you drive, we won't get back to the nick before the weekend.'

'All right. Well, after I graduated, I moved up to London, went to work for a firm just off Temple Lane. One of my first times in the Old Bailey, I was assisting counsel; we were defending this bloke on a charge of sexual assault. And my boss got him off, basically, by making out the activity that had taken place was by mutual consent. He intimidated the victim, tied her in knots, left her in tears by the end. And the jury came back, not guilty. Afterwards, when we were having a drink to celebrate, I said to him, how can you do that, how can you work so hard, use all your skill, everything you've learned, to help that bastard get off? You know he did it, I know he did it. What about justice, what about doing what's right? And you know what he said? He said, ideals are fine, but they don't pay the school fees, son. Don't pay for the house in Surrey either. If you're going to get misty-eyed about the law, you should find yourself another career.'

'So what did you do?'

'I took his advice. He was right, I wasn't cut out for it. You can't believe in the law and make a career out of it as well. I applied to join the Met the very next week.'

'How did that go down at home?'

'My father said I was mad. My mother didn't say anything, which was worse.'

'You're a brave man.'

'I like to think I'm guided by my own principles.'

'Christ,' Charlie said. 'I'm sitting in the car with a unicorn. Watch out for that motorbike.'

226

CHAPTER THIRTY-NINE

Dr Goldstein was an odd-looking bloke, Charlie thought. He resembled a garden gnome, and wasn't a lot bigger. He'd had a stab at a goatee, not a very creditable one, but it made him look more medical. His glasses reflected the strip lights; it put Charlie off, made it harder to concentrate on what he was saying. And then there was his voice. It was irritating, made Charlie think of his first car. He'd drowned that thing in WD-40 and never stopped the squeaking; had to sell it in the end.

'We believe Sarah is suffering from dissociative amnesia,' Goldstein said. 'In cases like this, when the subject has been exposed to extreme violence, or threats of it, it's not uncommon. It helps a person cope by allowing them to temporarily forget the painful details of the experience they have gone through. A person may suppress those memories until they are ready to deal with them.'

'How long will that be?'

'Tomorrow. Or never.'

'Never? Haven't got that long.'

'I cannot assist you in the reordering of time,' Goldstein said, with a straight face, and Charlie wasn't sure if he was having a laugh.

'So her memory could be gone?' Grey said.

'A small part of it, yes. She has excellent recall of the events leading up to this episode, but nothing afterwards. In a few months, if she's having trouble functioning in her day-to-day life, or experiencing nightmares or flashbacks, she may need further professional help. I realise this is not what you want to hear.'

'No, not exactly,' Charlie said.

'One other thing. Because of the nature of the incident, and how she presented to us, I took the precaution of ordering a gas chromatography–mass spectrometry analysis.'

'Well, it's what I would have done,' Charlie said.

'What is that?' Grey said.

'It's the only reliable way to tell if someone has ingested benzodiazepines. A normal toxicology report will not detect them.'

'What's the English translation?' Charlie said.

'You have heard of Rohypnol? It's a date-rape drug.'

'I know what it is.'

'The analysis can detect the presence of the drug up to twenty-eight days post-ingestion.'

'And the test was positive?'

'It was. So regardless of the physical and emotional trauma, there are other contributing factors to her apparent amnesia.'

So the rag-over-the-face routine, Charlie thought, that was just for the benefit of the CCTV cameras, as they'd supposed. He wondered how the Rohypnol had got into her system. Usually, it was dissolved in someone's drink.

'Can I see her?' he said.

'I'm afraid not.'

'It's important, Doctor. Just a couple of questions. I won't distress her.'

'You misunderstand. You can't see her, because she isn't here. She's already discharged herself.'

'She's gone?'

'Her father was of the opinion that she would be better off at home. He said he was prepared to take care of Mrs Howlett and her son. So she signed herself out.'

'I see,' Charlie said.

'Your detectives were here yesterday and were given

permission to interview her. I assume that discussion proved unsatisfactory?'

'Pretty much.'

'Sorry I couldn't be of more help,' Goldstein said, and walked away.

'What do we tell the guv'nor?' Grey said, as they walked back across the car park.

'We don't tell him anything. We're not supposed to be here. There's a pile of paperwork on my desk and I should be preparing for court next week; I've got a double homicide from last year that's finally come to trial.'

They got in the car. Grey started the engine.

'So that's it?'

'That's it. What we do now is close the file and walk away. Not a word about me being down here. I'll get a proper bollocking if FONC finds out.'

'FONC?'

'DCI Fergus O'Neal Callaghan.'

'Well, I'm strictly three monkeys, guv. And anyway, it was a nice drive.'

'Yeah. Kent. Lovely, innit?'

He stared at the open fields, a horse taking shelter from the sun under a tree. 'What did you think, guv? About Goldstein.'

'I thought he looked a bit like Leon Trotsky, to be honest.'

'No, about what he said. You had a very thoughtful look when he was talking about memory loss being a defence mechanism.'

'Did I? Perhaps I was thinking about my brother.'

'Which one?'

'The little one. Well, he's big now, big enough. His name's Will. I was thinking it would have been better if he didn't remember as much as he does. He talks about the past all the time and it doesn't do him any good. Four months ago, he was in hospital. Drug overdose.'

'What, suicide attempt?'

'Don't think so. Although you'd have to say no addict has a long-term plan, do they?'

'He's a druggie?'

'Does that shock you?'

'I've not had much to do with that sort of thing. I mean, personally.'

'Takes all sorts. My other brother, Ben, says we should try and look out for him. But it's bloody hard to love him; he's turned into a right miserable bastard and he hates the rest of us, no matter what we do.'

'Not much you can do about it, I suppose.'

'Can't just give up on him.'

'Yeah, but some people, they get shot, they get tortured, or they're in a war, they spend the rest of their lives having nightmares and drinking too much. Other people, they just get on with it. Depends on their nature. My father, for instance.'

'What about him?'

'He was in the Falklands. Lost all his mates on the *Sheffield*, so my mother tells me. He never talks about it. I suppose that's his way of trying not to remember. That's how he gets on with it, like you say.'

'Well, I suppose there's something to be said for that.'

'Can't save everyone, guv. People have to save themselves.'

'Yeah,' Charlie said, 'I've heard that said.' That's where I go wrong, he thought. Ben used to call him Crusader Rabbit, told him he couldn't save the world. But saving the world was why he joined the Met: help the victims, bang up the bullies and the psychos.

But perhaps Grey and his brother were right. You had to let people work it out for themselves. For some the past was just the past; for other people it was a fence they spent the rest of their life trying to jump over.

Sarah thought Ollie would hardly have missed her – he'd never shown much outward affection towards her – so she wasn't prepared for her welcome when she saw him again. He had been so excited. She'd been so overwhelmed, she burst into tears. Now she wondered how she could ever have thought of leaving him like that.

It was clear to her now: wherever she went, Ollie would have to go too.

Sarah sat him down at the end of the table, put his dinner in front of him, spooned up a mouthful of mashed pumpkin, even stroked his hair as she fed him. She hadn't felt this way about him in such a long time.

She hated this, being here, in this house, after all that happened. She wanted to go back to Clapham, but they wouldn't let her, not the police, not the doctors. Her father was tiptoeing around her. He didn't know what to do with her; nobody did.

Sarah wanted just to be left alone, but she couldn't be on her own, especially not here.

She felt him watching her from the doorway. 'Need a hand with him?'

She shook her head, wanted to scream at him, *No, I'm all right, get out of my face*, but if she started acting crazy, he might have her admitted back into hospital.

'No dizzy spells? The doctors said to watch for that.'

'I'm fine.'

'Is it coming back to you yet? Anything you remember, it might be important. For finding him, like.'

'Just let me feed Ollie, Dad.' She didn't want to remember. That was the last thing she wanted.

'Here, let me help.'

She twisted away from him and he put his hands in the air, *Okay, okay, I'll mind my own business.*

'They said you should be taking things easy like.'

'Can you make me a cup of tea?'

He started banging around in the kitchen, so eager to please, but he only made it worse with all his fussing. She got a damp cloth from the sink and wiped Ollie's face.

'The police rang, that inspector. What was his name? George. He wants to come and see you, just a follow-up, he said, see if you can remember anything.'

'What did you tell him?'

'I said I'd talk to you first, see how you were feeling.'

'I don't want to see him. I don't want to see anyone. Not yet.'

'They're only doing their job.'

'I said I don't want to!'

'All right. Okay. Easy, love. I'll tell them you're not feeling well, shall I?'

She tried to pick Ollie up and screamed and clutched at her side. Her dad came rushing forward and she pushed him away with her other hand.

'Just my ribs,' she said.

'Here, let me,' he said.

'Take him into the other room, then. I'll put a DVD on for him.'

He put Ollie on the carpet in front of the television and she found *Peppa Pig*.

'You don't know what a scare you gave me,' he said.

'You've told me.'

'I knew it was him all along. I told the coppers, but no, they wouldn't listen to me. I'll bloody kill him if I find him first.'

'What good would that do?'

'They reckon he had someone helping him. If only you could remember who it was.'

Sarah put her hands over her ears and screamed. He raised both his hands, waving them frantically to get her to stop.

'All right, all right, I'm sorry, I won't ask you about it any more. You're safe home now, no one's going to hurt you here, that's all that matters.'

She could feel him staring at her. Why wouldn't he just leave her alone?

'I told that nanny of yours you won't be needing her any more. I don't know what you can do with the house, we'll have

232

to go and see a solicitor. I don't know what the law is about these things.'

'I don't want to sell Clapham.'

'You're going to need a while to get better. Not just your ribs and the stitches and everything, but your nerves and that. It's a terrible thing he's put you through. Time's the great healer, like they say. I'll look after you here. No one can hurt you now, not with me around.'

'I want to go home,' she said.

'What do you mean, go home? This is your home. Can't go back there the state you're in. What are you going to do, banging around in that big house all on your own? Besides, you'll need a hand with Ollie.'

She shook her head. 'I'm going home. Tomorrow.'

'But what if he comes back?' His face crumpled. There were tears in his eyes, and he started to shake, his hands balled into fists at his sides. 'I'm doing my best here, all right? I'm only trying to help. When they said you were missing . . . I don't know what I'd do without you.'

Ollie was walking in circles around the living room. He banged into the coffee table and screamed. 'Oh, Ollie,' Sarah said. She tried to scoop him up in her arms, but she couldn't; she clutched at her ribs again, gasped at the pain.

'You should take it easy,' her father said. 'You've been through a terrible experience.'

He came up behind her and put his arms around her, hugged her. She could smell the wool of his cardigan, felt his stubble on her cheek.

The plates were still on the coffee table from last night, where she had eaten her dinner in front of the television. She picked up a knife, twisted around and pointed it between his eyes. 'Don't you touch me,' she said. 'Don't you ever fucking touch me.'

He backed up as far as the door. It was only a dinner knife, she thought, what damage did he think she was going

233

to do with that? So much for *I'm going to kill Danny if I find him.*

His face was white. She supposed he'd never thought she'd ever do something like that, not his little girl. 'Put the knife down, Sar. You're not thinking right.'

Something has changed in me, Sarah thought. I'm not the same, I'll never be the same. How can I be? Poor little Ollie was lying on his back, kicking his legs, screaming. He knew something was wrong.

She put the knife down and knelt next to him. After a while, she got him quiet. But the way he looked at her, it was scary. All the psychologists in the world couldn't work her out, but Ollie knew.

He knew she'd come undone.

CHAPTER FORTY

When he got to Arlington House, Julia was standing in the covered entrance, smoking, looking fidgety. Christ, Charlie thought, she looks old, my little sister. Scrawny and thin and too much make-up. What has she been doing to herself? Can't be good for the baby.

Her face lit up when she saw him, though, and it gave him a bit of a lift. These days only the spaniel looked like that when he walked in, and maybe Lovejoy. He wished he could see more of Jules, but it was hard. Even when he could get time off work, she always had the Missing Link sitting there next to her, scowling and making snide remarks about Arsenal missing out on the Champions League.

'Long time no see,' she said, and gave him a bear hug.

'Watch out for your baby bump,' he said.

She patted her tummy. 'Carrying bigger than I was with Rom. They reckon it's a girl.'

She saw him looking at her cigarette and ground it out under her heel. 'I know I shouldn't. I've cut down, honest I have.'

'Shouldn't be doing it at all really.'

'I know, I know, everyone tells me. After Mum's birthday's out of the way, I'll give up. Promise. Can't face Michael and Will and give up in the same week.'

'Be better for Rom as well.'

'I know. I'm thinking of buying one of them vapes.'

'They're no good for you either.'

'I know, but I've tried everything else. How are you, Charlie?'

'All right.'

'I keep saying to Tel, I wonder how Charlie is. Rom's always asking, when's Uncle Charlie coming down to see us?'

'Chained to the wheel, Jules.'

'You look like you could do with a holiday,' she said.

'Been busier than a monkey trying to screw a football.'

'When is it any different?' she said. 'I saw on the news about those two women that got abducted. Thought that would be one of yours.'

'Yeah, I get all the good ones.'

'They don't pay you enough.'

'If I'd wanted to make money, I would have transferred into the drug squad. That was a joke, in case you're wearing a wire. So, never expected to see you. You just up for the day?'

'Yeah, came up to see Will. Haven't seen him in I don't know how long. Michael's down as well, reckons he's staying until the party.'

'Well, he gets free accommodation and all the wine and wafers he can eat.' Charlie looked through the glass, saw them all sitting in a grim little circle in the foyer. It looked like not one of them had a thing to say to each other. His family were like strangers trapped in a lift.

'How is he, our Michael?'

'Not changed. Still waiting to get headhunted by God for one of the top jobs.'

'Well, he'd make a good Pope. Always liked wearing hats. How is Rom? Doesn't still support Watford, does he?'

'What can you do, they're his dad's team.'

'Is he staying out of hospital?'

Julia shook her head. 'Not really. Been in three times since you seen him last.'

'Why didn't you tell me?'

'If I rang you every time he has a turn, I'd have no battery left on my phone. I try not to let him see how it gets me down. He's so behind at school. What kind of life is he going to have, Charlie?'

He watched Rom through the glass, slumped in a plastic chair, playing games on his iPad with a surgical mask on his face.

'He's tough,' Charlie said. 'He'll get through it.'

'No, he's not tough. He's got no choice. There's a difference.'

'I should get down and spend more time with him.'

'I asked him what he wanted to be when he grew up. He said he wanted to be a cop like you.'

'Well, get that idea out of his head. He should go into something that's less work and pays better, like stacking shelves at Tesco.'

'He thinks you've got a gun; he keeps saying, when is Uncle Charlie going to show me his gun?'

'He's been watching too many American cop shows. I wouldn't mind a gun, though.'

'For the villains, like.'

'No, but it would be brilliant for getting through the traffic in Holborn. Show a few of those Uber drivers a thing or two.'

'Heard you've got Will staying at your place.'

'Yeah, Ben organised it. Nice of him.'

'What do you make of him, then?' Jules said.

'Well, I was a bit shocked when I first saw him. He's a right bloody mess, isn't he, even for this family.'

'How's it been, him living with you?'

'I haven't seen much of him, tell you the truth. I've been at work. When I get home, we have a quick family chat and he storms out and goes down the boozer. Been lovely.'

'Still, that's Will, isn't it? He's always been a bit loose.'

'Has he? I don't remember.'

'Emotional. Up and down. Always messing around with pills and stuff.'

'I don't think he's messing around now. I think he takes drug-taking fairly seriously.'

'Well, we're all addicted to something,' Jules said, putting her Benson & Hedges back in her bag. 'Even you.'

'Me?'

'You're addicted to your job. Don't know what you'd do if people stopped murdering each other. You'd go mental.'

'Well, no fear of that. Last time I looked, people are proper loving it. Even the gangbangers are wearing stab vests these days.'

The family were watching them through the glass, waiting for him to make his grand entrance. He wasn't eager to get in there, which was sad.

'Ben told me what he'd done. I mean, dropping Will at your gaff without asking you. I thought that was a bit cheeky, know what I mean. But that's Ben. Not the same since he got that girlfriend.'

'Who is this mysterious siren?'

'I don't know. If she lasts longer than six weeks, I'll ask. As it is . . . well, you know Ben, could be all over tomorrow.'

'Is he here?' He peered into the foyer.

'He's gone. He dropped Will off then said he had to get back to work.'

'He doesn't work Fridays. He goes to the gym, then has lunch until two in the morning.'

'I'm only telling you what he said.'

'I see your Tel's dressed for the occasion. What's the look, Eminem does Brighton, or is he opening a chapter of the Crips in Sussex?'

'Leave him alone, Charlie. Tel does his best.'

'Is he working?'

'Can't at the moment. You know he's had a health scare?'

'You don't have to whisper, they can't hear us out here.'

'Well, he doesn't want anyone to know.'

'Know what?'

'He had to have one of his testicles removed.'

Charlie wanted to say, *so there is a God*, but he kept the thought to himself. It wasn't very charitable, and Tel was his brother-in-law after all.

'When did that happen then?'

'Couple of months ago. He's not told anyone. He thought people would think it was funny, make jokes.'

'People wouldn't make fun of something like that,' Charlie said. 'Well, maybe we would. Has he got the all clear?'

'It was benighted, they said.'

'Benign.'

'Yeah, that. Anyway, everything's all right down there now. First thing he did when he got home from hospital was—'

'La la la, Jules, already way too much information. Anyway, we'd better go in, can't put this off all day.'

It was cool inside the atrium after the concrete heat of the car park. Michael was sitting at the head of the circle, in the chair nearest the door. Will was sunk into one of the purple plush armchairs, looking as if he was ready for a nap. Tel was chewing gum and fiddling with his knock-off Rolex.

Rom put his iPad down and jumped up. 'Uncle Charlie!'

'Hello, Rom. Still got your Watford shirt on, then?'

'Dad says we're going to make the top four this year.'

'I got some bad news about that and the Easter Bunny, but we'll leave it for now.'

Rom landed a playful punch to his arm. Tel nodded and Michael stood up and shook hands, a little more formally.

Ma was sitting next to Will, frowning at the television. 'Hello, Ma,' Charlie said, and there was a look of panic on her face, the expression people got when they saw someone at a party whose name they should know and they were trying to stall for time.

There was another, older bloke sitting next to Ma. Charlie thought it was one of the residents until he stood up and shook hands. 'You don't remember me, do you?' he said. 'I'm your Uncle Bill.'

'You come all the way down from South Shields?'

'Well, not every day my sister turns seventy.'

'That's a long way.'

'I met him at the station in Leeds,' Michael said. 'We came

down on the train together. He's staying with me at the presbytery over in Hackney.'

'Good to see you again, Bill.'

'We've got a lot in common, you and me,' Bill said.

'How do you work that out, then?'

'We're both called the Old Bill.'

He had a good old laugh about that, and Michael joined in with a smile that looked more like a grimace. Tel didn't get the joke, but Charlie couldn't be bothered explaining it.

The television was on and they were all staring at it, an American daytime chat show. Ellen DeGeneres was interviewing Denzel Washington. 'There's too many blacks on television,' Ma said.

Michael shook his head at him: *Leave it, Charlie.*

'They're taking English people's jobs.'

'He's American, Ma.'

'Taking American jobs then.'

'Denzel Washington *is* American.'

'That's why I voted for Brexit,' Ma said.

Another shake of the head from Michael.

'Want a cup of tea?' he said.

Not another bloody cup of tea, Charlie thought. There was a dispenser in the corner. He didn't want any, but he went over with him. Michael was right. What was the point of arguing with someone with Alzheimer's? Might as well talk to Jacob Rees-Mogg. Rom hung on to his leg all the way across. Charlie wondered if he was feeling for where he hid his gun.

'I don't know why you bother, Charlie,' Michael said. 'You'll not change her now.'

'I can't help myself. It's like listening to the old man.'

'Whatever her opinions, she did her best raising us all. Do you want tea, coffee?'

'Out of a machine? No, thanks.'

'You're going to be there for her birthday, though? It could be her last.'

'Did you know there's a world shortage of guilt? They say the Catholics have cornered the market. Even Jewish mothers are running low because of you lot.'

'It's not much to ask. She says you haven't been to see her for months.'

'Check the register. Look, I've just walked through the door. Give me a break. Rom, I got you a programme from the Arsenal–Watford game last season. Want to come and have a look?'

He headed back to the magic circle. Will had fallen asleep, snoring in his chair like a bear with apnoea. Tel was checking his phone and Jules had turned the TV to another channel, a David Attenborough documentary about penguins.

He sat down with Rom, a little bit away from the others, and they read every page of the match programme. Rom thought it was the game Watford had won 2–1 and Charlie didn't want to disillusion him.

As he was leaving, his Uncle Bill followed him outside. He took his arm and led him towards the car park, out of view of the others. 'I just wanted to say, I never had any idea.'

'Any idea about what?'

'What you kids went through when you were little. What *she* went through. I never realised back then what he was like, your father.'

'He got arrested for assault three times. Once the cops even came to our house and took him away. You didn't know?'

'Val . . . your mum . . . she never told me, never told any of us.'

'I suppose she was ashamed. Whenever she had a black eye, she wouldn't go out, she'd send me or Michael down the shops for her.'

'It's not her that should have been ashamed.'

'Yeah, but that's not how it works, is it? So when did you find out?'

'Only last year. I was shocked. I feel terrible about it.'

241

'Well, nothing any of us can do about it now. All water under the fridge, as they say.' Charlie patted him on the shoulder; he couldn't think of anything else to say.

Bill started to tear up. Charlie felt embarrassed. He didn't want the poor bastard to feel bad. If he had known, what could he have done about it? The old man would have torn him up like an empty packet of cornflakes. The police and family services had done sod all; why did he think he could have changed anything?

'It's all right,' he said. 'No harm done. We all turned out all right in the end.' He looked at Bill and he could see him thinking, well, that's not bloody true.

'The thing is, we all live our lives in such isolation, don't we? Take it easy, Charlie.' Bill patted his cheek and went back inside.

His Nokia rang as he was about to head home for the day. It was Halpin.

'Charlie, this may be nothing, but I thought I'd let you know.'

'What have you got?'

'I've had a report that a local man has gone missing not far from where we found Sarah Howlett.'

Charlie sat up straighter in his chair. 'What makes you think the disappearance is connected?'

'There wasn't anything at first. It just didn't feel right, if you know what I mean. So I took a closer look.'

'Who is this bloke?'

'His name's John Trescothick. He's a panel beater, works in Sevenoaks, IC1, twenty-five years old, single. We've checked him out, couple of speeding fines but that's it as far as his record goes.'

'How long has he been missing?'

'The day we found Mrs Howlett, he didn't show up for work. His mates thought maybe he'd pulled or he'd had a big night somewhere and was sleeping it off. His boss didn't get worried until the next day, when he still wasn't answering his phone, so he went out to the place he rents, other side of Hever. Anyway, when he got there, he saw Trescothick's Border collie in the back yard, said it was fair going off, hadn't been fed. He knew there must be something wrong, because he reckons Trescothick lives for that dog. He contacted the local station; the constable there followed normal procedures, thought he'd show up eventually with an embarrassed grin on his face. By the time this was escalated, he'd been missing about forty-eight hours.'

'They went back to his house?'

'The local sergeant went with a couple of officers, checked it out. He said there was no sign of forced entry, but his work van was gone.'

'What does his boss say?'

'Just that Trescothick's a regular bloke, been working for him for a couple of years, squeaky clean. He says it's totally unlike him to take off, never been late all the time he's worked for him. We spoke to the other employees. When he left work the previous night, he said he was going home to walk the dog.'

'Girlfriend?'

'Broke up with her a couple of months ago.'

'Drugs?'

'He wasn't much of a party boy. He didn't even smoke.'

'You've spoken to his family, friends?'

'Parents live in Essex, in Brentwood. They say he calls them every weekend. They hadn't seen him for a few weeks, but they reckon he's a good lad. Got a sister, married, lives up in Liverpool. Sees his mates at the weekend; they go into Sevenoaks for a few pints. They can't think of any reason he'd have to take off.'

'So there's nothing to connect this to Sarah Howlett?'

'That's what I was getting to. There's this one thing. I was thumbing through one of the statements my lads took at the auto repair shop. Something stood out.' Charlie heard him rustling pages on the other end of the line. 'Here it is. One of the other panel beaters, he said that the day Trescothick went missing, they were on their tea break and he told him he'd seen a van broken down on the way to work. Said he'd stopped to see if he could help and the driver, this woman, she was acting weird.'

'Anything else?'

'That's all he can remember. He didn't think anything of it at the time, didn't even put it in his original statement; remembered it later and rang up the station to tell them. It was just chat, he said.'

'Can you send me the files? I wouldn't mind taking a look. Unofficially, at this stage.'

'If you think it might be useful. How's the young lady?'

'She discharged herself, went home to her dad's place. She hasn't remembered anything more.'

'Poor lass. Look, I've handed the case over to MISPERs, we've done as much as we can our end. But I'll copy you in on everything we have.'

Charlie put the Nokia on his desk and powered up his computer. The DCI had told him not to spend any more man hours on this, so he supposed he would have to satisfy his curiosity on his own time.

CHAPTER FORTY-ONE

Sarah waited until her dad had gone down the shops for milk and the paper. Ollie was asleep. She went to the shed at the bottom of the garden. It was dark inside, and there was a strong smell of earth and motor oil. He had his garden tools on hooks on the walls, lined up in neat rows like soldiers on parade. But that was him, wasn't it, a place for everything and everything in its place.

It was easy to find what she was looking for. It was in one of the drawers, with the rest of the camping stuff. It looked like it had never been used. She remembered when he'd bought it. He pretended he liked all that outdoors stuff, never missed Bear Grylls on television, but truth was, he didn't even like going down the beach in case he got sand in his shoes.

She knew he'd never use it and surely never thought she would, especially not all these years later.

'Can't believe you don't have a plasma TV,' Ben said. 'What century are we living in? This is like staring through the wrong end of a telescope.'

'You were the one who wanted to come to my gaff and watch it,' Charlie said.

'I'm just saying.'

'I don't need a plasma because I'm hardly ever home.'

'Look at us, 2–1 up against PSG,' Will said. 'If we can beat this lot, the Europa League's going to be a cakewalk.'

'It's a friendly, Will, it don't mean anything. Half their first team's still sunning themselves by the pool and Neymar's off in the duty-free buying a diamond-encrusted iPhone cover.'

'Where is this being played again?'

'Singapore.'

'What they all doing out there?'

'They're on holiday.'

'I thought this was the International Champions Cup.'

'They call it that,' Ben said, 'because it sounds better than the European Football Teams Raking in a Bit of Extra Dosh from the Asians Trophy.'

'Why do we do this to ourselves?' Charlie said. 'We could beat this lot 10–0 and it wouldn't matter. First game of the season we play Man City, and we all know what's going to happen then.'

'This Guendouzi geezer looks lively.'

'I can't pronounce any of the names,' Will said. 'The only one I can pronounce is Ramsey. Good English name, that.'

'He's Welsh.'

'That's English enough. They're not going to make up a chant about that Greek bloke, are they, if they can't even say his name.'

'It was dead easy when I was growing up,' Charlie said. 'I could recite the whole Arsenal team. None of them had more than two syllables in their names: Adams, Parlour, Thomas. These days you need to be proper cosmopolitan.'

'Cosmopolitan?' Will said. 'You need a degree in linguistics to remember the team sheet.'

'It's boring, this,' Charlie said. 'You can see none of these blokes want to be there. They're all thinking about getting down the club after and picking up a WAG.'

'You don't pick up a WAG,' Ben said. 'They're not a WAG until they've slept with a player.'

'How many times do you have to sleep with a Premier League footballer until they make you a full-on WAG, then?'

'How should I know? I've never been out with one.'

Charlie got up and went to the refrigerator. 'Anyone want a Lagunitas?'

'Thought you'd never ask,' Will said.

'So what are you doing these days, Will?' Ben said.

'You know what I'm doing. Fuck all.'

'Sorry I asked.'

'Go on, say it: why don't I get off my arse and get a job?'

'Why don't you get off your arse and get a job?' Ben said.

'Are we going to watch the football, or is this one of those intervention things?'

'Simply a casual enquiry after your general health and well-being.'

'It's like this: someone in the family has to be the rank failure. We've already got one superstar.'

'I wouldn't go that far,' Ben said, but Will wasn't looking at him. The expression on his face. 'You mean Charlie?' he said.

'Don't see your face in the papers,' Will said to him.

'Bloody glory hunter,' Ben said under his breath.

'Charlie's like one of those American TV cops,' Will said, 'all gnarled and nasty-looking. The *Mirror* made it sound like you found those missing women all on your own.'

'We only found one of them,' Charlie said. 'The other one threw herself in front of a delivery van. Before that, we didn't have a clue where she was.'

'That's not the way they do it on *Law & Order*,' Ben said. 'It's all DNA and getting some plonker to waive his Miranda rights, whatever they are.'

'Yeah, well, we don't have such a good scriptwriter.'

'Don't you ever get nightmares? I mean, some of the things you see, it's got to mess with your head. All that gratuitous violence.'

'I grew up with gratuitous violence.'

'Maybe it was good for you.'

'How's that, then?'

'Well, you got desensitised. Maybe that's why you love

all this blood and guts; doesn't matter to you, you've seen it all before.'

'That's a very cynical viewpoint, Ben.'

'You thrived on it,' Will said.

'I what?'

'The old man used to take you to football games; he never took any of us, did he? You were his golden-haired boy.'

'He hated me.'

'I didn't notice. Did you, Ben?'

Charlie thought he must be winding him up, but Will looked like he was dead serious. 'Wait a minute,' he said, 'you don't remember the fist fight we had on the doorstep when I caught him hitting Ma?'

'He was always whacking her. I don't remember one time like it was any special occasion. All I know is I never went to the Arsenal and you did.'

'You should have asked him, if you wanted to go so much.'

'I didn't like to draw attention to myself. It was like sticking your head out of a foxhole in a firefight.'

'Maybe he thought you were too little. It was no tea party down the North Bank in those days. It wasn't safe.'

'How come he took you, then?' Ben said.

Good question, Charlie thought. He hadn't ever asked himself that before.

Will necked his beer. 'All I'm saying is, it's good that one of us did something with their lives.'

'I've got a job as well,' Ben said.

'That's not a job. A job is doing something for other people, serving a need. All you do is make a shitload of dirty money.'

'It was my dirty money that got you here.'

Ben's phone rang and he glanced quickly at the screen. Without a word, he got up and went outside. Charlie flopped down on the couch next to Will.

'What's that all about then?' Will said.

'No idea.'

'That wouldn't be work ringing him on a weekend.'

'He doesn't even work on weekdays, never mind weekends.'

Charlie could see Ben through the kitchen window, looking animated and preening at his reflection in the glass.

'It's a woman,' Will said. 'Look at him.'

'First time I've ever seen him leave a football match to talk to a woman,' Charlie said.

'What's happened to my brother while I've been away? Did you ring up the agency and get a replacement?'

When Ben came back in, his cheeks were shining. He grabbed his beer and sat down on the sofa as if nothing had happened.

'Well, come on then,' Charlie said.

'Nothing. Just work.'

'Bollocks,' Will said. 'That was a woman.'

'Were you eavesdropping?'

'Why would I want to listen in on your stupid jabber? I could tell by your face.'

Ben shook his head and took a long swallow of his beer. 'It was nothing.'

It was too a woman, Charlie thought. He knew Ben's tells well enough by now: the lip-chewing, the weird attempt at face-blanking. For someone who'd made a career out of banking, he was a surprisingly bad liar.

'What is this, an interrogation?' Ben said when he saw them both staring at him. 'Put me under a bright light and hit me with a phone book, why don't you?'

'No one uses phone books any more,' Charlie said. 'Where are we going to get one of those anyway? That's why they give us proper interrogation manuals. They're nine hundred pages thick, bloody perfect.'

They turned their attention back to the TV. The new French bloke, Lacazette, scored his second with a header. 'That's it, then,' Will said. 'Game over. Who wants another beer to celebrate?'

'I'm okay,' Ben said.

Will went to the refrigerator. He'd been going two for one since the game started. He already had a bit of a lean; a couple more and he'd be staggering.

'How many's that?' Charlie said.

'Sorry, am I drinking too many of your precious beers?'

'Just saying. It's only lunchtime.'

'Shall I have some milk instead?'

'Never mind. Knock yourself out.'

'You sure it's the murder squad you're in, not the fun police? Can't smoke, can't drink, it's like being back in rehab.'

They both turned around at that. 'I didn't know you'd been in rehab,' Ben said.

'You think I actually like being me?'

'It's good you went to rehab,' Charlie said.

'It's good, is it? Good that I'm trying not to be such a fuck-up and embarrassing you all?' He tossed the empty bottle at Charlie. 'Here, you have your precious Lagunitas, I'll go and get my own.'

He went out, leaving the door open behind him.

There was a long silence. They both stared at the screen.

'You were acting a bit like his mother,' Ben said.

'He's not going to do any better down the boozer. They want actual money for their beers down there.' He saw Ben's expression. 'You been giving him money?'

'He's got to live.'

'He's got severe dependency issues. What are you thinking?' Charlie got to his feet. 'Come on, we'd better find him before he gets into trouble. Start a fight in a phone box, our little brother.'

'What's the point?'

'We can't just leave him.'

'Yes, we can. We buy him a few beers, listen to his shit, then put him on the plane after Ma's party. Simple.'

'He's our brother, Ben. We have to help him.'

'It's not your job to save him, Charlie. There's no big talk we can give him that's going to make him see the light, no grand gesture that's going to lead to epiphany. He's a mess, and the only person that can stop him being a mess is him.'

'It's just such a bloody waste. He's a good-looking lad under all that hair, and he's not stupid. He was always getting prizes for art at school; he could probably get himself a job in graphic design or something and make some decent money.'

'He could, Charlie, but he's not going to. We all know what's going to happen. He'll come to the Arlington for Ma's birthday, piss in the pot plants in the atrium, feel up one of the nurses and pass out in the car on the way home. Then he'll go back to Sydney and do some more drugs, and one day we'll get a phone call to say we're another brother short. You'll feel guilty about it, because that's in your nature. I won't, because I'm a pragmatist. And that will be that. I should set up on the end of Southend Pier as a fortune-teller.'

'So we just turn our backs, do we? He's family, Ben.'

'You are not your brother's keeper, Charlie. It's his choice.'

'But it's not, though, is it? He can't help himself. He's addicted.'

'Or is he addicted so he doesn't have to help himself?'

'You reckon?'

'That's what it looks like to me.'

'Is that true what he said about me being the old man's favourite?' Charlie said.

Ben shrugged.

'So that was how you saw it too?'

'Everyone has a different view of things growing up, don't they?'

That's a yes, then, Charlie thought. 'I'm going after Will,' he said. 'Coming?'

'Just finishing my beer.' Ben stopped, distracted by a clear free kick on the edge of the box. 'Still can't believe you haven't got a proper TV,' he said.

***

Fenton's team were on call, and they had taken over most of the incident room. There had been another stabbing in Tottenham,

251

and staffers were busy at the banks of computers, bringing HOLMES up to speed. There was a briefing under way at the other end of the room, Fenton's squad sitting or standing around in a half-circle. The inside DS was still busy pinning crime-scene photographs on the board. Charlie felt a twinge of jealousy. Nothing like a knifing on one of the estates, couple of late nights and then bang up a pair of brainless scrotes, dead easy. Handball it to the CPS, thanks very much, by the numbers.

He thought he'd come into the office, catch up on some paperwork, then head home again. He had promised to take Will out for a spot of dinner and a few drinks, make a Saturday night of it.

The DCI was right, there was plenty for him to do. His team still had thirteen live murder and manslaughter investigations, some with the CPS on trial, other long-running investigations that still had not been closed. A Romanian illegal sleeping in an alley next to the Harp just off Trafalgar Square had been found stabbed to death and they still hadn't made an arrest. It was unlikely now that they ever would. He had to collate witness statements and forensic reports for the CPS for the stabbing in Bermondsey, and next week he had to be at the Old Bailey with family members when the man who had killed their son in a drive-by shooting was sentenced. Then there was a stack of overtime forms to sign.

All part of life's rich tapestry.

He was surprised to find Grey at his desk, staring at CCTV footage.

'Haven't you got a home to go to?'

'Something was bothering me.'

'And?'

'Take a look at this, guv.'

Charlie pulled a chair towards him and sat down. He looked at the numbers on the top right-hand corner of the screen; the footage was from Wednesday night, the concourse at Charing Cross.

'You do realise the DCI has closed this down?' he said.

'I can't help it,' Grey said. 'This is bugging me.'

'Go on, then.'

'I was thinking about what the skipper said, how he thought Howlett must have got out of the cab outside the Coal Hole, then doubled back to Charing Cross station.'

'What about it?'

'We didn't have time to check that. So I found the footage. I gave him five minutes tops, ten minutes if he stopped to listen to a busker or went into Sainsbury's for a Diet Coke and a packet of crisps. Nothing. He's not on here.'

'What are you thinking?'

'There's this, though, sixteen minutes after he first got into the cab. This bloke here.'

Charlie scanned the grainy images on the screen. You didn't realise how many blokes there were in London going around in hoodies until you started looking for them. But Grey wasn't pointing to any of them.

'Looks nothing like him. What's he wearing?' Charlie took a closer look at the screen: track pants, rain jacket, beanie.

'What makes you think that's him?'

'Howlett was limping when he got on and off the Underground. This guy is trying not to. But look here, he's favouring that right leg, he can't help himself. You can see he's struggling. What if he went into a toilet somewhere, got changed, then came back to the station? The Coal Hole's only just over the road from where he jumped out. That would account for the time lag. This bloke goes over to the ticket machines, looks like he pays cash.'

'Can we see where he went?'

Grey opened another file, fast-forwarded a few minutes.

'He's headed towards the gates.'

'He must have caught the train to Westbridge,' Charlie said.

'Well, that's what it looks like. But we never confirmed that.'

253

Charlie shrugged. The DCI would have a fit if he knew he was still worrying about this.

'I checked the timetable,' Grey said. 'I did make one massive assumption, that the train was running on time. Then I checked to see if we'd pulled the CCTV for all the stations on the line.'

'And did we?'

'Mac and Lube are nothing if not thorough.' He scrolled through the video files. 'First I checked Westbridge. Nothing. He didn't get off there.'

'Really?'

'Nope.'

'Well, maybe he got changed again. Put his black hoody back on.'

'No, because I took a drive back out to Kent, collected CCTV from a few other stations. I found this.'

Grey opened another file. A train pulled in, a handful of passengers stepped off, and there he was, in his beanie and his stupid pants, limping towards the exit.

'This isn't Westbridge?'

'Dalston.'

'That's two stops before Westbridge. It doesn't make any sense.'

'That's what I thought.'

'Perhaps there was someone outside the station waiting for him in a car.'

'I thought that too, so I checked the CCTV. No one. He turned left and kept walking.'

'They might have been in the car park.'

'Could be. We could send someone down to get more CCTV. Get vision from the high street as well, see if he went that way. The DCI wouldn't like it, though.'

'The DCI doesn't have to know. Pull up a map for me, Matt.' Charlie leaned in, pointed to the screen. 'Sarah Howlett was found right over here. That's mad. He's miles away.'

'Not as the crow flies.'

'A crow can't drive a Transit van.'

'Well, I thought I should show you, guv. It was niggling at me, is all.'

Charlie swivelled on the chair. 'I had a strange call yesterday from that bloke Halpin at Linton Spa. He had a local geezer go missing around the same time we found Sarah Howlett. Come and have a look.'

Grey followed him across the incident room. Halpin had emailed him the files and Charlie scrolled through them, found the map he was looking for. Halpin had scanned the route that Trescothick took to work every day and had circled the ANPR handshakes for the three days before he went missing.

'Who is this MISPER?' Grey said.

'His name's Trescothick, he's a panel beater, no criminal record, no history of mental illness, no connections to the underworld. A taxpayer. Look at the ANPR, same time every morning, about the same time every night.'

'Nothing between there and Sevenoaks,' Grey said, pointing to the screen.

'That's because he took the A road most of the way, but right here, see, there's a B road; his mates said he always came off here. There was less traffic and he reckoned it was quicker.'

'You think this has got something to do with Sarah Howlett?'

'In usual circumstances, no, except for one thing. Trescothick mentioned to one of his mates that he came across a van, broken down, on his way to work that morning.'

'What sort of van?'

'He didn't say. It might mean nothing, or it could be a bomb going off. We'd look a bit silly if we stuck our fingers in our ears and pretended we didn't hear it, just to keep our boss happy.'

Grey brought up Google Maps and checked the distances on the screen, using his fingers as calipers. 'If this is the route Trescothick took to work, the closest point to Dalston station is this stretch of road here. That's about three miles. Take over

255

an hour to walk that. You'd have to know the area; it was dark.'

'That's the thing, isn't it? Howlett must know the area. If he's got a map and a torch, he could do it easily enough.'

'What do you think he was up to?'

'He was trying to throw us off the scent. He gets off here, along the high street, takes this footpath around the castle, down the towpath, five minutes and he's in the fields heading out of town. You follow the track along here, eventually you get to the railway bridge, go underneath to the bridle path. Not a house or a road the whole way. No one's going to see you.' Charlie put the map on maximum zoom. 'And right here is where the bridle path connects to the B road.'

'Why would anyone do that?'

'Because they couldn't use their car. Because they were under surveillance and they couldn't get a lift because cabs and Ubers have GPS and we can find out exactly where the drivers have dropped their fares.'

'But Sarah Howlett was found over here, nearly ten miles away.'

'I know. Doesn't make sense.'

'So what do we do?'

'If I had the manpower and the authorisation, I would contact all the people who live along this stretch of road and ask them about their neighbours, see if they'd seen or heard anything. They're all just small farms, can't be more than a dozen or so. Trouble is, I don't have the resources, and I still have a mountain of paperwork to get through, and my family life is barmy, what with my brother over from Australia and my mum's birthday party tomorrow.'

'I'll do it.'

'You're not getting paid for this.'

'Won't take long. If nothing comes of it, I'll give you a ring and then go home.'

As he walked to the lifts, Charlie thought: I promised Ben I would be at the party tomorrow. Please don't find anything.

The DCI is right: it's a happy ending right now, best leave happy endings alone.

'Well, this is nice,' Will said. 'Last time you and me had a meal was down the chippie in Walthamstow. Now here we are in some fancy Spanish place eating fried lark's tongues.'

'It's tapas, mate. You must have it in Australia.'

'I can never afford anything like that. I'm glad we're on your coin. Look at this, couple of bits of fish roe for seven quid. The roe used to be the cheap stuff they chucked in the fryer for when you only had change left after you'd come out of the pub. That is extortion, that is.'

'Well, I'm paying, so stop complaining.'

They were at the Angel. Charlie had decided to make the most of his night off. They'd started with a couple of drinks at the Compton, and he had slowed down after that. But Will had got the taste and was still packing them away. Charlie hoped this wasn't going to get ugly.

Will gulped down his cocktail.

'Steady.'

'Lolly water. What is it anyway?'

'Bourbon, Campari and vermouth.'

'Well, that should do the job. Makes a change from sniffing glue. That was a joke, by the way.'

'Was it?'

'Take life too serious, that's your problem.'

'That's a nice jacket you got on,' Charlie said. 'Looks like an Incotex. I've got one just like it.'

'Okay, so I borrowed it. Big deal.'

'You could have asked me first.'

'You weren't around to ask.'

'And Marni sneakers.'

'They're a bit big on me. Can you get a size smaller next time?' Will looked around, tugged at his beard. 'Jeez, things are changing around here.'

'Not that much. You haven't been away that long.'

'Long enough.'

'You miss it?'

'A bit.'

'You must like it over there. Australia.'

'Not really. Never have.'

'Why did you go there, then?'

'It was as far away as I could get without starting to come back.'

'Right. Look, don't sugar-coat things, Will. Feel free to say what you mean.'

'Well, it's the truth.'

Charlie was about to say, was it anything to do with Uncle Pat, but he stopped himself. No good was going to come from talking about that.

'Go on, say it,' Will said.

'Say what?'

'You were going to ask me if it had anything to do with Uncle Pat.'

'More or less.'

'You want to know if he bummed me after choir practice?'

'Did he?'

'For what it's worth, you can't blame all your little brother's problems on that hypocritical bastard.' The waiter brought their food. Will frowned. 'All these bits and pieces. I wouldn't mind a steak.' He held out his glass. 'Another one of these, kind sir.'

'You didn't answer my question,' Charlie said, after the waiter had moved away.

'Well, it's not like it's any of your business.'

'Of course it's my business. You're my little brother.'

'It stopped being your business the day you walked out of home.'

'I was out of school. I had my own life to live.'

'Well, fine, and now you're living it. It's a bit late to worry about little Will, isn't it? I appreciate the thought and all, but fuck off.'

The waiter arrived with Will's cocktail. Will downed half of it in one swallow.

'We're still family,' Charlie said.

'Well, there's families and families. We got the short straw with ours.'

'Did we?'

'You know we did. Great drop of booze, this. Might start making them for myself when I get home.'

'And where is home?'

Will made a face. 'It varies. I'll sort something out when I get back.'

'You still doing meth?'

'What's it to you?'

'It's not good for you.'

'On the contrary, the only problem with drugs is that they wear off. Still trying to watch out for your little brother. Admirable.'

'Yeah, but not easy.'

'I remember when I was a kid, you belted Billy Donachy, biggest kid in the school, because his brother was bullying me. Took on the meanest prick in the borough on my account. God, you were my hero, did you know that? I got out of so many hidings growing up because of you; everyone was shit scared of you. Then one day you left home and I said to Ben, when's Charlie coming back, and he said he isn't, he's gone. Couldn't believe it.'

'I only moved a mile away.'

'We needed you at home.'

'You know why I couldn't stay.'

'It was all right for you, you were tough like the old man. Me. What was I? A little bit artistic. No wonder I'm like I am.' He finished his drink and waved a hand at the waiter for another.

'Slow down,' Charlie said.

'What are you, Mary Poppins?'

'Look, Will, none of us had it easy. But sooner or later you have to grow up.'

'That waiter's deliberately ignoring me.'

'The past is the past. It doesn't have to be the future.'

'You're wasted in the police, you should be working for Hallmark.' Will pushed his plate away. He'd hardly eaten anything. 'You don't understand, do you? Some of us can't get over it.'

'You don't want to.'

Wrong thing to say.

'Really?' Will leaned across the table. 'Tell that waiter to stick his fancy drink up his arse and insert the straw sideways.' He slammed the empty glass on the table and walked out.

Charlie stood up, thought about following him, then sat down again. There was nothing more to say that wouldn't make it worse.

A few people looked over, glanced away when he caught them staring. He was tossing up whether to pay the bill and leave or order another beer when his Nokia buzzed in his pocket.

It was Grey. 'I think I've found something interesting,' he said.

CHAPTER FORTY-TWO

It was quiet when he got back to the nick: a few tired-looking detectives staring at computer monitors, a couple of staffers inputting HOLMES data. They were mostly Fenton's people; his own crew were all on a well-earned rest.

Grey was waiting for him, fiddling idly with the mouse, a shy smile on his face. Charlie knew that look: he'd found something. He didn't know whether to be pleased or horrified.

'How did you go?' he said.

Grey pushed a list of names across the desk; he'd put lines through half of them. 'I haven't gone through the whole list yet, some of them are away.' He put a finger on a name near the bottom. 'This is the one I think you should take a look at.'

'Geoffrey and Jeanette Williams,' Charlie read.

'They own this little farm here. Bought it about five years ago. He's an absentee owner, spends most of his time in France these days, describes himself as semi-retired.'

'You spoke to him?'

'Got his number from the local estate agent. They've been trying to sell the farm for him.'

'What did he have to say that was so interesting?'

'Not much. He hasn't been back to the farm for a couple of months, flies over every now and then to make sure it's still there, I suppose. Must be nice to have that much money.'

'And?'

'Before he retired, half retired, guess where he worked?'

'Not Dillon and Rowe?'

'Same office as our Mr Howlett.' Grey brought up a Google Map visual of the B road that passed the farm. 'You can't see the farmhouse from the road, it's on the other side of the hill. You get to it along this private track.'

'If Howlett knew this Geoffrey Williams, then he probably knew the farm was empty. Perhaps Williams talked about it in the office, how he was going to live abroad but couldn't sell his little hobby place in Kent.'

'You think that's where they've hidden the van?'

'It's possible. Trescothick drives past this place to and from work every day. Maybe on Wednesday he saw something on his way home and stopped to have a look.'

Charlie picked up the phone. He didn't expect to get Halpin on a Saturday night, but he picked up straight away. 'It's Charlie from Essex Road,' he said.

'Have you found something?'

'I wonder if your boys might extend a courtesy,' Charlie said. 'There's a farm out by Fernoak. Reckon you could send a car to have a look for us.'

'What are we looking for?'

'John Trescothick.'

'Right. I'll send a patrol out. I'll give you a call if we find anything.'

Tomorrow was Sunday. Charlie hoped nothing came up to make him miss his mum's birthday.

CHAPTER FORTY-THREE

Sarah carried Ollie up to his bedroom. He was a dead weight in her arms, and she wondered how much longer she could do this. The poor little mite, where would he be without her?

She couldn't imagine her father looking after him if she wasn't around. The look strangers got on their faces when they saw him; most people didn't understand. He wouldn't be able to deal with it.

People could be so cruel.

She sat on his bed in the dark, looking at the teddy bear light on his windowsill flickering pink, blue and green on the ceiling. He liked the music it played; sometimes it was the only thing that got him to sleep.

She brushed back a damp lock of his hair. What was wrong with her? She wasn't supposed to feel like this. What sort of mother resented her own little boy? It wasn't his fault. He didn't ask for this either.

Sarah started to close her eyes and then jerked awake again; couldn't rest since she'd come home, not without the drugs they had given her. Every time she fell asleep, she heard the screams again.

She stood up and went into her own bedroom and shut the door. She turned on the night light beside the bed and got under the quilt, still in her leggings and T-shirt.

He was still downstairs, watching some game show on television, shouting out the answers, jeering at the contestants when they got the answers wrong.

263

She had vowed to herself once that she was never coming back here. But everything she had tried had gone wrong. It was hopeless.

She thought she'd finally done it this time, when she and Ania were driving out of London. They had been laughing at how easy it all was and Ania said, here, have some vodka, celebrate your new life! The roofies must have already been dissolved in the bottle.

She didn't know if she had the strength to try again. What was the point anyway? It was like being in a spiderweb: the harder she struggled, the more entangled she got.

Now she understood why her mother had done what she did, why she'd left her behind. She'd done the same, hadn't she? She had tried to tell herself that what she was doing was different, but it wasn't. Ollie needed his mum every bit as much as she had needed hers. He might not show it, but he knew what went on.

It had been wrong to leave him behind. She wouldn't ever make that mistake again.

Sarah heard her father turn the television off and start moving around downstairs, putting cups in the dishwasher, plates back on the shelves. She pulled the quilt up to her chin. It's okay, she thought. He had promised he wouldn't start all that up again.

Everything had been different after her mum left; he'd changed. Perhaps he'd always been like that and Mum protected her from him; or maybe it was losing Mum that did it to him. She would never know, and she didn't really care.

She didn't have many memories of her mum, just that one time she had taken her to the zoo. She could still hear her if she closed her eyes: *How about we go and play with the bears, Sar.* She'd pretended to pick her up and throw her into the cage, and she'd screamed like she really thought she'd do it.

She looked at the bears she had around her room. She had names for all of them. The tatty brown one was Miss Beatrice; her mum had given it to her before she left, said it had been hers

264

when she was a kid. It was only a couple of years ago that she found out that was her grandmother's name – Beatrice.

She didn't even know where the bear had come from. She thought it might have been her mum's once.

Then there was Pooky, Fudge, Wally, Fenton, Sprocket and Mr Wadsworth Smith. Wadsworth was named after her favourite teacher when she was in her first year at school.

She used to have picnics with them all when she was a little girl. Her mum would sit down with her on a rug in the living room and help her put out all the little cups and saucers and plates.

The picnics became a lot posher when they moved out of London. She remembered how her father took her to Hamleys and told her she could have anything she wanted in the whole shop. All she had wanted was a bear, and he bought her five. Even as a kid, she thought that was extravagant.

He had said, *don't worry, lovey, we're rich now, we can afford it*, but it had scared her a bit.

She would tell her bears things no one else knew; each one had their own special secret they were guarding. Mr Wadsworth Smith was the first one she told, and she made him promise not to tell the other bears, but of course he did. She never told him the really bad things again, because he couldn't be trusted to keep a secret. But Miss Beatrice was discreet, and so she told her everything; perhaps that was why she looked so old and tired.

She'd missed them, especially Miss Beatrice. Danny wouldn't let her have them at their house. He wanted the place to look like the magazines, not like a set from *Sesame Street*. That was what he said. The lights went out downstairs. Her mouth was dry. He came up the stairs and stopped on the landing. She could hear him thinking, hear him trying to make up his mind.

She reached under the pillow and felt for the knife.

The worst thing is when you know they're there, when the fear is so bad you start to gag. You know that if you can't stop, you'll choke. You tell yourself it's not really happening; try and pull yourself into the dark.

It gets so that you're not really in your body any more, like you're floating on the ceiling, watching yourself down there, all curled up into a ball. That way you don't feel anything. Knowing what's about to happen, before you can escape out of your body, that's what really does your head in.

So you keep swallowing it down, the bile, as he gets closer. In your mind, you run away, think about other things. You go to another place, a place far away where he can't find you, no one can. You pull the darkness over your head like a blanket. Please. Just leave me alone.

He gets closer and you can hear him breathing, hot and fast. He stinks. You're trapped, and he's right there, outside the door and there's no way of getting away.

'Sarah,' she hears him whisper. 'Sarah, are you awake?'

He is outside the door. You pull the covers over your head. Perhaps if he thinks you're asleep, he will go away and leave you be.

'Sarah?' The door opens and you see his shadow in the doorway. You keep quite still. The door inches open and he comes in.

CHAPTER FORTY-FOUR

Birdsong, flashing blue lights, police tape strung across the gates. It wasn't the way most people started their Sunday mornings, Charlie thought. Some hadn't even got home yet; Will, for example.

He hadn't been back at his gaff an hour when Halpin had rung him; the two officers he'd sent over to the farm had found enough to make Halpin request a proper search team, crime unit and police divers for first light.

The press had got wind somehow; a cordon had been set up at the end of the road that led to the farm, and already there were two television vans parked on the verge near the gate, one local and one from the BBC.

It looked like a nice place. He could make out a bungalow with pebble-dashed walls, a chicken shed with a corrugated roof, a grain store with rammed earth walls. A real gentleman's farm, nothing too rural, like mud or pigs.

The crime-scene techs were at work along a fifty-yard stretch of the road that led up to the farm, some of them on hands and knees searching the undergrowth. Uniforms were doing a sweep of the place. Halpin had taken down a stretch of fence to bring in a mobile crane, which was manoeuvring into position at the edge of the dam.

Charlie had a forensic suit and overshoes in the boot. He put them on and walked down towards the cordon. Halpin pulled back the hood on his white coveralls, ducked under the tape to greet him. 'Charlie,' he said. 'Looks like you were right.'

'Did you find the van?' Charlie said.

'No sign of it yet, or Mr Trescothick either. But we did find a few other things.'

He walked Charlie back up the private road. He pointed to the trampled grass either side of the road and a tyre print in the mud. 'The rain last night didn't help, but we did find this. More significantly, we found a woman's bracelet and a monkey wrench over there in the long grass. Thing is, the wrench had blood on it.'

'Where is it?' Charlie said.

'In an evidence bag, back at the station. I've got an exhibits officer making sure it's all done right.'

He led the way across an open field to the dam. They stopped.

'Bugger me,' Charlie said.

There was an ancient Jeep half submerged in the black water, one door ajar, and up to its axles in the soft mud at the lip of the dam. There was a length of tow rope trailing from the back of it. There had been a lot of activity. Charlie didn't need a crime-scene tech to tell him there were at least two sets of tyre prints.

'It was pretty much invisible from the road,' Halpin said. 'It was only when my boys went over to take a look that they saw it.'

'What do you think?'

'Looks like someone used it to tow another vehicle up here. If there is another one down there, they must have used the jeep to push it in, then got themselves bogged.'

The SOCOs had set up duckboards next to the dam to prevent contamination of the scene. The crane was on the hard ground at the edge. Halpin led the way across the duckboards. Two techs were busy taking casts of the tyre- and footprints along the bank.

The dive team were all set, spare tanks lined up and safety lines rigged. Two of them were sharing a coffee from a thermos; the sergeant was feeding out line to the lad in the water.

'What's the visibility like down there?' Charlie asked him.

'Not great. Like trying to find a dead body in pea soup.'

'Sounds like my old mum's cooking,' Charlie muttered.

'We think they got the jeep from the shed up there, next to the farmhouse,' Halpin said. 'Somebody cut the wires to the burglar alarm and let themselves in with a crowbar.'

'What about the main house?'

Halpin shook his head. 'No sign of forced entry at the bungalow.'

Charlie's Nokia rang. It was Parm. She'd volunteered to go into the nick, even though it was a Sunday, to do a little bit of catch-up for him. She'd checked Daniel Howlett's phone records. Geoffrey Williams' number didn't appear on any of them in the last year. She'd also checked with HM Customs. Williams hadn't been in England since May.

'That about our Mr Williams?' Halpin said. 'I suppose you'd like a word with him.'

'It looks like he's in the clear. He's driving to London to be interviewed, but all accounts, he's as surprised about all this as the rest of us.'

He watched the diver slip under the surface. The water looked black and not very pleasant. Not a job he'd like to do with his claustrophobia; it would give him nightmares.

'If they brought Sarah Howlett here in the van,' Halpin said, 'how did she end up at the roundabout in Westbridge?'

The diver resurfaced; his sergeant squatted on his haunches on the bank, talking to him. He headed back up the duckboards. 'He's found a vehicle,' he said.

'Can he see a body?' Halpin asked.

'He can barely see his hand in front of his face.'

They had to reposition the crane, and when it was done, the diver went down a second time to secure the chains. It seemed to take an eternity. As Charlie waited for them to start the winch, he went through a hundred scenarios in his mind, trying to find one that fitted with what he knew. None of them gave him a warm, fuzzy feeling inside.

The crime-scene manager came over while they were waiting, said he'd like a word.

'We've been looking at the tyre tracks,' he said. 'As you can see, it looks like they've held the Dakar Rally in this part of the field, but what it is, it's just two sets of prints. One of them belongs to the jeep down there.'

'Footprints?'

'At least three different sets, I'd say.'

There was a shout. The dive team's sergeant gave the thumbs-up to the crane driver. The winch cranked to life. Charlie winced; the noise was deafening.

As they watched, a white van emerged from the water. Charlie felt the hairs rise on the back of his neck. The plates had been altered, but the wing mirror on the passenger side was missing, and he guessed that when they had it all the way out of the water, he would find a dent in the right front bumper.

'That's the one,' he said. His DCI was going to love this.

'Is this what you were hoping for?' Halpin said.

He wasn't sure that was the word he would have used. 'Dreading' might have been better.

Water streamed from the bonnet. The crime techs were waiting on the bank in their green wellingtons. As soon as the van was stable, they would check the interior.

'Ready?' Halpin asked.

'As I'll ever be,' Charlie said.

The crane hauled the van the rest of the way out and set it down on the bank. Two SOCOs went over and opened the driver's door. One of them looked up at Halpin. 'There's a body,' he said.

Charlie swore under his breath.

Two more techs opened the back door. They pointed at something lying in the back, then one of them turned and held up two fingers.

'They've found another one,' Charlie said.

'Well,' Halpin said. 'Weren't expecting that.'

270

CHAPTER FORTY-FIVE

Charlie drove through the cordon at the end of the lane. There were a few cars parked on the verge: rubberneckers out seeing what the fuss was about, a couple of TV crews. This wasn't Tottenham; murder wasn't something they saw a lot of on their way into town to do the shopping.

He clocked Grey, all suited up, standing outside the house talking to the crime-scene manager. Charlie got his own suit and overshoes from the boot and put them on. There was no scenario he could imagine for this; the only person who could tell them definitively what had happened at the farm was Sarah Howlett.

His mobile rang. It was Halpin.

'Ready for this?' Halpin said.

'Not really,' Charlie said. 'But tell me anyway.'

'We've found Mr Trescothick. His van was parked down a lane about half a mile from the roundabout in Westbridge. He was in the passenger seat. Been dead at least three days, the pathologist reckons.' He gave him the rest of what he knew.

'Wounds?'

'Two skull fractures, blunt object.'

'Poor bloke.'

'Talk about wrong place, wrong time. Have you found Mrs Howlett?'

'Not yet. I'll keep you posted.'

Charlie closed his eyes and played it through in his head; now at least they knew how Sarah had got to the Westbridge roundabout from the farm. He felt sorry for Trescothick; sometimes life just wasn't bloody fair.

Grey saw him and headed over.

'Well,' Charlie said. 'This is nice.' He offered Grey half of his muffin.

'No, thanks, guv.'

'It's blueberry and white chocolate.'

'Feeling a bit nauseous, actually.'

'You'll get over it. Lead the way.'

Charlie remembered the last time he was here, the little shrine to Sarah in the hallway. It seemed quite poignant in the light of this morning's events.

'How did you get in?'

'After you called, I drove straight up here with DC Khan. When we didn't get an answer, we tried around the back. The door needed a little persuasion.'

'You broke in? That's illegal, that is.'

'I had reason to believe it was a life-threatening situation.'

'And why did you think that?'

'I thought you'd kill me if I didn't do it.'

'Yes, I would have. Well done.'

They got to the top of the stairs. Most of the SOCOs were in the bedroom on the right. It was immediately apparent why.

'What happened in Kent, guv?'

'I don't know exactly, Sergeant. We found the van at the bottom of Williams' dam. Daniel Howlett and a woman I believe to be our mysterious siren from Croydon were both deceased inside.'

'What about Trescothick?'

'Also deceased, I'm afraid. They've just found him in Westbridge. Someone walking their dog happened on his van about the same time we were dredging the dam.'

'She must have driven his van all the way from the farm.'

'Looks that way.'

'Do we know how they died?'

272

'Seems all three of them had been bludgeoned to death. In here?'

Tony Jones lay crumpled against the wall in the corner of the bedroom. His cardigan was covered in a gelatinous mess of blackened blood; God knows how many times he'd been stabbed, but it was the sort of thing pathologists liked to call a frenzied attack.

'Alas, poor Tony,' Charlie said. 'I knew him. A man of infinite jest.' He turned to Grey. 'What's that stuck in his mouth?'

'It's a teddy bear, guv.'

'Well, that's a bit excessive, innit?'

The CS manager had followed them up the stairs. 'I'd say someone didn't like him very much,' he said over Charlie's shoulder.

'There's even blood splatter on the ceiling.'

'You can paint a whole room with the blood of an average adult male,' he said, 'and still have some left over for a second coat.'

'I'll remember that when I'm redecorating. Christ, this looks like the first dry-land shark attack in history. Do we have the murder weapon?'

Grey shook his head.

'The pathologist said the blade had a serrated edge,' he said.
'Where is he?'

'He left a few minutes before you got here, guv. He said thirty-one stab wounds, give or take.'

'Time of death?'

'Rough estimate, twelve to sixteen hours.'

'Last night, then. No sign of the little boy?'

Grey shook his head. 'How could she do this to her own father?'

'You know your trouble, Matt?'

'Guv?'

'You come from a good home. Where was the little boy when all this was going on?'

'In his bedroom, I think, sir.'

'This isn't his bedroom?'

Grey nodded at the door. There was a picture of a teddy bear, and underneath, *SARAH'S ROOM*.

Charlie clocked the bed. It had been slept in, and Tony was still in his cardigan and jeans. That meant he'd come in here before he went to bed.

He put on gloves and picked up one of the bears from the dressing table. He pressed its stomach; it played 'The Teddy Bears' Picnic'. He looked at the tag on its stomach: *Milwood Wildlife Park, £15.99*.

He went back downstairs to the kitchen. There was a child's bowl on the kitchen worktop, a mess of half-eaten cereal in it. The TV was on, a cartoon channel. 'She fed the kid his breakfast in front of the TV before she left.'

'Like it was any normal morning.'

Grey went into the laundry. 'Guv.' One of the technicians was putting bloodstained pyjamas in an evidence bag. 'Looks like she got changed after she was done.'

'I do like a tidy psychopath,' Charlie said.

'You reckon she slept here all night with her father's body in the bedroom?'

'Looks like it.'

His Nokia rang. It was the DCI.

'Good morning, sir,' Charlie said.

'Nothing good about it. Come and talk to me.'

'Soon as I get back to the nick, sir.'

'No, now. I'm in my car, outside.'

He was sitting behind the wheel of his Merc, tapping his fingers on the console; didn't even look at Charlie, kept staring straight ahead like he couldn't bear to look at him. 'Four dead bodies, Charlie,' he said when he got in.

'I didn't *want* to be part of a multiple homicide.'

'It's always you it happens to, though, isn't it?'

'Can't help bad luck.'

274

'So they say. What do we have?'

'I suggest we issue an arrest warrant for Sarah Howlett in relation to the three bodies found this morning in Kent. She is also my main suspect in her father's homicide.'

The DCI nodded slowly, pursed his lips. 'I thought this was all tidied away.' The look on his face, Charlie thought: sadness, puzzlement, irritation. 'Why?'

'I don't know. I'm hoping she'll be able to tell us. I am now convinced the original abduction was staged, but after that, the water gets a bit murky.'

'Where is she?'

'She could well be out of the country by now. Stansted and Southend are just down the road. I've put out an alert for her, and I'll get her picture to the media.'

'If she's done a runner, she'll show up sooner or later and we'll get to the bottom of it.'

'Due respect, sir, you said that about Daniel Howlett.'

'You reckon she'll harm the kid?'

'I bloody hope not.'

'Fact is, no telling what she'll do, is there?'

'There is one glimmer of hope.'

'I was hoping there would be.'

'It looks like she didn't run off straight after the murder. She may not even be trying to escape any more. She could still be close by.'

'Find her, Charlie. No more bodies in the morgue. All right?'

After he drove away, Charlie called the skipper, asked him to check the ANPR cameras for the A414. Then he called Grey over. 'Let's get in the car,' he said.

'Back to the nick, guv?'

'Not yet. I'll tell you where we're going when I hear back from the skipper.'

***

One of the uniforms flagged them down when they reached the cordon at the end of the lane. There was a woman with him; she

275

looked distraught. He had hold of her arm while he spoke into the radio on his vest.

'That's Jackie Jones,' Grey said.

'Stop the car,' Charlie said, and got out. 'Jackie, it's DI George. We spoke a couple of days ago.' He nodded to the uniform: *I got this*.

'Has he hurt her?' Jackie said.

Interesting question. 'I'm afraid I have some bad news about your father. Why don't we go and sit in the patrol car over here?' He led her across the road; there was a local X5 parked up the verge. He sat her down in the back. She was shaking.

'What's happened?' she said. 'No one will tell me.'

'I'm afraid you'd better prepare yourself for a shock, Jackie.'

'Is she going to be all right?'

'It's not Sarah, Jackie. It's your father.'

She looked confused. 'Dad? What do you mean?'

Charlie shook his head.

'He's dead?'

'I'm sorry.'

She gave a little laugh. 'Jesus. How?'

'He was stabbed.'

'Stabbed? What, someone broke in?'

'There's no sign of forced entry. The person we'd most like to speak to about this is your sister. Do you know where she is?'

'Sarah. You think *Sarah* did it?'

'When was the last time you spoke to her?'

'I haven't. Not since all this happened. I went down to see her when she was in hospital, but Dad wouldn't let me near her. Wouldn't take my phone calls, neither.' She looked dazed. 'Sarah?'

'It does look that way.'

Jackie put her face in her hands and wailed. Charlie signalled to a uniform standing to one side. He was about to let her take over when Jackie said, 'I should have known.'

'What should you have known?'

'I shouldn't have let her stay with him. It's my fault.'

276

'How is it your fault?'

'He was interfering with her for years. Why do you think I got out?'

'Interfering with her? You mean sexually?'

'Didn't you see her bedroom? Do you think she wanted it that way?'

'Why didn't you tell us this before?'

'Look, we never even talked about it with each other. I never wanted anyone to know, neither did she.'

I wonder if it would have made any difference, Charlie thought. If I'd known.

'Even Oliver,' she said.

'What about him?'

'What do you think?' Jackie said.

Charlie stared at her. He still didn't get it.

'Why do you think she married Danny? You really think Oliver was his?' She curled up on the seat and howled.

'Get another ambulance down here,' Charlie said to the uniform. He felt bad leaving her with it, but that was part of the job, and anyway, he had to find Sarah.

He took out his Nokia, rang the skipper at Essex Road. 'How are we doing on the ANPR?'

'We've got a hit for Tony Jones's car on the A414 fifty-three minutes ago.'

'Result. Did you talk to Parm?'

'She's gone back through the GPS on Sarah Howlett's phone. She goes to Milwood on average once a month.'

'Ring the local station, ask them to send a couple of squad cars. I'll meet them there.' He ran back to his car. 'Get the blue light from under the seat, Matt, give it the full drama.'

'Where are we going?' Grey said.

'It's Sunday, Matt. We're going for a day out at the zoo.'

Grey gunned the engine. 'I don't get it. Surely she'd just run?'

'I don't think she's thinking about that any more,' Charlie

said, gripping the seat as they hurtled down the country lane. 'I think she's given up. This is about Oliver now. We have to stop her hurting the kid.'

CHAPTER FORTY-SIX

There was a queue to get in, and the woman behind the ticket desk looked outraged when Charlie shoved his way to the front. She was only a little mollified when he showed her his warrant card. The skipper had sent through the file image of Sarah Howlett, and Charlie held his phone up to her.

'Have you seen this woman this morning?'

She squinted at it.

'She had a little kid with her. He's about four. Probably in a pushchair.'

'We get a lot of mothers with kids,' she said.

'Have a closer look,' Charlie said.

Grey came running in from the car park, out of breath. 'Found the car,' he said. 'She's here.'

Charlie forgot about the ticket woman and followed him outside. 'Get the park manager, tell him what's happening. The uniforms should be here any minute. I'll go check the park.'

He ran through the entrance holding up his warrant card, set off along one of the nature paths. I've got the wrong gear on for this, he thought.

He stopped in front of a billboard with a map of the park on it. There were pictures of animals and facilities and tuck shops picked out with large yellow arrows. You didn't have to be Einstein to know where she'd gone, he thought. It would have to be the bears, wouldn't it?

It was a grey day; there weren't many people. The air was so thick, Sarah felt like she was suffocating. She took Ollie out of the pushchair and lifted him into the sling. There was no sign of the bears. Perhaps they were sleeping. It was that kind of weather.

'It would be nice to stay here for ever and ever, wouldn't it?' she said to Ollie. Her shoulders ached. He was so heavy in the sling; she wouldn't be able to carry him around like this much longer anyway.

She held Ollie's face, kissed the top of his head. She wondered what went on in his little mind, how much he understood.

'I wanted to get away from everything, even you. I was a bad mummy, wasn't I? I was going to leave you behind. You shouldn't love me, you know. I know you do, but you shouldn't.'

She felt for the hunting knife in the changing bag over her shoulder.

'Everyone lets you down in this world, Ollie. They say they love you, but they don't, not really. Grandad did stuff he shouldn't have, that's why I had to punish him, it was the only way I could make him stop. Your daddy wasn't a nice daddy either, not really. You don't even miss him, do you?'

Ollie was a different boy when he was still. So quiet.

'You're like me,' she said to him. 'You were behind the barn door when they were handing out the luck. I wish I was better for you. But I can't be, Ollie, I can't do it, not even for you. I'm in a lot of trouble. I've done some really bad things.'

She made her way to the middle of the rope bridge, balanced herself, looking down for the bears.

'You think you can change your life, but you can't. The same things keep happening over and over. People don't ever do what they should, they all let you down in the end.'

Ollie pointed at something in the trees.

'There she is. I can see him now too. Look what sharp teeth he's got!' She tickled him under the ribs. 'All the better to eat you with!'

Ollie wriggled in her arms.

'Shall we go down and play?'

CHAPTER FORTY-SEVEN

Charlie saw her on the bridge, her and the boy; she was carrying him in a sling around her neck. He saw her pull out a knife.

'Don't do it,' he said aloud, 'please don't do it.'

She'd seen him; she must have thought, bloke in a suit, on his own, only one thing this can be. She moved into the middle of the bridge, steadying herself against the rope mesh with her free hand.

She started sawing at the rope.

He remembered what the pathologist had told Grey: *The murder weapon had a serrated edge.* He understood now what this was all about, what she was planning to do.

He started running.

She cut away enough of the rope that she could squeeze through. He thought she'd fall, but somehow she kept her balance, steadied herself. Then she jumped. It was eight feet down into the enclosure; she landed on her feet then went forward onto her knees.

He heard Grey calling out to him.

Charlie turned around. 'Go and get one of the keepers, tell them there's someone in the bear enclosure.'

He ran to the bridge and looked down. Sarah was still on her knees; she must have hurt her ankle in the fall. The little boy was screaming, frantically waving his arms and legs. Was he hurt? He couldn't tell from here. Sarah wasn't taking any notice of him.

Charlie leaned through the hole in the mesh. 'Sarah!'

She looked up, smiled. He knew it was too late to stop this now.

She got to her feet, limped towards the bears' exercise pit. She looked back over her shoulder once, shook her head at him. *Nothing you can do now*, her face seemed to say.

There was a man and woman at the other side of the bridge with their faces up against the fence; they'd seen what had happened. The man pulled out his mobile phone. Oh yeah, make sure you've got something to post on Snapchat, that's the important thing.

Charlie looked around, hoped to see Grey with a couple of keepers with nets, stun guns, anything, but there was no sign of him. He was on his own now. He looked at the hole in the mesh. It made no sense going down there, but what else could he do? He couldn't just stand there and watch.

With any luck, the bears were all asleep. He just needed a few minutes for Grey to find the keepers, that was all. But then, almost on cue, the woman on the other side of the bridge started screaming and pointing. No prizes for guessing what she was pointing at, he thought.

He heard something crashing through the trees. It didn't look all that big from up here, didn't even look very fierce. It was lumbering towards the tyre swing. Then it stopped, curious, sensing something was wrong, its nose working the scents in the air.

It associates people with the keepers who give it food, Charlie thought. Its next instinct, when it discovers it's not dinner time, will be to protect its territory. It had already spotted Sarah and Oliver. Puzzled, it padded up and down, watching them.

Sarah had seen it too. She started walking towards it, talking to it; God knows what she was saying. Ollie was shouting at the top of his voice, not words, just sounds. Was he scared, excited? Charlie couldn't make out from here.

He remembered what Lovejoy had said to him: *Don't go getting into any scrapes without me. Remember to wait for backup this time.*

Yeah, but Lovejoy, there is no backup, there's a kid down there and I can't stand here and watch him get eaten, can I?

'Fuck,' Charlie said, and clambered through the hole. He hung there a minute; he really didn't want to do this. He looked over his shoulder; Grey, where the hell are you?

And then, because there was really no choice, he jumped.

He landed heavily and rolled; well, there was his suit ruined along with his Fratelli Rossettis. He stood up gingerly. Twisted his knee when he'd landed, not as nimble as he used to be.

There was no time to work out strategy.

He'd barely got to his feet when he saw the bear run at her. It knocked her off her feet and then stood over her like it was wondering what to make of her. Ollie was yelling. The sling had come off and he was lying on the ground, flapping like a beached fish.

Sarah tried to get up and reached out a hand towards him. She still hadn't made a sound. The bear knocked her down again and raked her back with its claws. She screamed then all right. She got up and started to run, and it bounded after her like it was just a game, then brought up a massive claw and swiped at her. She gave another blood-chilling scream.

Charlie ran over and grabbed the little boy, picked him up in one movement and headed back towards the bridge. Now what? he thought. It's seven, eight feet, I can't get back up there. He stopped and turned around, looking for another way out. There was an eight-foot electrical fence, no way over that either. Ollie was wriggling and trying to get away, slapping at his face, screaming at the top of his voice.

He remembered there were two bears. The other one could be anywhere.

He looked around, saw Grey on the other side of the fence, running along the path with two keepers in green overalls. They were carrying long poles and one of them was fumbling with a set of keys. They still had to get through a set of double gates; he could be hamburger meat by the time they reached him.

Then he saw it. It looked like it was the male – it was much bigger than the other one – and when it saw Charlie, it rose up on its hind legs and roared. You don't need to convince me who's the alpha out of the two of us, Charlie thought. You win, mate.

He turned around and ran, blindly, back across the enclosure. He could hear people screaming and shouting. His knee was killing him. He stumbled and went down. Ollie wriggled out of his arms. Christ, it was like trying to wrestle an octopus.

He made for the bears' play equipment – the tyre swing, a climbing frame: no sanctuary there. He saw people watching him through the fence. By the looks on their faces, he knew the bear was just about on him.

He looked over his shoulder, wished that he hadn't. Papa Bear hadn't even picked up any kind of speed; he was just kind of lumbering along, taking his time because he could. Charlie went down again, and that was it, he knew it was all over. Ollie was still fighting him, and he couldn't hold him any more. The bear stood over him, raised one huge paw in the air to strike, and all Charlie could think of to do was throw his body over Ollie's and brace himself for the pain.

When it didn't come, he dared another look. He heard the bear snarling in frustration and saw it backing away. The keepers were fending it off with long poles.

He glanced up and clocked Grey on his knees by the rope bridge; gasping for breath like he'd just run a marathon. Then he looked around for Sarah, but he could see already that it was too late.

CHAPTER FORTY-EIGHT

Charlie drove to Arlington House, found a spot in the car park as far from the doors as he could get. He'd need a minute before he went in there. He checked his face in the rear-view mirror. There was a smear of blood on his forehead; where had that come from? His suit was history: there was a tear in the knee of his trousers, and they had mud all over them. It looked like he'd played football in his shoes.

Hopefully they'd all seen it on the news. He wasn't expecting a hero's welcome exactly, but it would be nice if they could make allowances.

He got out of the car, went over to the bushes and threw up.

Delayed reaction, he thought. When he'd done, he felt faint. He'd kill for a cigarette right now. His hands were shaking, so he put them in his pockets. Perhaps no one would notice.

He went up to the entrance, checked his watch: only an hour and a half late. Someone was yelling his name. He turned around. It was Ben. He looked like he'd just got off the catwalk at the BRIT Awards; he was wearing a designer-label electric-blue suit and Charlie could just about see his own reflection in his shoes.

'Where have you been?'

'Got held up,' Charlie said.

'All the trouble I went to. You promised me you'd be here.'

'Sorry, mate. Didn't you get my messages?'

'Got your messages, yeah. But message is not the same thing as showing up, is it? You always do this.'

Charlie looked over his shoulder. Ben's black X5 was parked a couple of bays down, and there was a girl in the passenger seat watching them through the window. She looked like a Chelsea WAG, all blonde hair and Botox.

'Who's that?'

'That's Delilah.'

'You brought a girl to a family thing?'

'She wanted to come. She said she wanted to put faces to names. She even wanted to meet you.'

'Well, she can meet me now.'

'No, we'll do dinner next week, when you've actually got time off, do it properly. You all right? Look at the state of you. What happened to your suit?'

'I got attacked by a bear.'

'Very funny.'

Charlie sagged against the wall.

'Mate, you don't look too good.'

'I'll be all right. Did it all go off okay?'

'No, it was a complete disaster.'

'Because I wasn't here?'

'Hardly. Jules and Tel had this big fight – she walked out and Tel went after her across the car park, and that was the last we saw of either of them.'

'What about Rom?'

'She took him with her. Ma fell asleep before we even cut the cake, and she kept calling Michael Liam. Then she went on and on about "Where's your dad, he should be here, he likes cake." So the four of us, and Uncle Bill, sat around singing "Happy Birthday", and when we finished, she wanted to know whose birthday it was.'

'What do you mean, the four of you? Where was Will?'

'I don't know, I thought you were going to bring him.'

'I thought he was coming with you. I haven't seen him since the other night.'

'What happened the other night?'

'We went out to dinner and we had a row.'

'Great. Well, I don't know how to explain this to Delilah. When her mum had her birthday, it was at a restaurant in the Bayswater Road and they had two hundred guests.'

'Perhaps Delilah invited a lot of her school friends.'

'Hilarious.' Ben turned and walked back to the car.

'You going to see the Arsenal next week?' Charlie shouted after him.

'Yeah, I'll call you,' he said.

'Well, well, look what the cat dragged in,' Michael said when Charlie walked into the foyer. 'Almost literally, I'd say. Didn't see the need to dress up for the occasion?'

'I got attacked by a bear.'

'Was that the best you could come up with?'

'Any cake left?'

'We gave it to the staff for their afternoon tea.'

'How's Ma?'

'I think you'll find she's asleep. You should still go in and say happy birthday.'

'I will. Thanks.'

'Sad about Will.'

'His choice, I suppose.'

'I shall pray for him. With God's help we may yet bring him back into the flock.'

'If the flock is hiding some alcohol and hard drugs in the corner of the paddock, I'm sure he'll be there.'

Michael shook his head. 'Always the joker.'

'I know you're dying to get into it, but I've already had a proper bollocking from Ben.'

'Sometimes you act like your job is the most important thing in the world.'

'And we all know that's you, right?'

'I don't miss my own mother's birthday party.'

'Did you meet Ben's new girlfriend? What's she like?'

'He seems very keen on her.'

'Get out of here. Serious?'

'Never believe you know the last thing about any human heart, Charlie.'

'Henry James.'

'Very good. You were always erudite.'

'Thanks. Well, it was nice catching up again. You take it easy.'

'Go with God, Charlie.'

'I will, as long as he wants to go with me. I'll look in on Ma now.'

He went down the carpeted corridor to her room. The door was ajar. She was lying on the bed, still in her slacks and print blouse, her hands folded on her chest. It reminded him of one of those tombs of some ancient queen in Westminster Abbey.

Her birthday cards were lined up on the dresser beside her bed, next to a bit of cake wrapped in a napkin. He knew who the cards were from without having to look inside: the one with Mother Mary on the front, that had to be Michael's; the jokey one was Jules; the one that said thanks for being my mum – now that took him off guard. He opened it up and there was Ben's name at the bottom.

Any human heart, as Michael had said.

She was snoring softly, all wrung out after a busy afternoon of having to stay awake and remember who her family was.

'Poor old thing,' he murmured and sat down next to the bed.

One of the nurses came in. 'Oh, hello,' she said. 'You must be Charlie.'

'That would be me. The prodigal son.'

'Such a nice party. Pity you weren't here.'

Charlie let the silent accusation hang. He didn't have the energy to argue his case, and besides, the nurses looked after her like she was their own; it was good they cared so much about her. But this one was young, and she wouldn't let it go.

'Where were you anyway?' she said.

Charlie was about to tell her, but just remembering made him feel nauseous again, and he ran into the en suite and threw up a second time in the sink. He held tight to the edge, afraid that if he didn't, he would sink right through the floor. Thinking you're about to die will do that to you, he thought.

When he came out, the nurse was gone. That will make a nice story for the staff room later, he thought.

Ma was still asleep. He went to the bottom drawer in her dresser, found Mr Rocastle and put him in a plastic bag. No point in leaving him there. Okay, he supposed Will was right, it had been a pretty shitty childhood. But not all of it had been bad, and if you didn't hang on to the good bits, you'd go crazy.

CHAPTER FORTY-NINE

Lovejoy sat in Howard's overstuffed armchair with her left foot on a stool. She'd been asleep. She'd left the back door open because he'd called ahead and said he was coming. Couldn't do that where he lived.

The spaniel did a few laps of the living room when he saw him, then jumped up, perfect height and timing, got Charlie in the groin. Having inflicted maximum pain, he jumped back onto Lovejoy's lap, threw himself on his back and went to sleep with his feet in the air.

'Wish I could do that,' Charlie said.

'What, sprawl all over my lap?'

He didn't know what to say to that. She'd never flirted with him before and it took him off balance. 'Go to sleep straight away,' he said.

'Sleeping is what cocker spaniels do best. For them, it's an art form. How was your day?'

'Same old, same old. Have you watched the news?'

'No, I got sick of watching TV in the hospital. Nice to sit here and listen to music.'

Just as well, Charlie thought. The news was leading with mobile-phone footage of a police detective legging it across a wildlife enclosure holding a four-year-old with a brown bear in hot pursuit. Apparently it had got tens of thousands of views on YouTube already.

'Who are you listening to?'

'Mumford and Sons.'

'Don't know this one. Funny name. Not really his sons, are they? They should have called themselves Mumford and his Dodgy Mates. Much better name.'

'What happened to your suit? There's mud all over it.'

'I fell over running after a suspect.'

'Did you catch them?'

'Sort of.'

'I hope you were being careful. Is DS Grey making sure you don't get in any scrapes?'

'He's a regular mother hen.'

'Good. At least I know I don't have to worry about you, guv.'

'No, he takes good care. Won't even let me pour my own coffee in case I burn myself.'

'You're wearing trainers.'

'My shoes got ruined.'

'Let me guess, running after a suspect?'

'Had to borrow a pair back at the station. Wes's gym gear was all that fitted.'

'It was nice of you to drop by. There'll be talk if you keep doing this.'

'I came to see Charlie, not you.' He took a bone out of his pocket. 'I got this at the pet shop.'

Charlie opened one eye and was immediately awake. He sprang off her lap, dancing on his toes to get to it.

'Is that beef?'

'It's not human, if that's what you're implying.'

'He's allergic to beef.'

'Let him have it, Lovejoy. You can see he's wasting away to a shadow.' Charlie gave him the bone and he grabbed it with his teeth and hid behind one of Howard's boxes to enjoy it in peace.

'Where's your dad?'

'He's gone down the park, meet his man.'

'His man?'

'You know, his contact. His dealer. He's run out of herb.'

'You shouldn't be telling me this. It's better if I don't know.'

'It's only a little bit of grass, nothing to worry about. It's not like he's importing cocaine in a shipping container, is it?'

'You'll tell me if he starts doing that, though, won't you? Talking of that, have you been smoking some of his stuff?'

'Only for medicinal purposes,' she said. 'You'd rather I get hooked on the drugs they gave me at the hospital?'

So that was why she was being so familiar, Charlie thought. I've caught her out. She's high as a kite.

He watched Charlie gnawing contentedly at his bone. You'd never know his history to look at him. 'Can't believe that's the same dog,' he said.

'All he needed was a proper home.'

'Lucky dogs have short memories, I suppose.'

'It's not the damage, it's the dog. How's your brother?'

'No idea. He's disappeared. He didn't make it to Ma's birthday party, and that was the entire reason Ben brought him over. Lost cause, I suppose.'

'I can't imagine you having a brother like that.'

'Sometimes I can't imagine it either. I'd think I was adopted, but my old man didn't want the kids he did have, so he wouldn't have taken on anyone else's.'

'Has it been good? Seeing Will again.'

'No, not really.' Charlie sat down, started going through Howard's selection of vinyl. Must be worth a fortune. He had early Stooges, even the Sex Pistols. Like owning a piece of the True Cross, that was.

'He bothers you.'

'It bothers me that he remembers everything so different to how I do. He said I was the favourite in the family. How could I have been the favourite? The old man used to belt me black and blue like everyone else.'

'Some kids, they'd rather get a belting than get ignored. Perhaps he was jealous.'

'Don't talk mad.'

'That's not the thing, though, is it?'

'No. It's not. It was something else he said.'

'What was that?'

'He said I was just like the old man. You know what? I spent every day of the last eighteen years, ever since I left home, trying not to be like him. Not in any way. And he goes and says that.'

'You're not like him, guv.'

'You don't know that, Lovejoy. I'm your guv'nor, we work together. But you don't know what I'm really like.'

'I think I do. I think the whole team does. Charlie here does.'

'He's a spaniel. It's his job to be nice to people.' He held up one of the records. 'What's he doing with the Carpenters?'

'Must have been one of Mum's.'

He stood up. 'Better head back. Bit of paperwork to tidy up.'

'I won't be seeing you on the news tonight, will I, guv?'

'Me? Not a chance.'

'Good. Thanks for coming by. Sorry about your suit.'

'Say hi to your dad. Though he probably already is.'

'Charlie, come here, you've got something on your collar.'

'Where?'

He leaned over and she grabbed his lapel, pulled him towards her and kissed him.

Charlie stared at her. 'What was that for?'

She'd coloured up. 'Shouldn't have done that,' she said. 'You'll have to transfer me out of the squad now.'

He mumbled something and left.

He sat in the car, feeling a bit dazed. That shouldn't have happened, she was dead right. But he had to admit, it had put the shine on a proper shite day. The Nokia buzzed in his pocket. DS Grey.

'Where are you, Matt?'

'Still at the hospital. Bad news. Sarah Howlett didn't make it.'

'What about the boy?'

'Social services have picked him up. I guess it's up to them to look out for him now.'

That's lovely for him, Charlie thought. Probably a good thing that he'd never really understand any of it.

'Thanks, Matt,' he said and hung up.

Well, he'd better get back to the nick and see the DCI. He and Catlin had been fielding the media all day. It was a massive body count for one missing persons job. Last thing the DCI had said to him, the Met would be forced either to sack him or give him a medal for bravery, and Catlin thought that sacking him would be a bad PR move.

He clocked Lovejoy's old man coming up the street in his old donkey jacket, shuffling like a tramp. You'd never know he was a millionaire by the look of him. Charlie supposed he was rich in a lot of other ways, too. He was coming home to a family, of sorts. He had a daughter, and a spaniel, stuff going on.

As he drove back to Essex Road, Charlie dared another look at himself in the rear-view mirror. Not everyone's cup of tea, but it was nice to think he might still be someone's. *Something on your collar.* He put the radio on, sang along with Tom Walker, 'Leave a Light On'.

One day perhaps he would have someone leave a light on for him.

ACKNOWLEDGEMENTS

First of all, a huge thank you to Krystyna Green, my editor at Little, Brown, for your boundless support and enthusiasm in dragging Charlie George into the light of day. He'd never have made it out of uniform and into Serious Crimes without you.

Special thanks also to my desk editor, Rebecca Sheppard, for your endless patience waiting for me to come down from the writers' garret to answer your emails and making sure that I always stay on schedule. Not an easy job. You are wonderfully good at it.

To Penny Isaac, my copy editor, for your diligence in poring through the manuscript and making sure I didn't any words out.

There is one person who does all the structural editing, crossing out and ripping up of pages before it ever gets as far as the publisher. Thanks so much, Lise, I really couldn't write Charlie without you. You're my guiding light in so many ways.

To Annie, my sister-in-law, thanks for always going into my local bookshop and rearranging all the shelves so that Charlie George is always above Martina Cole and Ian Rankin on the bestsellers.

To the real Charlie George, who will probably never read this, but who I had the great pleasure to meet on the Arsenal Legends tour. It was players like you who made people like me and DI George fall in love with football when we were kids.

To Charlie and George, our two cocker spaniels. Thanks for the naming rights.

And finally, to my mother, who today would have got her telegram from the Queen. Thanks for all the stories.